BURNING STREAMS
The Books of Joy – Volume One

Alexis Brooks de Vita

BURNING STREAMS
The Books of Joy – Volume One

DOUBLE DRAGON

CHAPTER ONE
WILLOW FRONDS AND WISTERIA VINES

The white Jaguar glided into the clearing as though the women had entered a sinister fairy tale. The house shuddered before them in waves of sunlight, an ancient girl-woman roused suddenly from sleep, a sphinx curled in on secrets.

I'm getting fanciful, Eva thought as she rose from her cousin's Jaguar to face the wreck of all their dreams.

Staring at the house, Eva felt that it stirred. Its unfocused gaze met her own. Light shimmered on vines parted like braids on a head thrown back to peer drowsily at her, revealing rotted planks, broken steps, and staggered bits of insect-bored wood. Willow fronds and wisteria vines framed the wisdom and ignorance that softened the house's unearthly facade.

Why do I feel I know you? The house seemed uncannily familiar to Eva, painfully charming in its degenerated state. Cockeyed with skewed windows, wild with tangled growth like sleep-matted locks, nursing unhealed wounds and hurtful secrets, the house exuded welcome, hope, and hideousness in equal measure. Clearly, it was still standing only because it was too far north to get the full blast of Hurricanes Ike or Katrina.

But what was that horrid stone growth, like a lumpy gray goiter, that met the wraparound porch on one side and scuttled like a bug toward the back?

"Welcome to Mississippi," Charley said. Eva's cousin Charlotte had slipped out of the idling car and come upon her like a wraith. Thin as a specter and silent as a ghost, was Charley.

Suddenly upright in the heavy air, Eva weaved and steadied herself against the car. When had she last eaten? She had been in such a hurry to get here, to reach the site of both their ancestry and their new beginnings, that she had worked herself into a frenzy of map-reading, catnapping, and hours behind the wheel when Charley could drive no longer.

For three days, Eva, Charley, and Eva's daughter Anastasia had trekked from Los Angeles into the Deep South. First, the Southwestern deserts burned them dry of the salty waters of their coastal birth. Then, they'd marveled all along the Atchafalaya highway at the miles of dying swampland and lingered in Louisiana, determined to feed what little revenue they could, in one day and night, into the oil-ravaged community. Now, what was left of Mississippi's vine-canopied woods, logged to aridity along the major highways, and its Blues and Civil Rights signposts the closer they got to the plantation, all called up unfamiliar memories as if from primordial waters.

Perhaps Eva could do her dissertation on ancestral memory in African American literature here, under the ever-present weight of a history of people in chains, hung from trees, blasted by rifles, gnawed by scavengers. Was this intuitive empathy what Eva's beckoning Southern ancestry had given her? Could that be what she had just thrown aside a lifetime of achievement to discover?

And how did Charley feel now that hope had slammed into reality?

Time to turn around and head back to L.A., Eva fretted. But, "It can't really be this bad," was what she said.

It was the heat, so wet and heavy. The fistful of braids that tended to migrate from the nape of her neck to a ballerina's topknot tugged at her scalp. Blood sucked empty of oxygen struggled to reach her brain. *I'm going to faint,* Eva thought.

"Girl, get a grip," Charley quipped, stolid as always.

What have I led them into? Eva never would have imagined abandoning everything she had worked for to chase the illusion of an ancestral home. It was Charley who had said, "Let's just go do it, Eva. My treat." As if it were a trip to the Santa Monica Pier.

So Eva had joyfully dropped it all, the lecture hall of upturned student faces and the pen-tapping, mumbling professors. She had even let go of that elusive dissertation that vanished like a mirage each time she approached it, touched it, tried to reduce it to black words on a white page. What did Eva know about ancestry? No more than she knew about her lonely, lovely daughter, whom she had just hurt once more by snatching her out of an excellent university to drag her to this mosquito-ridden backwater.

"Can we go back to earlier, more hopeful times?" Eva had asked Anastasia and Charley when she told them of her inheritance. She meant Los Angeles and its disemboweling success. Exile from the old neighborhood. Swallowed fear. The desire to flee.

Which was what they'd done. Having shot from poverty into that disillusioned class of the African American elite, the three women had come away, escaped, so to speak, in search of meaning. But what could this wreck of a plantation mansion, this disaster of history long past, possibly *mean*?

What could the house mean now, echoing her own questions back to Eva in its unstill repose? "Go back. More hopeful?"

"It wants us," Eva babbled. "So why do I feel like this is our last chance to get away from it?"

The exhausted city women escaping to a home they had never known were, Eva decided, the house's destiny. They had not suspected what pulled them here. But the house had known and waited. Like a lonely old lady caught unaware by visitors, the house self-consciously gathered its frayed foliage and fragmented bits. It would be rude to turn and leave just yet.

Charley had no more patience. "Say what?"

Eva felt a light touch. A hand slid around her waist. Eva turned. Of course, the embrace came from gentle Anastasia.

"Thank you, Anastasia," her mother said. "I needed that."

Anastasia's voice was a whisper. "Let's get you out of this heat. You don't look all right."

Charley said, "You're dizzy as a betsy bug, Eva. You haven't eaten more than three bites together in as many days. In this heat, that can't be healthy. Let's go get us some grub. Everything'll look better on a full stomach. Even this nonsense."

Eva sensed real rage boiling up. Nonsense, Charley called it. Really, there was no answering Charley sometimes. No dealing with her, either. "I'm not hungry. You go ahead."

"Oh, come on, Eva. You know that gas station we passed at the turn-off from the main road to come here? I bet they have some of that down home food out of somebody's grandmama's kitchen that you've developed such a taste for." Charley's tone took on the smile that Eva refused to turn and see. "Some of that peach and rhubarb cobbler? Or maybe that fried okra dripping with green pepper sauce?"

Anastasia laughed. It was true that, the deeper South the women had ventured, the more their tastes had leapt to embrace wildly regional foods their minds could not remember.

To lighten her discouraged mood, Eva bantered back. "Or maybe some of that alligator sausage you took such a liking to in Baton Rouge. I swear, Charley, I didn't think we'd ever get you away from that Cajun fisherman. And don't tell me it was money and a job he was looking for, from you."

The palpable pain that shot across Charley's face and left it shut against her shocked Eva. What had Charley heard in the meaningless tease?

Anastasia stepped in to pacify aunt and mother. "I'll go with you, Aunt Charley." She slid onto the Jaguar's back seat.

Charley balked. "*She's* going? What does that mean? We're *all* going. I know you don't think I'm leaving you here alone."

Eva shook her head. "Charley, thank you for trying to save me from this moment. But you know perfectly well I did this to us, and I'm going to have to assess the situation on my own."

Charley snorted. The sound was profoundly rude and jarred Eva out of her slump. "As-*sess*," Charley hissed. "You blew it. What else is there to as-*sess*?"

Eva had to admit that this was a down-to-earth, admirably healthy approach to the mess she had landed them in. And she should be counting her blessings that Charley initiated it. As the financial backer of this misadventure, Charley had arguably the most right to be upset.

As an investment broker, Charley not only understood money but had amassed a worth that translated into what seemed a constant supply of cash and bargaining clout. It was always Charley who made it seem they could do almost anything.

Maybe this was a hopeful sign.

Hopeful? Charley was going to tell Eva to give it up. She'd say Eva should have listened to that attorney, the executor of their deceased relative's estate.

And why hadn't Eva listened to him?

Because she hadn't trusted him. It was clear that he and the real estate agent handling the property hadn't expected her to take an interest in her windfall. Some city woman out in California? They'd expected her to unload her inheritance on the first buyer they could snag. They were floored when she wanted to know more about the place.

They hadn't told her anything more than, "We can sell it to developers for you. It's got a fresh water source untouched by the Gulf oil spill and plenty of land for employee housing."

Eva suspected she knew what that meant. She'd read about the endemic poverty of the South exploited by overnight plants and factory towns that left ecological destruction and epidemic cancer in their wake.

She would not be part of it. That she promised herself. But how to persuade Charley not to sell?

Like an irrelevant flash in a daydream came the thought, *Where is that fresh running water they told me about? And why is this air so heavy with unshed rain?* And then Eva knew she had the answer.

Assess. Just like she'd said a minute ago. Slow down, calm down, pick up her courage, and take a look at the place.

Alone. Without worrying about Anastasia's future or Charley's investment. Or even her own dissertation.

Confront the house questioning only its own merit. And take it from there.

Now Eva turned to Charley with a smile. "You're wasting gas. It might be okay to buy peach and rhubarb cobbler from that gas station, but I'm not sure you want to trust their fuel."

Charley wasn't reconciled. "I know you ain't crazy enough to think I'm leaving your big-city self out here in the swamp with snakes and alligators. Get in the car, Eva."

Exhaustion and exasperation struck. Eva let go of the Jaguar's hood and sank to the weedy pebbles that ran in a U before what used to be the house's verandah. She reached gingerly from the safety of the low growth on the driveway across the border into the thicker grasses.

"What are you doing?" Charley screeched and bent to slap at her outstretched hand as if Eva were a child. "Playing in the dirt. Or are you faint? Get up out of there, Eva."

Eva snatched her hand from under her cousin's. "Charley, stop. I'm just trying to get a stick or something to fend off snakes. You're the one worried about them."

"Well, no need to go looking for them. Get up and come with me," Charley huffed. Eva rose and followed her obediently, always the younger cousin trailing behind.

She was alarmed to realize that she wobbled as she walked. She plastered herself against the car's rear end as Charley opened the trunk and fished inside.

"Here," Charley pronounced, wielding an unfurled umbrella at the ground. "I think I read somewhere about somebody opening an umbrella on a snake about to strike. It hit the metal rods with its fangs and knocked itself out. You try it."

Eva took the weapon. "Thank goodness we're isolated out here. You're not really going to make me carry this thing, are you?"

"Open it up fast, like this." Charley reached for it, to demonstrate.

Eva jerked the umbrella away. "Charley, leave."

At last, Charley smiled back. "Something sweet and something spicy?" she called as she dipped into the driver's seat.

Eva glowered. "You going for food or boyfriends?" she snapped and then, as always, wondered if she'd been too saucy in front of Anastasia.

But as the dusty white Jaguar, one of the original English makes-nothing *parvenu* for Charley-pulled forward around the U and surged through the dangling green canopy, Anastasia waved gaily at her mother from the front passenger seat. When had she shifted her seat from the back?

"She must have seen how the argument was going and figured I would be the winner," Eva mumbled. "Got into the front just like that. How does she know these things?" And when had Anastasia become such a silent reactor to all that went on in her mother's life, shifting her own plans without a murmur as her mother's circumstances made change necessary?

Absently, Eva shunted the umbrella open and shut at the pebbled driveway, fussing a bit when the button on the umbrella's handle stuck. *"En garde,"* she challenged, wandering toward the house. Really. Could a human being possibly have reflexes fast enough to stun a leaping snake?

"Seems to me that thing'll do you more good if you raise it over your head," a voice said.

Eva shrieked and dropped the umbrella.

"I'm sorry, ma'am. I didn't mean to scare you." The baritone voice drifted from the doorway of the sleepy, feminine house. Eva's first ridiculous thought was that she expected the house to sound girlish and wise like Anastasia.

Her second thought was that she was not alone out here, so far from everyone and anything. So far from help. "You didn't scare me," she announced shakily. She bent to retrieve the fallen umbrella.

"You screamed," the voice accused.

To her dismay, Eva found herself unable to rise. Stunned by the weakness in her knees, she wobbled to a sedately seated position on the pebbles.

Still the dizziness would not pass. Eva looked beseechingly toward the shadows separating themselves deep in the porch's interior. There, a man's broad shoulders tapered to a slender waist as he moved like liquid through lightening darkness, coming toward her.

Eva thought, *I must get up. I must get away. It's not safe to sit here, waiting for him.*

But she couldn't even remain upright.

I'm not really going to faint, am I? Eva demanded of herself in her distress as the blinding sunlight swam into green and then into black.

Eva roused to find herself flying through shifting darkness in strong arms. Dreamily, she thought that her father was alive again, and she must be a little girl, and those bulky shapes that loomed and receded all around them in the glaring dark were like monsters in a carnival spook house. But she was safe in a strong embrace and would never fear again.

It seemed a long time later that Eva came to fully enough to sit up. She gave a little cry of panic. She could see nothing. But as soon as the humiliating sound escaped her, a voice near her said, "It's all right. I'll get this lit in just a minute. You're okay."

Where was she? With what strange man that she didn't know?

14

Bright flashes of scenes outside the house lit her mind and left her head throbbing. The intruder had stepped gracefully, swiftly toward her as she sank under sunlight, his worried face suddenly close to hers, his pillowy bronze lips whispering against her cheeks something she could not understand. Up close, he was older than she guessed when he said that boyish, countrified "ma'am," his walnut skin finely traced across his forehead and down the sides of his mouth.

Eva realized she had fainted. And he, this stranger, had picked her up and carried her into someplace dark and dank. She could hear water far off, dripping.

"Where am I?"

"It's all right."

Time to get control of this situation. "I'll decide that," Eva said with authority. "I asked you where I am."

She could feel more than see that he had turned sharply toward her, taking into consideration her mistrust. He was too close. She must have thrust her face up near his when she sat up. And he had not honored a stranger's need for space and backed away.

What could she do to get some distance, some sense of safety? Surely not lie down again, vulnerable.

Eva pressed her palms behind her into the floor to get her bearings and scoot away from the man's intrusive warmth. Her hands sank into something thick beneath her. A sleeping bag? Yes, buoyed up from the floor on a mattress and what felt like the height of a box spring.

15

Eva gasped. Had some strange, strong man picked her up bodily and taken her to the place where he slept? Her sudden, unwanted attraction toward this man whose strength reminded her of the safety she'd felt in her father's arms was attacked by a sense of danger.

His behavior was inexcusably intimate. What was going on here?

A scratching sound, and a sliver of light flared beneath the man's pensive face. Up so close, alone together in sudden fiery light, his beauty, still and sculpted, was astonishing. Chiseled edges sharpened the curve of his lips and rounded nostrils. That little dip plummeting from nose to upper lip was a river flowing from breath to speech. Too private, too promising, to be exposed.

He pursed his lips, thinking. He turned to her, parting those lips to speak. For no reason that Eva could imagine, it occurred to her that his full lips must feel like cushions of dry warmth, his breath moist between them.

Eva slapped herself mentally and snapped out of this uncalled-for reverie. Lightheaded and fantasizing in the midst of obvious peril! She had been kidnapped by some nut, and it would do her no good that he was handsome if he. . . .

What was he planning to do with her?

"Where have you brought me?" she said sharply at precisely the same time that he said, "I've brought you into your own house. Don't worry."

Firelight in his glass-domed kerosene lamp-she had only seen such rustic things in supermarkets and thought they were curios, but he was *using* his-

burned in his smoky irises. Was he thinking what his eyes seemed to say that he was thinking?

Did he really have trouble fixing his gaze on her eyes instead of letting it drop to the sunburned skin exposed from neck to bra, freed by the thinnest, skimpiest shirt she owned? Would her expanses of thin limbs, bronzed by travel through desert and swamp, appeal to him? Or did he share many African American men's disdain for skinniness and dark skin?

What did he think of her? What would he think if. . . . Eva wailed at herself, *What's wrong with me?*

But was the same thing wrong with him? Why had he whispered with his lips to her skin?

Eva's mind reeled in the face of her battling feelings. She must get control of her wild thoughts. Could he tell what she was thinking? If the humiliating passion that had overcome her was not normal, was not even shared, what could this stranger possibly make of her trembling?

Angry with herself, Eva yanked her attention back to her predicament. "Into my house?" She looked around.

The dark beyond the stranger's slender, shapely silhouette was too thick to be penetrated by his lantern's scraggly wick. "A special part of your house. It's the coolest place I could think of, to get you out of that heat. I'll have to tell you about it." He smiled. The slow spread of his lips over his even teeth sent warmth and shame radiating from Eva's insides throughout her body.

Eva didn't believe in instant passion. "You'll tell me about my house? I think you'd better tell me about yourself, instead. Who *are* you?" Eva demanded with genuine outrage.

How dare he come into her ordered emotional existence and shatter it with careless gestures. Who did he think he was, breaking into her house, carrying her in like a fainting bride, and taking advantage of her lightheadedness to make her feel smitten?

"I'm listening," Eva said. Her tone was tough, but her heart slammed. Weren't mass murderers often charmers?

As proof of the stranger's dishonesty, now that the lantern was lit, she was sure this couldn't be a house. The dark was black and as thick as fog. Barely at the edges of it, the lantern cast hints of light upon the outthrust edges of mossy stones protruding all around them.

A dungeon?

Eva had heard of such things. Weirdos stalked women and trapped them in subterranean rooms and did sadistic things to them. Internet lovers met and tortured each other before burying each other's dismembered corpses in gardens.

Now Eva pictured this man lurking in the shadows of the verandah waiting to pick off her little family, all three of them one by one, extracting cries of pain and revelations about where to find their traveler's checks as he took his sweet time killing them. Why hadn't they brought guns in their backpacks?

And where was a door out of this stony chamber of horrors?

CHAPTER TWO
PINNED BUTTERFLY

"I don't think this room is in any house," Eva parried. She braced herself to rise.

She settled her hands firmly into the sleeping bag, dipping and swaying on the lumpy mattress and towering box spring, and hoisted her hips into the air. All the while, she looked frantically about her, straining to peer through the blanket of blackness. Vertigo brought her down again.

"Give me your hand," the man commanded. Suddenly he was up against her. His strong hand clamped about her fingers, tugging her to her feet.

Eva let out a full-throated cry. He released her, but it was too late for the freeing gesture to reassure her. Eva darted away from him into the mossy pitch.

Of course, outside the circle of his lantern's light, Eva couldn't see. She slammed hands first into a stone projected from the wall at face level. She gave a little animal whine.

She should have guessed it would come to this. She was trapped.

No, the rational woman argued from deep inside the panic-ridden mind. *He carried you in here without putting you down. Somewhere there is a door that is already open or, at least, easy to open and shut.*

Eva began to feel her way along the wall.

The man had not waited to watch this performance. He had come up behind her. "Eva," he said now. She jumped to face him.

"You know my name," she accused.

19

"Of course I know your name." Now a scowl disfigured his thought-etched brow, plunging the sublime whole of his face into a mask of impatience.

Eva screamed.

Startled, the stranger backed away. His amazement gave her time to turn away, begin a methodical escape. She could rescue herself.

"Where's the door?" Eva slapped the stones with the flat of her palms as she zigzagged along the wall, searching. She was prepared to perambulate the entire stone chamber, if she had to.

"Let me show you." The stranger's raised voice and the sharp sound of his steps on the stone flags alerted her to his renewed approach.

Eva flattened her back to the wall and faced him, ready to fight. She thought morosely, triumphantly, *You never think this will happen to you. How do you prepare to fight for your life one day?*

"Let me light the way." He stopped inches from her face. "The dark is making you panic, Eva. Stop running from me. I'm trying to show you the way out."

It was true that Eva had feared the dark, absurdly, mindlessly, since her parents' deaths. But how would he know that? Was her fear exaggerated now?

Or did he know this fact about her the same way he knew her name? Whoever he was, had he stalked her to the Deep South?

He came no closer but veered to one side, raised his lantern, and turned only barely to catch her eye, as if he suspected that something in his gaze was the problem between them. "Here." He reached his free hand toward her.

Eva thought he was reaching, innocently enough, for her arm. His reluctance to look directly at her, in the pitch pierced only by the feeblest flickers of his lamp, was probably to blame.

Whatever was at fault, the stranger's hand fell fully, unselfconsciously, upon her breast. Then it slid effortlessly down and around to cup her waist, as though it had followed this loving trail a thousand and one times.

One part of Eva's mind knew that the movement indicated nothing more than the stranger's assumption that his hand would fall on her upper arm and slide down to her elbow or wrist. He meant to take her arm and guide her out without confronting her face to face.

But the strength of his grasp and the deliberateness of his touch were heavy with suggestions of mutual want.

Stunned by the caress and humiliated by her own shocked pleasure, Eva could not suppress the thought that the chance embrace answered the questions she'd asked herself only moments before. *What would he think of me?*

Apparently as surprised as she, first by the smooth flow of his hand down long lean muscles and then by her stillness under such inexcusable contact, the stranger turned fully to face her.

His eyes searched hers. His mouth opened. To speak? To reassure? To deny the firm fit of his hand into the deepest curve of her torso?

What could he say? What would she say to him?

Eva felt as still as a pinned butterfly. Her mind raced to tell her to move, to speak, to fling away the offending hand that lingered, that would soon, very deliberately, pull her in closer.

He's already shown you that he can slide away your inhibitions, your concept of yourself as a civilized being, with one feint. Hadn't he just set her whole body moistly burning with his mindless caress?

She must act. She must think. If she didn't move, then something must happen. This stranger must kiss her. Or she would be the one. . . . What would she do?

"To your right, as you're facing me," he said softly, holding her eyes with his own in the lantern light.

Eva came to herself. Humiliated, driven away, forced to retreat from the discovery that she was desirable to this awesomely lovely man, Eva began to inch her body along the wall. Only as she moved did she discover that he had not, in fact, ever withdrawn his hand from her waist.

He had not sent her away. He had given her a choice.

Just as this thought struck her, the fumbling fingers of her right hand plunged into a void.

Or was it an open doorway? Had he told the truth? Told her how to escape this horrible room, this awful confrontation?

She stumbled into nothingness. Free. Delirious with relief at the thought that life, normalcy, order were all hers, Eva dashed forward.

"Watch out," the relentless stranger's voice warned just as her hands took the impact of the walls before her. Dazed, Eva touched the mossy rocks blocking her again. She was in a hallway of some sort.

"To your right, now," the stranger said close behind her again. "Are you all right? Look, let me help you."

Eva turned to the right and took off running.

"Listen, Eva. I'm not going to hurt you," she heard the intruder call.

She couldn't help but listen to the echoed statement again and again. The small distance she was able to put between them as she ran was no comfort to her. He had light. He knew where they were. She didn't.

But it was a safe guess that this was some kind of cave or dungeon located on the property. And to judge from the lamp, the sleeping bag, mattress, and box spring to raise him off the damp stones, he must have squatted here for some while. He would know where she was running long before she got there and figured it out herself.

Would he have truthfully told her how to escape him?

Just as this bleak thought destroyed her resolve, Eva emerged from the stone corridor into what looked like the lab of a mad country scientist.

Rough wood boards made up the walls and were hammered in tiers all around the room as shelves. Chinks in the unfinished wood let in shafts of sunlight where trapped dust motes whirled above the coated floor. The man couldn't have carried her this way very long ago, to judge from the unsettled dust. Eva only had to follow the path against his tread.

His call behind her spurred her into the disquieting room, where rusted iron hooks and hanging pots corroded along the ceiling and walls. What had this room been used to do? Eva shuddered to think and plunged through the entryway where his footprints led.

More darkness. Eva edged through it, bumping against shrouded relics that cracked and snapped from the impact of her thighs. She felt like a child running through a bad dream. She would never find the door in this blackness. Perhaps there was no door, no way out, no way back to everything she had known and discarded to come foolishly to this surreal place.

A door opened. The stranger stood to one side of it. He must have discarded his lantern, for he no longer carried it. He stood silently, watching Eva make for the way out he had provided.

Eva halted. Was he, the intruder, the trespasser, letting her out?

Just beyond him and the seductively opened door she saw the broken verandah, the beckoning vines, the encroaching forest beaten back with cut grass to welcome the new heir.

Eva shoved past the madman into the sunlight and leapt down the broken porch steps. Ahead, she saw Charley's car careen toward her through parted strands of mossy willow. Eva hit the pebbled drive, stumbled from the impact, and ran on, waving her arm to flag her cousin down.

Charley's car barreled to a purring roar beside her. Anastasia, blue eyes wide with alarm and dark with impending shock, tumbled out of the car and clutched her mother. "Get in," Charley shouted from behind the wheel. "Both of you. We've got to get out of here."

Eva didn't stop to wonder what might have brought her cousin and daughter skidding to her rescue in such a state of their own agitation. Their distress matched her own. She dove into the car's back seat, still holding Anastasia tightly.

The car lurched and stalled. Charley shouted, "Who is that fool?"

The tall man who had abducted Eva into the house's dungeon must have flown down the steps after her. He plastered his body against Charley's windshield.

"Wait," Anastasia called with rare authority. "Don't run over him, Aunt Charley. He's got something in his hand."

It was true. In this moment of riotous panic, the man had slapped his open palm against the front windshield on the passenger's side, where Eva would have been sitting if all things had been normal. But nothing was, so no one was in the front passenger seat to see what magic talisman he had used to arrest their flight.

Anastasia craned from the back, straining against her mother's protective grip to lean forward. "It's a card," Anastasia announced. "An ID card. Mommy, let go."

Charley stopped fumbling with the ignition while stomping at the brake, apparently thinking it was the gas pedal. "A card? What does it say?" she demanded of Anastasia as though the young woman were in league with their assailant.

"It says he's a faculty member," Anastasia reported and gently peeled her mother's fingers from her left shoulder. Thus freed, she rose slightly above the backrest of the front seat and peered more closely at the depths of the man's flattened palm. "At someplace called Cooper College," Anastasia pronounced. Now her conciliatory tone soured. "Whatever *that* is," she finished with full contempt, as though she had finally found the flaw in the man's deception.

"Cooper College?" Eva echoed. "I used to want to teach at Cooper."

At this, both Charley and Anastasia turned stunned eyes upon Eva.

Eva understood this look. How many times had she herself studied her companions recently, thinking, *I didn't know that about you. Was it important? How did I miss that?* Perhaps, Eva thought, looking at their sympathetic faces, drooped with sorrow as though she had been deeply wronged, she sounded just a bit more devastated than was necessary. Was this an inauspicious moment to try to explain about Cooper?

Before Eva could begin, Charley turned a glare on the stranger who strained to communicate through the solid pane. Her hostile gaze said that it was entirely his fault that Eva had not been hired to teach at Cooper College.

And now Charley's foot found the gas pedal at precisely the instant that she turned the key in the ignition. Charley gunned the powerful motor against the man's body.

But he stood his ground. Perhaps stupidly, for Anastasia said, "Look at him, Aunt Charley. What's his name, anyway?" as if it were only right to know someone's name before running him down.

"Dead meat," Charley said.

Anastasia's keen young eyes soon solved the enigma of his name. "He's Bo Wolfson," she read aloud.

The car lurched backward, away from him, a clear warning to get out of Charley's way.

"What's his problem?" Charley said, and then, "Good Lord," as she tried to pull the car far enough away from him to go around. "Do our people even name their children something like that? His mama must have, because nobody in his right mind would have gone out and changed his name to whatever you just said."

Charley's voice was calm now. Despite the problem of the man before them determined to be run over rather than run out on, Eva and Anastasia had nearly relaxed. Soon they would be out of here and find a hotel and have a shower and then a swim in the hotel pool. . . .

Eva tore her gaze from the frenzied faculty member of Cooper College to see a gaudy blue Cadillac swerve onto the U, spattered with thick mud from the rutted drive down their backcountry road. "You know these people?" Eva asked Charley incredulously. "Isn't this a private road?"

Charley had the car facing the entrance of the U driveway. She cried, "Not again. What's with these people?" and gunned the motor of the Jaguar with determination. "Would I know people like that in a place like this? That's the fool that chased us when we got to that gas station, honking his horn and skidding through the mud. I thought we lost him. I don't know nothing about him but that he better get out of my way." The Jaguar sprang at the oncoming vehicle.

The Cadillac's rapid glide ended in a spasm of gunning motor and spinning wheels flinging mud out of a little trench at the side of the driveway. Charley now emerged from her Jaguar wielding a cell phone. "Operator," she bellowed, a woman in control, "get me the local police."

A sweating man in a badly creased blue suit threw himself from the mired Cadillac waving a white handkerchief. "He's surrendered," Anastasia laughed, but the man was only snapping the cloth open to wipe his face.

He glared at Charley through the fluffy folds. Fresh perspiration followed the handkerchief's futile trail. "Ma'am," he croaked, "I dare say I gave you a bad fright, for which I am truly sorry. But I cannot fathom why you-uns would try to run me down."

"It's *you* who were chasing," Charley spat back, dramatically closing the phone.

Still inside Charley's car, Eva cringed. Coming here had not been a mistake. This was worse than a mistake. This was a descent into lunacy.

"Charley," she said gently and clearly, opening her door only wide enough to let her voice penetrate her cousin's argument. "Get in the car and let's get out of this toon town." She meant Looney Tunes, as in out of one's mind. Eva was pretty sure it was an "in" thing Anastasia's age group used to say.

Charley, no mother, didn't get it. She turned on Eva and bent down to make her point. "And go *where*, cousin? We're out here in the middle of your country acres you've never set eyes on before, tired, hungry, nowhere to turn unless we stumble

28

out to the interstate and crash into a hotel we didn't see coming, and you say let's get out of here. Where, pray tell, do you intend to go?"

Now the sweating man beamed. "Precisely," he proclaimed.

Charley glanced sharply at him as though she had forgotten what a threat he was. She got back into the car and reached for the ignition.

"Wait. Wait!" Bo Wolfson threw his pectorals across the hood of Charley's car again and flailed both arms against the windshield. The man in the rumpled suit frowned.

Charley started the engine. "Get off my car," she advised the prostrate Bo.

"Bo. Bo," the suited man said. "I think you better get away from that crazy woman's car. Son, she don't look none too stable to me."

Bo held his ground. "We need to talk," he mouthed through the windshield. "Let's sit down and discuss this. Let me tell you about my work."

The suited man yelled, "You ain't told them about yourself yet, Boye? No wonder they acting such a fool."

Bo glared over his shoulder at the man. Then he tapped the window, gazing earnestly in at Anastasia. "Please open the door and come out. We all need to just sit down and talk."

Anastasia turned to Charley. Charley said, "We can talk over the phone from Los Angeles. It's time to get out of here."

Eva said, "Charley, please. Let me just find out what these people have to say."

The car continued to run while Charley lowered Eva's window. "She's listening," Charley called to the men. "Talk fast."

Bo got started but was soon drowned out. Another car zoomed into the U. This was an old lavender Mercedes lovingly preserved and glistening with wax.

"Oh, look," Anastasia cried. "How pretty."

The Mercedes neatly skirted Bo and the trenched Cadillac and slid into place beside the antsy Jag. A tall woman the color and roundness of hazelnuts stepped from behind the wheel. She wore a lavender-gray silk suit touched with pearls at earlobes and neckline. She bestowed a calming smile all around.

Then she went after Eva. "Eva? Eva, is that you, baby?" the woman said, reaching for the handle of the Jaguar's passenger door. "Babygirl, I would know you anywhere. I swear you the spit of your mama."

The door was open and a hand arrested Eva's retracted arm before she knew quite what had happened. Beyond the welcoming woman, Eva saw that the blue-suited man radiated relief.

Bo looked tense and unhappy.

"What have these mens done to you?" the woman in the lavender-gray silk wanted to know. "You tell me, and I'll let them have it, child. Now you come on out of that car, and don't you be scared. I ain't going to let nothing happen to my cousin's baby."

She threw an admonition over her shoulder, eyes still fastened on Eva, to demonstrate her point. "Bo? Ham? Y'all back on off, now. You see how you-alls done scared these womenfolks to death. Don't make me say it twice, now." Though she had already voluntarily said it twice, the threat worked like a charm. The men backed away and eyed the women emerging from the Jaguar as if they were an invading enemy.

"That's better," the woman cooed. "Now let's us sit down and have some of this picnic I done prepared, and see can't we be civil and get to know one another. You know, it's been a long time since the Dennisons and the Wolfsons and the Johnsons was all together."

Eva and Charley shared a glance. Who were all those people?

"Well, we were born Dennisons," Eva said, "and I kept the name, even when I was married, which I guess you know. But who are all those other people, if I may ask?"

It was hard to respond in kind to this excessively genteel woman. But she rewarded Eva with a glorious smile, as if Eva had won first prize for a church recital. "Well, dear, that's what we're going to talk about. I'm your Aunt Portia, born a Johnson, but married to Mr. Hammond, here." She indicated the man from the blue Cadillac. "Everyone who's a family friend just calls my husband Uncle Ham. You must, too, babies."

Eva threw a look at the handsome, sinewy stranger who had carried her into the house's darkness. He studied his scuffed loafers.

Aunt Portia trilled, "And of course, you've met your cousin Bo, haven't you? Bo Wolfson? Well, he prefers to be called Bo. But actually, he's inherited

31

from both lines of the Wolfsons, and to top it all off, his full name is Boye."

Charley caught her breath. Eva couldn't tell without looking if the gasp was one of indignation or laughter. She turned to Charley, barely too late to intercept her cousin's explosion.

"In this day and age," Charley roared just as Eva said, "Miss Aunt Portia, did you say 'Boy'?"

Aunt Portia, grace itself, elected not to have heard the audacious Charley. She smiled and nodded gracefully at Eva. "Yes, my dear, I did. Now, when it comes to one's traditions, one must try to learn and understand and not just jump to taking offense." This was a good beginning, but Aunt Portia seemed content to close her explanation upon this cryptic note.

Anastasia took up the lacy gauntlet. "Well, Aunt Portia, I think I understand. My name is Anastasia, and I've struggled with its many personal meanings all my life. I've come to love my name because I feel I've had to live all its possibilities," Anastasia concluded in fluent California-ese.

Aunt Portia, joyous with pride, said to Eva, "Honey, is this your little girl? Oh, she does you so proud. She speaks so well. Don't she, Ham?"

The Cadillac man mopped his brow, mumbling, but managed to emerge from behind the sodden handkerchief with a hearty smile. "Yes, indeed, she does that, Miss Portia," he said robustly.

Eva began to understand why Bo's shoes might have become so fascinating to him just at this time. Whose idea had it been to saddle an intelligent African American man entering the new millennium with a name so representative of racial insult?

"You did say 'Boy,' Miss Aunt Portia?" Eva insisted.

"Honey, please. Just call me Aunt Portia. You don't have to use that old-fashioned Miss in front of all that. Y'all won't never get nothing said if it take you so long just to call my name," Aunt Portia demurred, but she was radiant with pleasure at Eva's efforts to be faultlessly correct.

What does one have to do to get a question answered around here? Eva wondered desperately.

Anastasia rescued them all. She turned directly to Bo. "So, Dr. Wolfson, the origin of your name must be intriguing. Do you know it?"

Bo, an inveterate college professor, raised his head to the challenge of answering an intelligently phrased question, no matter how embarrassing.

He crossed his arms and spread his legs slightly, as though addressing a lecture hall. "Anastasia, Boye is actually the name of one of our earliest ancestors on this plantation, in its heyday as a freepeople's hideout and community farm, before Emancipation. He's disappeared from local history, but he's become something of a legend in the few extant writings about the period."

Charley wanted to know, "What does all that mean?"

Aunt Portia clicked her tongue in exasperation. "Oh, that Bo," she lamented, as if he were a stubborn stain. "Forever carrying on about such nonsense. You would think a college professor would have more intelligent things to do. Did you all know that Bo here is a college professor? Of history and—what now, Bo?-African American Studies? Is that what they calling it these days?

Y'all know I can't keep all them politics straight in my head." And Aunt Portia shook her head in dismay at the college administration that would slap names on its departments without regard for apolitical citizens.

Charley turned in utter confusion to Bo. "What did she say?"

Bo said, "She doesn't want me to tell you the legends about the first Boye and the two families named Wolfson. The Dennisons were descended from the original owners of the plantation, and your fathers, Eva and Charley, were the last men to pass on that name in this family. The Johnsons are descended from an enslaved man who was made overseer. He had a bit of a magical reputation, sort of like John the Conquer in the African American folktales."

"I've read those stories," Anastasia said with interest.

Bo nodded, a gesture of approval as though she were the first student to answer a question in class. "The original Boye's descendants make up another special family from this plantation. The other family also had Boye's distinguishing traits, though they were not related by blood."

Aunt Portia snapped, "Boye, enough of that, now," so sharply that everyone turned to her, startled and distracted, just as Dr. Wolfson finished explaining. She turned on her heel so abruptly that she dug a hole in the dirt where she'd been standing before she stomped furiously to the trunk of her car. There she fumbled with her keys, jangling them and snatching them back from Uncle Ham when he tried to help her.

Eva wondered if she were the only one still paying attention when Bo said, "Both branches of the Wolfsons were rumored to be werewolves."

CHAPTER THREE
FAINT FIRST PROMISE

The woman in lavender-gray had prepared a picnic. As wicker baskets, white folding chairs and tables, and lacy cloths were lifted from the Mercedes's deep trunk, Eva wondered when Aunt Portia could have found time to put together this feast.

The suspicious strangers sat in the shade of the dangerously broken porch before two tables laden with deep-fried chicken, fluffy biscuits, cucumber sandwiches, potato salad, coleslaw, and pitchers of iced tea.

The suited man wiped his face and intoned grace. "Let our family be reunited in complete accord."

Anastasia slid a glance at her mother.

What did her daughter's look mean, Eva wondered. But there was no time to give the look much thought.

As soon as the two tables' worth of people had said, "Amen," the woman in lavender-gray said with feeling, "Now, who wants to go first?"

From the last names, Eva had guessed that these people were not necessarily all related to each other. But that Aunt Portia was-improbably enough-married to the man in the blue suit, however their attachment came about, puzzled her.

Eva was discomfited by this discovery. Aunt Portia was so elegant, and her husband, Uncle Ham, such a lout. Their intimacy indicated a disquieting lack of justice in the world. A marriage of convenience, perhaps?

"I'll speak first," Uncle Ham said loudly and smiled at Charley, who was not mollified by Aunt Portia's appearance on the scene. "Let me apologize sincerely for frightening you ladies. Of course, it should have occurred to me that three women traveling alone wouldn't know what to make of a man in hot pursuit."

Aunt Portia gave her husband a little glance of disapproval to indicate that his words were ill-chosen. He flushed darkly and contemplated his mound of potato salad.

"What I mean to say is," he began again, but he had blown his only chance.

Aunt Portia finished for him, "That he didn't mean to frighten y'all. We were all just so excited that you was coming, babies, and it didn't never cross nobody's mind you wouldn't be expecting us to meet y'all when you got here." She turned the full radiance of her loveliness upon the immoveable force of Charley. "You have been anticipated, my dears," Aunt Portia cooed.

Charley responded with one eyebrow peaked to within an inch of her hairline. She continued to sit as if on a hunger strike.

Anastasia said, "Thank you." Eva smiled at her.

Aunt Portia turned to contemplate Bo. "My dear, perhaps you should start," she coaxed.

Bo, like Charley, had sat as still as a stone, staring with hostility at his delectably full plate, slouching and pouting like a flat-bellied juvenile. Now he raised a glance to meet Aunt Portia's.

37

Whatever he saw there must have persuaded him. He turned to Eva. "Eva, cousin, I wanted to buy your house," he said. Eva noticed how careful he was to call her cousin and to make it clear he recognized that the house was her uncontested inheritance. Had he forgotten that touch in the dark?

Impossible. Was his recognition of some distant kinship between them meant to deny that incident? Cover it up in front of the others?

Reassure her that he hadn't meant anything by it?

"Everything that's happened that caused you confusion about our motives or your welcome has been because of my desire to buy this house," Bo admitted.

So that's what his touching and flirting was meant to accomplish, Eva thought. *To charm me out of my inheritance.*

How did she feel about this revelation? Maybe a little silly.

Maybe a lot. That touch on her breast, along the curves of her side, had been devastatingly sweet.

"And why do you want to buy it?" Eva made herself respond in kind, as aloof and business-like as Bo. Did he mean to tell her that he already knew of her discomfort with the real estate agent and the attorney who acted as executor of the estate? What had she ever said that might have let slip her dissatisfaction with those two?

"I know my uncle and my father tried to talk you out of keeping it," Bo confessed. "It must have all seemed suspect to you. That's my fault. I thought, from what little I know of people who've grown up outside the South, that you wouldn't want it. I thought it would be easier to just buy it off you."

Did he say the real estate agent and the attorney were his uncle and father? Eva was aghast.

But, "Easier than what?" Charley challenged him.

Bo flicked her a glance, looked at Eva, and then let his eyes settle back on Charley, evidently the irresistible force with which he must contend. "It's just that we didn't know what you might make of my real interest in the place."

He said this last with so much weight that Eva recalled her panic in the stone room and the unsettling intensity of his desire to calm her, to keep her. Her uneasiness returned.

Charley tilted her head to one side. "What is your real interest?" Now both eyebrows soared.

Bo looked at Eva. She would not look up at him but listened as he took a deep breath and sighed it out. Again Bo shifted his gaze to Charley. Charley glared.

Bo gave up and addressed Eva's bent head. "I wanted to show you, Eva. I was going to show you when I carried you inside."

Eva looked up and caught Anastasia's amazement. Eva looked down at her plate again.

Uncle Ham exploded. "You *carried* her inside? Boye, you done lost what's left of your mind? This here city woman don't know you. What you doing laying hands on her?" Ham rose, sputtering chicken bits and potato cream across everyone's plates in his ire.

Bo rallied but didn't rise to defend himself with his more muscular size. "I didn't have any choice,

Uncle Ham. She'd fainted. I carried her to where it was cool enough to revive her."

Portia's hand flew to cover her gasp. "Fainted? Oh, you poor thing." She reached to pour Eva some iced tea. "Bo got a point there, now, Uncle Ham. It's this heat, honey. I swear. I been borned here, myself, and even I can't take it sometimes. Have some more iced tea, baby. This'll cool you right off."

Uncle Ham did not relent. "Boye, watch your tone with me. You know you ain't in the right. You laid hands on a woman who don't know you from who-shot-John. Well, no wonder she all up in here acting so strange. How she know you ain't just laying in wait to take advantage?"

"Now, Ham." Aunt Portia slid a warning tilt into the tail end of her voice and a glance at large-eyed Anastasia. "No need to scare womens who is all alone out here in a new place, now."

"Well, excuse me, my dear, but these here is city womens, and they must know better'n anybody that it's the truth," Uncle Ham huffed. "That woman don't know this big fool. What'd she think, coming to with his hands all over her? Boye, your peoples raised you up in a barn?"

"That's enough, Ham." Portia must have decided to wrap up the debate. "Perhaps it's been an unfortunate first acquaintance. But when we recall our near relation to each other, and our deep happiness that our cousins have returned home, I'm sure all will be forgiven. In time."

Eva and Charley looked at each other. In time? In what kind of time? In time for what?

"Our mothers were second cousins, Eva, Charley." Aunt Portia must have decided to do the explaining herself. Fewer people could mess it up that way. "We're truly glad you've inherited the property and decided to return. It's best, all around. In time, you may consider allowing Bo to continue his work there." Aunt Portia shot a silencing glance at Bo.

But Bo would no longer be silenced. "In time? In time? Aunt Portia, you know perfectly well I don't have time."

Aunt Portia re-joined placidly, "Nor do you have a choice, seem to me, Bo."

"That's right," Uncle Ham mumbled with finality and shoved a buttered biscuit dangling a strip of chicken into his mouth.

"Please," Eva said turning fully to Bo. He looked suddenly so dejected. It struck her that one's childhood authority figures never really lose that impact of the universe having spoken, no matter how aged, pot-bellied, or gray-haired they get. It would not be an exaggeration to say that this erudite professor-of what, by the way?-looked like a cornered child. "Bo-is that your name?-what is your work? And can you help me see what it has to do with my inheriting the house?" Heavens. Maybe Aunt Portia's inclination to coax was contagious.

Bo looked up, surprised, as though he had not suspected that Eva could be conciliatory when she chose. Eva flushed at his full-faced stare, vulnerable and hopeful.

But oddly, Aunt Portia announced, "Not at the dinner table," and busied herself in the depths of one of her wicker baskets. "I've got us here some

41

pies, y'all. Sweet potato. Pecan. Uncle Ham, I know you want you some lemon cake after the day you've had." And Aunt Portia eased aloft a bright round confection above the cluttered table with such a look of pleading that even Charley, the stone, seemed moved.

"It's lovely, Aunt Portia," Charley said. "It was good of you to come prepared to feed us like this."

This homely exchange stirred old memories in Eva. She found herself mimicking forgotten niceties. "Yes, Aunt Portia. Uncle Ham. Cousin Bo. Thank you for preparing ahead to welcome us in such a-" she stumbled for a word "-generous way."

"Oh, please. It's nothing." As Aunt Portia sliced cake and pies and set hefty portions before everyone, she began to talk about how they were all related.

It had to do with the plantation. Apparently, the plantation tied the local African American elite together. Not elite because of wealth or education. There was, as far as Eva could understand, a degree of local notoriety one enjoyed simply for being descended from the plantation's original freepeople.

The enslaved had outwitted or driven out their enslavers and formed a small community of freemen and women even before the Civil War. Gradually, in the first half of the nineteen hundreds, as cotton farming by hand became an outmoded way to try to make a living, the community members began to move off to cities in search of jobs. Those who remained retained ties like family, though the original inhabitants had been related by forced interbreeding.

Much of this history was a surprise to Eva. No theories she had ever encountered proposed that African Americans had pride about or attachment to their history of recent enslavement, or escaping or outwitting that system. She wasn't sure how she felt about Aunt Portia's revelations.

And Eva, who had wanted to know about her ancestry, had not counted on how much such information might disturb her.

**

When she woke in the fullest darkness of the night, her face inches from the powdery layers of dust and ropey spiderwebs that coated absolutely everything in every room of this house, it was the watercolor image of those families of enslaved people, hidden in broad daylight, laboring for a light-skinned woman who was one of their own, that came to her.

The plantation had been a community of runaways pretending to be enslaved up until the Emancipation Proclamation supposedly freed them. The fake "white" woman who protected them by claiming to own them had apparently not been able to resist occasionally appearing in public with her obviously African husband, their growing number of brown-skinned children, and eventually their even darker grandchildren. The lynch raids that had terrorized the plantation when she was assumed to be a selfish, stubborn "white" spinster too proud to marry and share the wealth escalated over time to torture fests.

Awake in the dark, breathing the dust of centuries of neglect and terror, Eva wept.

There was no more sleeping. Somewhere downstairs, she knew that Bo Wolfson moved. She could not hear him. He had said that he would arrange his work to show to her in the morning.

How large was this house? How far away was that intense and disturbing man? What drove him?

He had begged to stay. They had sat together on the safest edge of the porch steps after the verandah was cleared of dishes and tables. They watched fireflies, mesmerized. Eva sent Anastasia like a child chasing after them.

Bo had talked of his work. "It's history, Eva, but history is us. It's alive. It's today. It's why we think the way we do, and who we are, and what will become of us." He stared into her face so close that she smelled sugary pecans on his breath.

Eva hadn't known what to say.

Bo swayed closer. Moonlight glinted in the earthen iris of his eye. "I don't know how to tell you how important this is. You don't know me. But I wish you would trust me." He thrust his desire at her with such force that she feared for an instant he would get up off the porch and go down on one knee.

"Please," he'd said, leaning in at her. Begging was the only word for it, though he didn't touch her, take her hand, yank her arm as it seemed he wanted to. "Let me stay here, near my work. I need to get it together. I need more time. I can show it to you." He'd turned wildly toward the wide front door.

Aunt Portia rested in one of the white folding chairs, lightly holding her husband's free hand as he smoked. She called into the low-voiced conversation, "Now that is a good idea, Bo. Eva, you listening? You all are womens alone. I myself am going to sleep much better knowing y'all got Bo here."

Uncle Ham muttered agreement.

Charley had already gone inside with a flashlight to clean up a space to sleep in. Aunt Portia had given up insisting that the three women accompany her to her own home or even that they accept her spotless towels and linen amidst this filth.

For Charley, clean, Eva was to discover, was a relative term. Charley apparently took the previously useless umbrella and beat three appallingly rotted beds in three dust-sealed rooms to drive out vermin. It seemed that Charley was far too proud to send Aunt Portia home not only for linens but even for brooms and mops, and too exhausted to travel the highway looking for a place to buy these herself.

After this exercise, Charley reappeared briefly on the verandah. From the glove compartment of the Jag, she had fished out a yellow bandana to cover her expensively clipped and dyed hair. But her black silk tank top and black linen slacks were gray with fine flying debris.

Charley whipped off the filthy rag, shook it so that dust flew all over Ham's battered suit, and retied it on her head. "That's better," she announced to no one in particular. "Bo, if there's really running water in that torture chamber you call a kitchen, you better show me how to pump it. Eva, Anastasia, we best follow this man to that outhouse while there's

45

still plenty of people here to get us to the hospital in case of snakebite. Then we can wash up fast as soon as I get the pump primed."

Eva turned and rose to do as her cousin bid. "Charley, Bo wants to stay the night."

Charley's snort had lost its sting. *She really is tired*, Eva thought.

"Then he better beat his own bed," Charley said and walked past them both down the porch steps. "Anastasia, anybody check for snakes before they let you loose to run in the grass? I swear. Am I the only person who remembers when all these Southern hospitals didn't take no colored?"

Aunt Portia laughed like running water. "Oh, all that's done with, baby," she assured Charley. "Yet and still, you right. Uncle Ham, get down there and see can't you help them find that outhouse."

Uncle Ham waved the glow of his cigarette at Bo. "Why me? I ain't used that thing since I was in britches. Whyn't you tell that lazy so-and-so get a move on and help these womens? He the one abusing their hospitality."

"Bo?" Aunt Portia said in that characteristic blend of warning and wheedling that lifted everything she said through two or three octaves before she was finished.

"I'm going." Bo pushed himself from the porch in deep thought and in focused pursuit of Eva.

Of course, he was intent on winning her to his cause, whatever it was, but his pursuit had nothing to do with her, as a woman. Bo wasn't thinking about Eva, she reminded herself. Awake now in the blackest and most hopeless slice of the night,

46

isolated from the world and from tomorrow, Eva wished he would.

Perhaps if, way down there as he worked through the night to organize whatever he was to present to her the next day, he would but think of her, lonely and searching for meaning, she would not feel so overwhelmed.

Bo was a part of something here. Of course, she was a part of it too, she argued with herself, or she would not have inherited this house when so many relations lived in the area.

But Bo *knew*. Eva had come here searching for something he had grown up *knowing*. It pained her, made her feel ridiculous, an intruder and a thief lying in the dark, in the stink, and in the sudden damp cocoon of the sunless Southern night, coating her rinsed skin and hastily brushed jeans with deeper layers of grime and antique filth.

She did not belong here. She was a stranger. And that man, slaving through the night to win her approval of his specialized knowledge and his life's work, branded her an outsider by his very efforts.

It's even worse than that.

Bo also knew Eva. He had stood with her in the dark and looked into her loneliness, the long stretch of years from her marriage through her divorce and all the sad and sobering self-revelations that had brought her to stillness beneath his heavy, wanting hand. He had looked and, she was sure, had seen her desire, her need. Her tremendous fear.

And he had let her go.

Without a word. Without a restraining touch. Without a question in his eyes at the table on the verandah. *Was it real? Did you feel it, too?*

47

Eva felt used and abandoned. The silliness, the pettiness of her young marriage to a meaningless stranger, a boy in her high school crowd who only distinguished himself by asking her to marry him, came back to her.

Charley had been so brave. Only an adolescent when her own parents died in the mysterious depths of the South, Charley had barely reached nominal adulthood when Eva's parents, too, succumbed to the lethal journey "home." Charley, an orphan, took care of Eva as though it had all been planned. As though she were thirty and not eighteen.

As the incredulous adolescent Eva threw herself against fate and railed against God and orphanhood, teen Charley picked up the ever-breaking pieces and insisted they fit back together.

When the shrieking pain of waking to find she had lived another day became dull hopelessness, Eva realized she had survived.

What had Charley sacrificed so that Eva could live again? Eva could not fathom it. Nor could she wrest any confessions of martyrdom from Charley. Their lives were secure. They had everything but their parents.

When the faceless boy at the back of Eva's high school crowd couldn't get her to go to prom with him, so he asked her to marry him instead, it made perfect sense to Eva. What possessed her to think that marrying that gangly, insecure boy would return to her the stable universe of her childhood?

In a matter of weeks, condemned to a life sentence of trying to get to know a schoolmate who meant less than nothing to her, Eva realized the enormity of her error. There seemed to be no escape. Her husband wasn't cruel. He wasn't neglectful. He was simply nothing more than a bad date.

It took years for the bad date to fossilize into screaming nightmares, pounding her words at a husband who retreated into stony, watchful silence. Just like that God who had killed her parents. When Anastasia was a toddler, Eva's neighbor and confidante pointed out to her how shatteringly simple it was to plan, to pack, and to flee a nonviolent man.

Charley welcomed her wiser cousin back home. Anastasia's father sullenly visited his little girl one evening per week for two years until, suddenly and without explanation, only his monthly support checks marked his awareness of her.

Did Anastasia forget that tinderbox ready to flare into explosive cruelty, the brittle embattled air of their apartment? She and Eva had jobs to land, nursery schools to enroll in, and college degrees to earn. Eva began to perceive her marriage as desertion of Charley, who had needed her to have a family. Eva ached over that youthful, thoughtless abandonment.

What had Charley done to survive? Eva couldn't remember Charley's having produced a date since her parents died and her fiancé abandoned her. What had happened to high school's most popular girl, the one sure to marry upon graduation? Eva had tried to become that fabled, fabulous Charley. Now she was a loner, just like the Charley she had returned to. Could Eva say she had loved any man after she left her husband?

Far from it. Eva was now appalled to realize that she had even, a handful of times, fed herself on someone else's loneliness. Taken him into her arms at a moment's notice and without the least shred of conscience.

Without fail, Eva had abandoned each of these rare encounters-as she had once done Charley and would never do again-when the craving to be held in a man's arms was satiated. Eva couldn't think of one time in her adult life she had actually said to a man, "I want to be with you."

How crushing now to look at her life and, and lying in a dust-coated bed in an historical ruin, listen for sounds of the man who had excited passions she didn't even believe in. It was one thing not to want. It was another to be incapable of doing anything about it.

What would happen to her if she couldn't free herself of this desire-not to be held, but to be held *by Bo*-by morning?

Eva suspected that a grievous wrong had been done her. Surely that handsome stranger, that distant cousin, that intellect-driven man pouring his heart into research in the bowels of her home in the middle of the night, oblivious to her existence, her needs, her loneliness, had foreseen all of this when he stared into her lantern-lit eyes.

Eva willed Bo to throw aside his research and come looking for her. If she were not terrified of his stone corridor, of his startled look as she appeared, frightened and agitated, in his doorway, she would do it herself.

He must come up. To show me his work. To ask me my opinion. Make an excuse, or come without one. Seek me out. She thought of the close grip his hand had on her waist in the dark and wished with all her heart that she had opened her lips to meet his. If she had, would he be here now? *Hold me.*

Would she be frightened of this house, of her rootlessness in this strange southern place, in Bo's arms? Or would she lie here satisfied, wanted and reassured, enjoying her rare treat of instant, brief intimacy and belonging, rich like dark chocolate?

Even as she yearned for it, Eva quailed. Unaccountably, she feared she might adore Bo. It seemed too late in life to lose control of her emotions. Eva hated emotional risks.

And what would such a dream-come-true-too-late as love in her forties, such a nightmare of emotional chaos, mean to Eva's ordered life, to the tight bond of family that she and Charley had built around Anastasia? Would Eva end up abandoning Charley again? Worse yet-this time, would she abandon Anastasia, too?

Eva wept until her eyes were too swollen to see clearly if that gray beyond the tatters of crumbling lace at the dirt-caked bedroom window was really the faint first promise of dawn.

CHAPTER FOUR
STONE PRISON

Morning brought muffled bird chatter and a burst of sunlight trapped in Anastasia's white eyelet camisole and pale jeans. She had gathered her ropes of frizzy braids into a ponytail that cascaded from the top of her head. Rousing to meet her daughter's enthusiastic greeting, Eva realized she must have slept, after all.

Eva was shamed, remembering her morbid sense of inconsequence in the small hours of the night. She now despised the memory of her desire to be thought of as a person-not a problem-by the man downstairs. How could she have been so unconcerned in those bleak moments for her daughter's adjustment to this atrocious place? Was she really so needy?

Eva tossed back her head and said stolidly, "You look like you've slept well, punkins." She followed this with a hearty smile. "Did the critters keep you up?"

Anastasia laughed. "Nothing could have kept me up." Then, frowning, "Does your room have 'critters'?"

It was Eva's turn to laugh. "Not that I know of. I think Charley did her umbrella thing to them." They spent the next twenty minutes outdoing each other's satires of the previous day's moving-in slapstick.

Soaking up grime-filtered sunshine and the radiance of Anastasia, it was hard to credit yesterday's loss and bewilderment, its series of stumbles and mistakes.

"What is it?" Anastasia asked.

Eva grimaced. "Oh, I was just thinking that we nearly gave up on this place as soon as we got here." They had nearly fled to any hotel on the road back to L.A. If they returned to L.A. with nothing now, they'd be in for roadside motels with homeless families peopling the lots as the three women searched want ads for whatever jobs and housing they could land at a moment's notice. Now that they'd survived the shock of arrival, it would be better-healthier-to tough it out.

Anastasia sparkled with her cold-water early morning wash, eager for the day's adventures. "It's like camping, but in a house. Do you remember camping with me when I was little?"

Eva's good humor stutter-stepped. Was Anastasia referring to the Rockies that linked the Southwestern reservations? She couldn't be.

Voice neutral, Eva asked, "Honey, what do you remember about camping?"

Anastasia's brow puckered and smoothed again. "Oh, the mountains. The ponies on the reservations. The jewelry seller's children I played with on Wolf Creek Pass."

Eva's voice came out firmer than she intended. "Anastasia, you were only a toddler. Still nursing. You can't possibly remember Wolf Creek Pass."

Laughter like the silver links of the river a solid mile below the unprotected two-lane mountain road. "Of course I do. Mommy, you were so afraid I'd fall off the side of that mountain." An indulgent shake of the head.

"It was a sheer drop."

"The other kids weren't afraid."

Eva quirked an eyebrow. "They were Apache. They're incapable of fearing heights."

Anastasia looked skeptical. "I thought that was Cherokees."

Under the sunny blast of Anastasia's joy, Eva had to let go of her shock that her daughter remembered that terrible time. *But she didn't understand it,* Eva reassured herself. *It's okay.*

The two of them were giggling and reframing their new life as the grandest of adventures when Charley knuckled the door, shoving it open.

Charley did not bring sunshine. "Who's for a drive to that wretched station at the end of the dirt path?"

"Good morning, cousin."

Anastasia grinned. "Isn't it great, Aunt Charley? I have the best feeling about this place."

Charley scowled. "Don't get me started."

Eva was determined to be encouraging. "I see you found clean clothes."

"That wasn't hard," Charley pointed out. "All you got to do is look for the one thing that don't look like nothing else around here, and you found something clean."

Eva left this sour observation alone.

"So does that mean that you and Mom'll be cleaning the place today?" Anastasia prompted and didn't wait for Charley's appalled reply. "Because I thought I'd go exploring. Doesn't this remind you of camping, Aunt Charley? I bet there are caves on our land and everything."

This was not a conversation Eva wanted to let continue. "Exploring? Punkins, I think all hands are needed in the house today to get this place under control. Charley, where'd you put my backpack last night? I need to get out of these things I've slept in. Did you two wash up in the kitchen at the pump?"

Charley's voice dripped contempt. "*I* did, but I don't recommend that *you* do. I wasn't half done when that fool professor tried to break down the door on my butt-naked behind."

Eva was open-mouthed. "Charley, don't tell me you locked him in that stone corridor."

"What else was I going to do? Take my sponge bath in front of him?"

Eva screamed with glee. Bo locked in the dungeon and banging to get free? Served him right for frightening her yesterday.

Anastasia shook her head. "You two," she said affectionately and disappeared.

Eva's backpack was on the wooden floor soft with the omnipresent coatings of dust on threads of undigested wool, too dry for moth larvae over the decades. Eva stripped off her jeans and the sleeveless cotton tee that had gotten her bitten to a resemblance of smallpox while sitting on the porch steps last night. Hadn't she sprayed on Charley's insect repellent? She'd have to remember to reapply it at sundown from now on.

In her haste to leave L.A., Eva had stuffed a crinkled white Indian cotton dress into her pack when she couldn't wedge in an extra pair of jeans. She pulled this on, tied it at breastbone and waist to secure the delicate bodice buttons, and wiggled out of her underwear. She slid on the clogs Charley had bought them all at the outset of the trip South, as protection against snakebites on their feet.

Eva bundled her dirty clothes onto her hip. "All right, Charley, lead the way. I'll do your laundry at the pump, too. Where's Anastasia? She must have dumped her dirty clothes somewhere."

Charley said nothing. She had already gone through Eva's bedroom door into the pitch of the hallway.

Following her cousin, Eva understood her silence. The bloody darkness of the house's viscera was awe-inspiring. Where did that hint of gore and fire come from?

As though tapped on the shoulder, Eva whirled to face the far end of the hall. She gasped and stumbled backward, catching herself against the roughly papered wall.

At the far end of the hallway was a breath-taking rosette of stained glass. Sunlight splintered the many-colored shards, spattering the upper hallway with a glow that tinted the gloom. How had that masterpiece of hand-fitted bits of precious glass survived in this abandoned farmhouse?

Like a sleepwalker, Eva drew toward this proof that the house had been a mansion at one time, an enslaver's showpiece. "Charley, enslaved people must have made that rosette. How did they-?"

Charley stopped her with a snatch at her wrist. Eva's bundle of dirty laundry tumbled to the floor. "Some other time, Eva. You come with me now. A little goal orientation, if you don't mind. Here. I got my laundry out of my backpack while you were mooning over the glass gallery."

Charley bent to retrieve Eva's dropped laundry. With two bundles of sweaty, female-smelling clothes pressed into Eva's arms, they turned from the swimming shapes at the end of the upper hall and made their way to the creaking staircase.

Charley clasped Eva's arm with one hand and the rail with her other, resisting the sweeping descent. "Isn't this thing dangerous?" Eva asked as they stepped into the slate-black curve.

"No more so than everything else you touch or bump into in this place. Come on. The bottom comes up at you just when you think this is the stairway to hell and will go on forever. Feel for it with your clog so you don't stub your toe."

Eva had assumed that Anastasia would be downstairs releasing Bo Wolfson from the stone dungeon. But when she and Charley emerged into what they had been told was the kitchen, no one was there. The door to the stone corridor was still barred.

Bo was not at the dungeon door making barely audible pleas to be released. The silence increased the eeriness of what Charley had called the house's "torture chamber."

Perhaps it had actually been a kitchen. But Eva, a professor of literature, had read about enslaved people hung from meat hooks in smokehouses and kitchens and was not to be mollified. This room certainly had enough rusted chains and iron hooks appended to ceiling and walls to cause the direst suspicions about its slaveholding activities.

"Those hooks and chains really did hold bundles of drying herbs and cured wild game, even when I was a boy." Bo Wolfson came into the room.

The door he used seemed to be hacked through the rough planks of an outside wall. "Of course, I'm not sure how old any of that stuff was, even when I was little."

"Where is it all now?" Eva wanted to know.

"I imagine that it was used or thrown out as the house changed hands over the years." Bo shrugged as he pulled the heavy outer door shut behind him.

"Leave that open," Charley demanded. "How'd you get outside, anyway?"

"Anastasia of the tender heart released me." The two women glanced at each other.

Eva went for the kitchen pump. "Do you know where my daughter is now? I'm going to wash up and do laundry. I might as well do hers, too, while I'm at it." Eva grasped the pump handle with her free hand and lifted it ponderously as high as she could. "Charley, did you really work this thing?"

Bo muscled Eva out of the way. "Let me. It takes some getting used to."

Charley sighed. "Might as well get this day on the road. I'm for shopping. I'll bring you people something back." And she was gone.

"What about Anastasia?" Eva called, meaning shouldn't they try to find her before they went their separate ways. There was no answer but the thump of the heavy front door.

Holding her dirty clothes, Eva realized she was standing in front of a strange man who had only yesterday caressed her breast in a dark dungeon. Now she wore nothing but a white cotton shift over expanses of sun-bronzed skin. Sunlight from the opened outer door flew in a dusty shaft through the room. Her body was probably silhouetted by it.

She felt vulnerable. Could she get away from Bo?

Centered away from the plank-lined walls cluttered with wooden, clay, and rust-covered bowls and cooking implements, stood a massive table circled by rough benches. Eva made her way to this refuge and eased herself onto a bench's edge.

She fumbled for the remnants of their conversation. "So, because this room was a kitchen when you were a boy, you assume it was a kitchen during enslavement times. Is that right? I thought they tended to have outdoor kitchens then."

By now, Bo had gotten spurts from the mouth of the pump to splatter into the tin washbasin at his feet. Each succeeding gush spat a softening wad of water against the metal.

Working the pump handle, Bo looked at Eva. "That's right. There is, in fact, a museum-quality kitchen out back, just through that door." Bo jerked his chin at the door through which he'd come.

"So you don't really know what this room was used for, when the house was in its slaveholding heyday."

Bo paused his pumping and wiped his brow with a bare, sweaty forearm. He considered Eva attentively. "I wouldn't say that. But what makes you question it?"

Eva shuddered a little. She couldn't help it. "The room itself. It's not just the hooks and chains on the walls and ceilings. It feels secretive in here. Hidden." She shrugged with frustration. "It's just a feeling."

Bo left the pump and made his way through the earthy darkness. Eva watched him move between the walls that encircled them like the rings of dead trees. He sat beside her. "What does it feel like, Eva?"

Eva didn't want to say. She didn't like to talk about feelings as though they were facts. Some of the decisions she regretted most in her life had been based on her feelings.

But to be truthful, she argued with herself, so had all of her best decisions.

"The problem with feelings," Bo said gently next to her, "is that once you've made a decision based on them, you never find out how right they were. Whatever else would have happened, whatever disaster has been averted. You just have to trust that you felt your way into doing the right thing."

Eva looked up sharply in the ray of light from the outer door that sliced the darkness and spotlighted them together on the bench. She could see Bo clearly now, so close in the pathway of the light. He had no right to invade her space like this. She stood up.

As soon as she did, she felt silly. Here she was, ready to flounce off in a dress that looked like underwear, because he'd hit an old sore spot. Eva argued with herself that Bo didn't know about her past. He couldn't have known what those words would mean to her.

She softened her voice. "Is there enough water in that pan to wash these clothes? And do you think I can have some privacy to wash up, myself?"

"Sure." The unsettling intimacy of the moment was broken. Bo was all business. "I have that display almost ready for you."

"Display?"

"My work. I'll just get back to it. You can close the door to the hallway." Bo indicated the ominous stone corridor. "You don't have to lock me in like your cousin did."

Eva smiled. "She just acts tough so people don't get the idea that they can take advantage of us. She's always had to be like that. Even when our parents were alive."

"Why?" Was it the darkness, or did his coal-dark irises soften and the pitch pupils open, inviting her to believe that she was understood? Distant relative or no, he was a stranger.

Eva decided to confide. "Our parents couldn't have understood Los Angeles, fresh out of Mississippi, as they were. Even then, when we were children, L.A. was changing fast. It was becoming something that had never existed anywhere else. They couldn't have caught up, even if they'd known they needed to. I guess, as the oldest, Charley always felt she had to look out for me."

Bo's voice was tender. "Whose parents died first, Eva?"

Eva had the odd feeling that Bo knew the answer to this question perfectly well. *Then why is he asking?* Could he just want to get her talking about personal things, to match the intimate attire?

If she stood still one moment longer, Eva had the feeling that Bo would stand, come near, and slip an arm around her waist to draw her close and comfort her. She felt her heart hammer.

Eva turned from him as if she hadn't heard. She had her dirty clothes and Charley's soaking in the circular bottom of the tin pan when she heard him get up and walk softly down the stone corridor.

Only then did she look around. He hadn't closed either door.

Eva left the clothes and leaned against the door to the corridor, closing it first. She considered sliding the splintery bolt but didn't. She'd laughed at Charley's locking Bo into the dungeon more out of spite than out of appreciation. She herself hated to feel locked into dark spaces.

Eva contemplated the door to the outer yard. Bo was in the dungeon. Charley was long gone and would return through the hallway from the front entrance. Only Anastasia was unaccounted for, and having her daughter come in on her washing up was the least of Eva's worries about her right now. Where on earth had that grown child gone?

Eva left the back door open to invite Anastasia in and to give herself a chance to enjoy that shaft of light. It promised hope and normalcy in this room and, therefore, in the whole house someday. Sunbathing, Eva fished for her muddy tee shirt and used it to wash her face and body under the dampening white shift.

When she was done, Bo still had not returned from the dungeon. Eva went to that door and opened it. Like a petrified child facing a nightmare, she stared along the stony plunge into blackness. She would not go down there alone. She left the door open and returned to the wash tin.

Might as well do the laundry. Was there really no soap?

The evening before, they had ended their trip to the outhouse with a group splash under the pump in the backyard. Charley had brought soapy disposable cloths to Eva and Anastasia in their dusty bedrooms before they fell asleep. The soapy smell had been washed away overnight by Eva's tears, and brushing her teeth with the tip end of her tee shirt had been radically dissatisfying.

She searched the shelves with her fingertips on tiptoe. She hated to touch anything. There were probably rats, droppings, silverfish. Cockroaches.

"Ready?" Bo said in the doorway, and Eva shrieked. "Do I make you nervous?" he asked with exasperation.

"No. No, not at all." Eva struggled to catch her breath.

"You scream almost every time I speak to you."

"You're always sneaking up and breaking into my thoughts," Eva accused.

Bo looked hurt. Eva relented. "I'm not used to hearing a man's voice outside the university," she admitted. "It's been a while since I spent time with anyone but Charley and Anastasia."

Bo looked thoughtful. He held out his hand. "Here. Let me escort you. I don't think you'll like the stone hallway. I'll help you get through it."

Eva considered his hand. "Come on," Bo coaxed, imitating Eva's tone of the night before on the porch. Eva smiled slightly up at him and slipped her hand into his.

They took off into the bulging blackness of the corridor. Their speed frightened Eva a little. She wondered how well Bo knew the walls, how he could calculate their twisting closeness, avoid them, without any light to help him see. The smell of mold

63

and moss encircled her, filled her. She began to panic.

"Bo, slow down!" She couldn't tell if he heard her.

She recognized the sensation overcoming her. It was like the fear of falling asleep when one was little and had seen a scary movie or been told a creepy story. It was fear of being lost in one's own mind.

The hall of stones was like that, Eva realized. It hadn't just been the faintness of yesterday, the disorientation of arriving at a mansion to find it was a ruin. Fear of financial disaster, career suicide, and snakes. This hallway had engendered its own fear in her yesterday and was doing it again.

This hallway, for Eva, brought on the sharp awareness of her dread of descending into her own fears. It suspended her in that helpless moment of realizing that the out-of-control experience ahead would not be real, but it would be no less terrifying and entrapping, for all that.

Eva tugged at Bo's hand, trying to slip loose her fingers. She would escape his insouciant dragging of her into hell and run back to that promise of sunlight in the murky kitchen. No. She would run past that slice of light into the full glare of daylight and normalcy just outside the massive kitchen door.

Bo's fingers clamped more firmly around her own. He threw words at her over his shoulder. The tone was cheery, but it was lost on her. "See that light? We're almost there, Eva!"

She didn't want to be almost there. She didn't want to go one step further. She didn't want to have to retrace one step more when he freed her from this trek and allowed her to leave this stone prison. "No!" Eva snatched at her hand in a desperate bid to escape.

They really were almost there. Eva could tell when it struck her that they had stopped flying between the stone walls, over the slippery stone floor, and she could see Bo's head, the curve of his neck, the delicate outline of his ears. The darkness of his shape was suddenly framed by faint kerosene light through the doorway behind him.

Eva's hands were free. She could escape. She could not go back into that room. She could not stay in here.

Eva stumbled back from Bo a step or two before she turned and ran.

Now she truly frightened herself. Why was this panic so overwhelming? Why hadn't she prepared herself for it, braced herself to get through it?

She hadn't suspected it.

As Eva thudded along the corridor, her clogs raising dull echoes that rebounded at her from the walls, she wondered at herself. What was there in this dank stone tunnel to frighten her so? Even as she felt it, why couldn't she resist it?

True to the goal she had set as they neared the stone room, Eva did not stop in the paltry slice of light through the kitchen door. Once she reached the kitchen, she hurled herself outdoors like a sprinter at the finish line. Perhaps she would never bear to go into that awful house again.

Where was she?

Looking around, Eva thought that this must be where she and Charley and Anastasia had followed Bo to find the outhouse the night before. Now she recognized nothing. It had been twilight, fast deepening. They could see little except where Bo had pointed Charley's flashlight.

Now, dry, bright, and burning in sunlight, the backyard expanse stretched to weedy patches that must have been gardens. Bare pebbly walkways were littered with small stone circles and clusters of fallen planks that must have been huts. Beyond all that, a jungle of grassy cropland ran to the border of a forest.

The sight of the decayed farm staggered Eva. She stopped, panting from exertion, and stared.

She had finally regained the ability to think methodically and had squatted by a stone fire circle to investigate its relics when Bo called to her softly from behind. "Eva? Can I talk with you, please?"

Guiltily, Eva rose and turned from the fire circle to face him. "Listen, Bo. Before you say anything more, I want you to know that I'm sorry. I know you stayed up all night preparing to show me your work, and I know it's very important to you. It's about your connection to this house, I think, and to the people who lived in it. Your ancestors-"

"And yours."

"-And mine," Eva admitted, "whom you grew up knowing about, and I didn't."

"That doesn't make them any less yours, Eva."

Eva shook her head. She felt impatient with his patronizing. "Please. I know all that. That's not what I'm saying."

Bo was silent. He watched her and waited. She thought of herself crying in bed the night before over those shared, faceless, emotionally entangled ancestors. How could she feel them and yet not know them?

But she was sure she did. Felt them and couldn't bear it. Didn't understand it.

"What are you saying, Eva?"

Eva studied Bo. Could she tell him about this tangle of superstitious emotions? Why risk it? "I'm saying I'm sorry you've worked so hard to show me something, and I just can't stand to go into that dungeon again to see it. I can't, Bo."

"Dungeon?"

Eva tensed. But Bo said nothing more. In the silence, she realized his tone had been concerned, not mocking.

"Doesn't it strike you that way, Bo?"

"I guess we're fundamentally different. I like it in there." His tone was conciliatory, almost apologetic.

Eva reacted poorly to this. She felt herself rising as if to a challenge. "Oh, I'm sure," she said with barely restrained sarcasm. Why was he baiting her? "What is there to like?"

Bo refused to take offense. Instead, he reached for her hand, as he had when he had led her into the tunnel a few minutes earlier. He tugged her close. "Let's sit down and talk, Eva. Okay?"

Eva resisted. "I'm not going inside that house. I can't right now. I can't explain. I've just had enough of the dust and cobwebs and. . . . Oh, I don't know how to describe it, Bo."

"The history," Bo said. "Everyone feels it. You heard Uncle Ham and Aunt Portia last night. They can't stand it, either, and they grew up with it."

67

Put that way, as their history, Eva's revulsion for the place shamed her. "You don't seem to feel it," she pointed out.

Bo smiled and shrugged. "I'm a particular case. Come on. We don't have to sit inside. Do you want to go back to the front porch?"

She really didn't. But maybe it was the best they could do in her thin white cotton. The very thought of being taken to the nearest coffee shop, unwashed and wearing what only Bo would be polite enough to pretend did not look like an undergarment, embarrassed her.

Eva thought of yesterday's parade of vehicles. "Not to the front porch. Is there nowhere else?"

"I may have a place," Bo said slowly. "Let me know, when we get there, if it's not all right."

Eva was relieved by Bo's sensitivity. And she had decided to admire his resistance to so much as glancing at her other than keeping his firm gaze fixed on her eyes, despite what must be the nearly transparent quality of her cotton shift in this sunlight.

Eva followed Bo more trustingly than she would have thought herself capable of just a week ago. She did not wonder where they were going until they arrived in a bower of willow and wild rose vines.

A stone seat curved up from a mossy knoll in the midst of the scented curtain. Once seated, a winged angel rose before them above a square marble slab in the ground.

Eva gave a start and touched Bo's arm, as if for reassurance. She stared, petrified. Then she laughed at herself. "What's wrong with me?" she asked, eyes still fixed on the statue. "I thought-I could have *sworn*-that statue moved."

Bo took her hand again wordlessly when she released his arm. "There's much here to make one question what's real, Eva."

Did he really say that? She should ask, to be certain. But must she take her eyes off this glorious statue?

Staring at the opalescent angel, Eva felt she had perhaps discovered the reason for her coming here. "What did you say?" Eva shook her hand free and pointed. "Look, Bo. Doesn't it seem to *move*?"

"Is it an illusion?" His voice was hushed.

"You're the expert on this place. You tell me." When he said nothing, Eva shook her head in awe. "How does it do that? Seem to move like that? Just stone."

Even now that she was prepared for the trick, she could still swear to the gentle fluttering of fine gold and silver-tipped feathers in the angel's wings, as though it only seemed to alight but soon would lift again in soundless flight.

Bo took her face in one hand and turned her to him. She was jolted by the strength in his fingers, the power running like a current beneath his smooth earthy skin, the firmness of his unsmiling mouth. He was so solid, so still, compared to the ethereal, flickering vision of the angel. She wanted to turn back to it, but he held her cheeks and eyes.

"Do you see it?" The urgency of his voice stirred that deep fear she'd just escaped.

"See what?" Eva was equally cautious and breathless.

Bo waited a heartbeat too long before he answered. Eva used the instant of his uncertainty to pry his fingers from her face.

As soon as she had done so, she turned back with yearning for another glimpse of that magical, sparkling illusion of otherworldliness in the angel. To see-no, to *feel*-again that giddy magic as the angel scintillated in its incipient flight. It would burst from the constraints of the real world and free her, with it. Their inner beings would be freed.

But the illusion was gone. There was nothing of the statue now but expertly carved stone.

CHAPTER FIVE
TO TAKE UP THE CAUSE

Eva heard and winced at the irritation in her voice as she snapped, "She was just a crazy old lady."

Eva hadn't meant to be so harsh. But, she defended herself, the old woman was her great-great-great aunt, too. Eva's scathing dismissal of the woman's writings affected her as deeply as it did Bo.

But had Eva inserted enough greats? Quickly, Eva counted back five generations on her fingers. All the way back to forty years before the Civil War! Why, the woman who was Bo's great academic find was Eva's own age, forty-four, when the Civil War broke out and she began to compose her odd collection of stories. Forty-four was old for an enslaved African woman in those brutal days.

For some reason, it was the similarity of their ages that staggered Eva. She tended not to think of real people when she thought back so far, and certainly never to compare them to herself. The experiences her ancestors endured were so clouded and grotesque that they defied reality. Not real people raped, branded, mutilated, beginning and ending each venture limping the lush wooded roads naked in chained coffles as gentlefolk rode mindlessly by. Such images seared the mind and were gone before shock could set in. Denial.

Eva knew she had just lashed out unfairly at Bo in her outrage and rejection of the relationship he had thrust at her. The reality of this lonely, mad old woman feverishly scribbling her ravings tore at Eva's sense of self. She would not be descended, even obliquely, from such as Great-Great-Great-Aunt Baby Joy. Eva refused to claim this historical atrocity.

How tragic to be senile and alone, convinced that one's insanity could ever matter to a violent and powerful world.

Eva condescended, not daring to look at the hurt on Bo's face, "Of course, what this old woman wrote matters to *you*. *You're* her descendant. You're nostalgic for a sense of ancestry. But such nonsense is of no interest to academia."

Eva heard herself pontificating, a trick she'd learned at the California university she'd fled. She hated herself for it. *At least say* we, she scolded herself. *Say it matters to* us!

But she said nothing more. And the pronouncement silenced Bo. Was that why she'd done it? Guiltily, angrily, Eva picked at the fluted china coffee cup before her. She could not grasp it in her shaking fingers. She plunged her clenched hands into her lap.

Bo reached around the curve of the little table that separated them. His fingers dove after Eva's and dug between them to interlace in the warmth on her thighs. She had to look at him.

"Don't do that," he pleaded.

"Do what?" Challengingly.

"Don't leave me behind with this, alone," Bo said.

"What do you mean, 'behind'?"

"You know what I mean." Bo's voice was low. "I brought you into my work, into my world, and you're walking out and leaving me alone with everything I've opened up to you. Don't, Eva. You know better than this. Say something. Give me something back."

Eva assured herself that she didn't have to take this drama from him. Shouldn't take it. There were people at neighboring tables starting to stare.

She couldn't be quite sure why they were staring. Perhaps the clothes Bo had materialized with looked as odd on her to these Southern suburbanites as she had feared they would before she put them on. From nowhere-probably that notorious corner gas station-Bo had produced a flowered cotton skirt, a sullen burgundy peasant blouse, gaudy skinny sandals, and a suspiciously skimpy bra and panties set.

Still flustered by her view of the stone angel, Eva had retreated to the kitchen torture chamber to swirl her own and Charley's clothes in dirty water. She was spreading them on the front porch rail to roast in the morning shade when a silver Volvo pulled up into the U driveway. She was unaware that Bo had gone until he emerged.

When Eva first saw the offered clothes, she had not wanted to try them on. How silly of Bo. This costume reminded her of one of Anastasia's fantasy experiments.

But Bo's hinted reward of a cup of coffee at a real cafe was too much to resist. Eva had barely re-entered the house's dark kitchen before she'd flung off the white shift, pulled the ridiculous Gypsy costume on, and found herself transformed.

How good to be out of jeans and yet casually, effortlessly dressed. How delicious to feel so feminine in the pouting colors and flamboyant flowers!

How embarrassing to be so intimately flattered by the thoughtless gift.

Completely humiliated by her joy and eagerness to win Bo's approving smile, Eva had ridden beside him in the Volvo, buoyant. Now and then, as they flowed toward the edge of what Bo considered a tourist town, Eva wondered about Anastasia and Charley's whereabouts. Where could they have gotten off to, and what would they think if they returned to the abandoned house and found Eva gone?

White lace tablecloths and curtains at the Tea Party Cafe fluttered against buttercup-bright walls where were scattered oil paintings of local houses and gardens. Mismatched bookcases displayed antique novels, diaries, and cut glass vases of fresh flowers.

Eva dispensed with all guilt about her escape from her new house's filth and decay by deciding to buy something creamy and crusty to take back to her cousin and daughter. This little breakfast escapade was going to be delightful.

But as soon as their coffee and pastries were on the tiny table, Bo started in on his project. Eva was supportive until Bo described the great work he had lurking in her house's dungeon.

"Let me get this straight," she eventually interrupted him. "A besieged African American spinster spent the Civil War years recording her visitations with an angel who brought her ancestors back to life to tell her about themselves. Saving this-creation?-for posterity is your great project."

74

Bo regarded her and said nothing. He didn't need to speak. His disappointment was clear enough.

Because he hesitated before he defended himself, Eva filled the silence with an intensified attack. "And you seriously think that the academic world will want to read this garbled account with the uneven grammar and spelling that even you have trouble deciphering. Bo! You've been locked up in that dungeon too long. Come out and breathe the air, for heaven's sake."

It was at this point that she'd denounced the old woman as crazy and then realized, with an agonized sense of kinship, that Great-Great-Great-Aunt Baby Joy had been exactly her own age when she'd started her delusional journal entries.

Now Eva couldn't help looking down into her brightly flowered lap where Bo's slender fingers entrapped her own.

Here she was, dressed like a masquerading teenager in a cafe that her parents could never have entered by the front door just a generation ago, ridiculing that childless lunatic for her harmless fantasies.

It was Bo who said, "Let's get out of here." With his free hand, he gathered up the four bags of pastries they'd collected as he talked, one new set for each time the waitress had approached to hint that they had occupied their table a long time. With his other hand, Bo led Eva through the tables of staring guests to the belled glass door, as though she could not have found her own way.

Or as though he knew how hurt and frightened she felt, Eva thought to herself as they got into his car. The existence of Baby Joy's composition profoundly disturbed her.

Should she read it? Could she?

Why should she? She already knew it was trash, the psychotic inventions of a woman raised in secrecy and fear.

How mind-eroding Baby Joy's existence must have been, knowing that life depended on her mother's denial of her, her siblings, and her father, and knowing that such renunciation was almost useless, anyway. Hiding in that stone chamber from the sporadic lynch raids at night, smelling the smoky scent of human bodies burning, filling the house. Hearing the screams of the people who had raised her, as they were caught and killed.

Surely this horrific childhood was the reason Baby Joy had grown into a woman who created a world of angels and powerful magic people who could fly out of enslavement, poison enslavers with impunity, transform into wild beasts, and rampage to their hearts' content. Not folklore come to life. Lunacy.

The whole thing was so horribly sad. Of course, Eva would never read it.

Eva hung her head as the car drew her back to that historic trap she must learn to call home. She hadn't realized she was weeping until Bo reached for her hand again. "You're tired, babygirl. We're both tired."

Weeping twice in twenty-four hours. What was this move doing to her?

And poor Bo. Eva hadn't given his fatigue a thought. But surely he could not have slept more than an hour or two before dawn. "Did you sleep at all?" Eva asked him tentatively.

Bo shrugged and said nothing.

"Will you sleep now?"

"I might as well."

The finality of his tone worried her. But Eva decided to ask nothing further just yet. She knew whatever she said would degenerate into her deep distaste for the very idea of his preserving that madwoman's efforts at entertaining herself.

It was indecent. It was unfair. It was unkind of Bo to expose an old woman's insanity to the academic community.

He should have left that poor spinster to her fantasies and her pain, in privacy. He should have burned those papers as soon as he understood what they were.

Perhaps Eva would persuade him.

Perhaps she would put him out and burn them, herself. They were her property, after all, weren't they?

Eva got out of the car as it swung to a stop, silent with her resolve. This afternoon Bo would sleep. This evening, she would invite him to whatever Charley helped them scavenge for dinner. And during dessert, Eva would explain that Bo needed to return to his own home-wherever that was-and leave behind everything he had found in her house.

And by tomorrow evening, Great-Great-Great-Aunt Baby Joy's distorted legacy would be no more.

Laughter burst from the massive front door of the house before Charley emerged from it, leading a team of teenagers. *Friends for Anastasia!* Eva thought happily. Then she noticed that they were all headscarved and shaking out brooms, dustpans, and dry rags. A cleaning team.

"Hey!" Eva called.

The group looked straightforwardly at her and Bo, waved, and waited to shake hands, smile, and make introductions. Close up in the shade of the verandah, they were a gorgeously open-faced bunch. They all seemed to know Bo already. Of course, Eva thought. Country living and plantation distant relatives. How could she forget?

They were polite, eager, warm-hearted, and ready to get back to work. What was Charley paying them?

As Bo descended the porch steps to make his way around the house, one of the freshest-faced teens gently pulled at Eva's puffy sleeve. Eva turned to her.

The smooth-skinned young woman gestured at the spot on the rail where Charley's and Eva's underwear had been drying between thick slabs of jeans. The underwear was gone.

"I put *those things* away in your bedroom," the teen whispered conspiratorially to Eva. "Y'all don't *never* want to leave *those things* out round here. This here conjure country. Folks know how to use things like that against you."

Eva stared. Was this girl telling her that her panties had been in danger of kidnap for purposes of voodoo? "Thank you," was all Eva managed to say before the young conspirator vanished back through the front door.

Eva looked desperately about for Bo. Sleepy or not, he could explain this kind of thing. He was heading around the far corner of the house, making for the kitchen door to his dungeon, no doubt. Eva rushed to catch up.

But it was Charley who collared Bo before he could disappear. "Bo, you probably know how to find that plumber your uncle Ham said he'd get out here today." Coming from Charley, it sounded like an accusation. "Drive down and tell him we're waiting. I want a flushing toilet in before dark."

Bo turned without a word and headed back to his car. "Charley, he hasn't slept," Eva said in his defense.

Charley lifted an eyebrow. "How would you know that?" She ran a disapproving glance up and down Eva's costume.

Eva turned and flounced after Bo. "Let me drive," she said before he slid behind the wheel.

She really wanted to ask where Anastasia might be, Eva thought to herself as they pulled out of the drive. But Bo's mumbled instructions about navigating the tortuous country backroads seemed to be all he could manage without drifting into sleepy ramblings. He was, indeed, sound asleep by the time they pulled up at the junkyard that proclaimed itself a plumbing establishment.

The plumber was hearty in his welcome and effusive in his assurances that he'd be right out. "I'm plumb happy-" Eva accused him silently of using that ridiculous phrase deliberately and did not smile "-that you all done showed up. Y'all wanna choose the fixings?" Eva realized he meant "fixtures" and followed him into his warehouse.

She was thrilled to find an antique pink porcelain set, complete with a claw-footed tub newly re-enameled inside and with a pull chain for flushing the toilet. She chose it and waited in the idling Volvo for the huge man and his liquid-jointed assistants to load it on a truck and take off ahead of her.

Following, Eva chided herself for making fun of his English. He was probably another distant relative. And anyway, they certainly needed his goodwill if they were going to make that house habitable.

Bo slept on the drive back to the house. Eva had wanted to question him more closely about where Anastasia said she'd be going. But she hated to force him to waken, given his hopeful overwork throughout the night and her plans to destroy it all.

Eva convinced herself that Anastasia would be among Charley's team of industrious teens. But when they reached the house and she had tugged Bo by the arm out of his car, she scouted the smiling faces hauling uncovered furniture out onto the mown front lawn and realized Anastasia's was not among them.

Now Eva was worried. This was unfamiliar territory. Despite her irritation with Charley's obsession, there probably were snakes. Eva hated to think of the many misadventures that could greet Anastasia out exploring the southern countryside. Anastasia's insouciance was notorious in L.A.

Eva hunted down Charley, who had trailed the plumber and his men to the kitchen.

"What do you think, Eva?" Charley said as soon as she caught sight of her cousin. "They say they can make this whole kitchen into a bathroom, but I think that would be a waste. Though I guess it *would* be a treat to bathe with a fire going in the fireplace, in the winter. But they say they can run the water to this pantry here for a little bathroom, and that would free up the kitchen to be made into a real kitchen. Don't you think that's the way to go?"

"Yes, Charley. But tell me. Have you seen Anastasia?"

"Not since this morning. Okay, Mr. Jackson. Let's go with the pantry. Did you say it has a door that opens to the hall? I've seen those old houses where the bathroom opens into the kitchen, and I won't stand for none of that."

The plumber's team was busy digging a pit for a septic tank near the outhouse and far from the backyard pump and well. As soon as Eva approached them, they began to gesticulate toward the woods and explain in a warm pool of mellifluously Southern accents how difficult it was to gauge where to dig without unearthing bones from the old burying pits. Eva recoiled with horror when she realized they were referring to burial grounds for the enslaved. Was history really such a part of daily life here?

Eva assured the young plumbers that she, unlike Charley, had not come to check on the progress of their work. She was looking for her daughter.

Questioning them about a nymph of Anastasia's description produced quantities of appreciative commentary but no information. No one had seen her, as much as they would, apparently, all have liked to.

Discouraged, Eva returned to the house and contemplated the black descent into stone, where

Bo had retreated to rest like a minotaur in his labyrinth. She should have wakened him and questioned him in the car. Could she follow him and question him now?

She must.

Bravely, Eva went to Charley to demand a flashlight. The plumber absently handed her one of the two strapped to his tool belt, and she rushed back to the stony corridor before she could lose her nerve.

Eva flicked on the circular beam and descended into her personal chaos.

Eva had meant to hurry, hoped to rush behind the light. But she could not. Instead, she discovered that the best she could do was creep in the wake of the illuminated stones, studying sets of them, lumps of them, before she passed over and went on her way.

Lichen clung to the curving steel-colored surfaces. Dampness seeped from the earth beneath. And still that endless trickle sounded from somewhere near. *Drip. Drop.*

Behind the light, Eva felt herself slip into that place beyond thought that roused and came to the forefront of her mind in this stone hallway. She was so profoundly alone in here. She remembered other times, younger times, before words had come into her mind to shape her thoughts with order, reason, and to people her imagination with those who could have heard and understood, saving her from solitude.

She was lonely when her parents died.

Even now she could hear their voices murmuring in the space between the echoes that

82

rose from the stones. *Eva wasn't. . . . Eva didn't. . . . Eva, where. . . ? Honey. . . .* Whatever could be the point of such cruelty as her mind inflicted upon her with these fleeting memories?

Eva had suspected that something like this might happen again. She accused herself of poor planning for having let Bo sleep in the car. Why hadn't she just wakened him and asked him what her daughter might have said before disappearing?

But speaking of poor planning. Whatever could be the reason that this cavelike passageway had been built? Perhaps if she knew, she would not be so vulnerable to the tricks her mind played on her in here, Eva reasoned with herself. Storage space? It seemed too damp. A cooler for fresh game in the winter? She must ask Bo if he knew why the stone corridor had been built.

Then suddenly Eva remembered the picture Bo had painted just that morning of the enslaved people running to hide from patrollers and lynch mobs in the house's fortress of stone. But that was later, a century or more after the house had been built.

All the while Eva thought, studied the stones in passing, and chatted with herself in her mind, the echoing voices about her sharpened, clarified. Were not her parents' any more. *He lied. . . . She tried. . . . They ran. . . . We died. . . .*

A small gasp escaped Eva. She silenced the cries that wanted to follow. She would not panic. These sounds were a trick of fatigue and darkness. There were probably studies about such things. *Alone. . . . The children be crying. . . . Why they doing this to us?*

Don't leave me behind. . . .

That was nothing but a memory of what Bo had said to her earlier, Eva decided with a twinge of hysterical relief. Nevertheless, it was horrible to hear it bouncing off the stones about her head.

And it was fascinating. Against her will and better judgment, Eva listened. She strained now to make out the syllables of the rising, falling, senseless sounds. Whose voices could those possibly be? They must be someone's she had known, even long ago as a child, or they could not be surfacing from her mind like this, she told herself against the feeling of eavesdropping.

Words bubbled up from the hectic whispers. *Mother! . . . Angel? . . . Rose. . . .*

Were these names or nouns, things or people she might have yearned for? Eva tried to think of the role these words might have played in her life. Loss. Hope. Beauty?

She had scraped her childhood memories to the barest skeletons by the time she found herself at the minotaur's lair. *It's like a mythical beast should live here,* Eva thought. *What is it about this house that makes me think such fantastic things? No wonder this house drove Baby Joy crazy.*

Bo had left no light burning. Eva's tiny circle guided her into the chamber. She was shaken by her experiences in the corridor and disoriented, like a sleepwalker. She felt unsure anymore of why she had come. She made her way cautiously over to a still form on the floor.

It was Bo. The edge of her circle of light hinted at his sleep-smoothed brow, the curve of his bronze cheekbones, and the soft stillness of sharply outlined lips.

Why am I so antagonistic toward him? Seeing Bo helpless in sleep, remembering his disappointment at her disapproval of his project, his reaching for her hand, caught at her. In her own shaken state, troubled by the violent reality of the voices she'd fought through to get down the corridor, Eva could appreciate loneliness. It occurred to her that Bo's great project must be waiting for her in this room.

I'll make it up to him for being so dismissive earlier today. I'll take an interest, see what he's doing before I wake him to ask about Anastasia. Eva turned, swinging her beam of light to see.

Ugly stones bulged out from the walls at her. Blackened mossy masses loomed in her feeble light. Eva didn't want to see. "But how will I find his work without looking around me in this room?" she asked herself aloud and shuddered with aversion. She did not want to be here, did not want to see these still massive stones squatting about her, piling up to hem her in.

Frightened, the very walls seemed to whisper.

There, Eva announced to herself with knee-weakening relief. That ugly mass just over there, *That must be Bo's project,* huddling in the corner farthest from where he lay.

Timidly, Eva moved from the crossroads of the chamber's threshold, from which she could still escape, committing herself to an entry into this most awful of rooms.

What are those? Coffins?

It seemed, from where Eva stood, that rows and rows of wooden planks lined the floor with

85

something glistening just above their splintery surfaces. *Mass graves unearthed in this dungeon? Is that what the place is? A homemade mausoleum? No wonder it's so disturbing.*

But from their talk in the cafe, Eva had thought that Bo wanted to show her Baby Joy's writings.

Come. Come see. Our past, your future, the world's only reality.

Why were the voices now so sinister?

Eva's teeth began to chatter. Yet she drew nearer the rows and rows of wood.

Again relief weakened her. Her first impression of coffins must have been a depth deception. Perhaps the piles of stones confused the eye, from a distance in the dark, creating optical illusions of everything they dwarfed in the room. For, up closer now, Eva could see that the rows of wooden planks rested on the chamber's stone floor. The shiny stuff on their surfaces was neither water nor slime, but glass. Beneath the glass, pressed protectively into the drying wood of the planks that raised them from the damp floor, were sheets and sheets, stretched side by side, of aged, cracked brown paper.

So this is Baby Joy's work. Or only a fraction of it?

Heedless of her skirt against the damp stones, Eva squatted close to see. She shone her brave little light onto the defiant work of years. *How long did it take Joy to write all this? And I don't think this is everything. Look at those wooden trunks cowering in the far corner. How can Bo stand to go over there and get the sheets out to press them?*

He is a good boy, a voice from the corridor whispered, *to take up the cause. Evil child, why do you deny him?*

Shaking in her hand, Eva's flashlight yet caught and illuminated mountainous squiggles of aged homemade ink faded to a brown only slightly darker than that of the rough paper upon which they'd been penned. The unpleasant accusations of the voices that had followed her, apparently, from the hallway, were becoming hard to shut out. Eva's teeth began to chatter faster, rattling her whole body with her growing fear that, in this room, she was unbalanced.

Trembling, afraid and unwilling to read what Baby Joy claimed to have transcribed from the spirits of dead people, Eva crouched and fought with herself. For the longest, she could not bring herself to make out any of the faded, looping words.

Will these be the written words of those vicious voices in the hall? I don't want to know what they have to say. If I believed in evil spirits. . . . Of course, I don't, but I don't want to read this.

Hear me, Eva had just perceived on the page where her flashlight beam rested as the lesser of two evils, as she could not bear to swing it upward and risk seeing the craggy, brooding stones, when Bo's sleep-heavy voice called to her.

"Eva? Baby, is that you in here? Come over here, Eva. Come here."

Eva whirled to look at him, relief and fear distorting her face. *Not alone. I don't want to feel alone in this hellish room.*

Bo's barely opened eyes glittered, reflecting the edge of Eva's beam. He watched her with remarkable calm, as if he were not surprised to see her here, in this room she couldn't even enter with his help. *Doesn't he wonder how I got here alone?*

He knows we brought you. Go to him, Eva.

Terrified now, wanting only to ask about her daughter and beg for an escort out of his stone maze, Eva rose and picked her way over to Bo.

She kept the light from his eyes and therefore didn't see when he propped himself up on one elbow to reach for her.

The warm touch in the cool dampness startled her. She jumped and gasped.

"You're afraid." Bo's voice was soothing. "There's no need. Come sit with me here on the sleeping bag."

Eva relented and felt herself pulled down beside Bo's body. She felt the flat muscles of his abdomen twist and ripple against her hip. He had reached behind himself for something. He brought it forward onto Eva's lap. She felt the hard corners of a large three-ring binder.

"Some of Baby Joy's work," Bo said and sat up against her back. His chest pressed to hold her up, as though to support her like a chair. He could read over her shoulder, if she chose to look into the collection now. *I don't want to read this now, in here. Will I hear those damnable voices, if I read this? Will they follow me out of here? Do they come from this awful collection? Was Baby Joy haunted as well as insane? Evil spirits. . . .*

Eva sat with her back against Bo, facing his glass-covered display. Could she ask him about the voices and the incessantly dripping water? Did he not hear the sounds that plagued his stone retreat? What would he say if she told him that she had been

88

pursued in here by menacing voices that said devastatingly sad things?

He will tell me I'm crazy, Eva thought, *and maybe I am. But I'm not ready to hear that just yet.* She opened the notebook and shone her beam onto its first page. *A table of contents? A journal section. Story titles. How many stories are in this one notebook?* Eva began to turn the crisp pages.

The first pages were charts of births and relationships. *These must be the names of people who lived here. What a goldmine of historical information.* Eva turned to Bo, his face stopping her cheek at her shoulder. "Why have you only charted the names of women, Bo?"

Bo murmured at her ear, "Baby Joy only wrote women's stories. Those are the dates I could be sure of, because of the incidents Joy describes."

"All the way back to the early seventeen hundreds?"

But Bo said nothing in reply to this. Instead, his hand came gently, faintly around her waist, settled into a comfortable place, and pressed her back against him. "You've stopped shaking, Eva. Do you feel better, close to me?"

Yes, she felt better. But she wished he would stir, rise from the sleeping bag, offer to take her back toward the sunlight.

Eva had been brave to come in here, and braver still to stay and take a look at Bo's beloved project. But it was unreasonable to think that this stillness, this dark, this silence interrupted only by odd whispery echoes and the drip of stale water wouldn't begin to wear on her. Perhaps she should take this notebook and go.

But she still had to ask about Anastasia.

Eva turned toward Bo, clutching the huge plastic notebook to her chest. She leaned close and whispered, "Bo, I need to ask you about my daughter."

So close, Eva was startled to realize that a warm, sweetish smell came from Bo's skin, like a baby's. Attracted and curious, she leaned closer.

It had to have been the darkness. The silence. The aloneness.

Bo turned toward her, probably to answer, to ask what she wanted to know. But his hand fell upon her ankle and from there moved swiftly upward, under her skirt and out again over her hip, up her back, and to her shoulder as he lay down so that she curved close over him.

CHAPTER SIX
POWER AND TENDERNESS

Bo's searching fingers startled Eva and seared her out of her mist of fear and curiosity. His touch, demanding and restless, left on her skin a trail of fine lifted hairs and in her mind flashes of intimacy, images of embraces urgent and sweating shared between them, two rational people swept up in unreasoning need.

Now the voices in her mind and from all along the walls seemed to murmur of the void opened by passion. *Trust me. . . . Let me. . . . Wait for me. . . .* Eva responded frantically to both the voices and Bo when she cried out, "No! Don't."

Silence, wet and heavy, oppressed her as the barrage of echoes abruptly ceased. She heard herself and Bo panting in the sudden quiet.

Then one lone voice took up the chant. *Did anyone ever love me? Will you?*

Where did that voice come from? Surely not Bo.

And Eva hoped desperately that it had not come from her. Had she spoken aloud? She was losing her mind in this place. She must get out.

Eva was amazed to realize that she had not yet pulled back from Bo. His hand still rested on her shoulder, weighting her with his insistence that she come closer. She wished he would let go.

Lying beneath her like this, holding her still in the sightless dark, their faces almost touched. Eva smelled the mild sweetness of Bo's skin, the slight sharpness of his breath from sleeping, and felt the moist warmth of his mouth as he spoke now almost against her lips. "Are you afraid?"

Inanely, Eva insisted, "I asked you about my daughter."

Alone. Don't leave me alone.

Who said that? "Do you hear?" Eva asked.

The bulky notebook pressed them apart. Holding it, Eva's arm was caught between the pointed plastic corners and the swelling, dipping flow of the valley from Bo's chest to his abdomen. She felt his heartbeat, her arm pressed and released by the rise and fall of his breathing. *I remember. . . .*

Bo shifted. The movement brought his leg to the inside of her knee, brought their bodies closer, though she couldn't tell how. He seemed everywhere, his comforting warmth, the promise of power and tenderness if she put down the notebook and nothing more was between them.

Are you afraid? Don't fear me. Surely he had spoken this time. Those were some of the very words she had heard him say only an instant ago.

It must be Bo whispering, must have been him all along. And yet, Eva thought with returning panic, the voice was not quite his own. Perhaps heavy with sleep? Weighted with deep feeling?

For her. Bo desired her. Eva shuddered. She never gave herself to men who made her feel vulnerable. Never.

Eva's involuntary movement dislodged Bo's light hold on her. His hand fell from her shoulder but returned to her ankle. He slipped off the sandal he had bought her just that morning. Then his fingers started up the rise along her leg more slowly.

I will never hurt you.

Her eyes had adjusted to the darkness enough so that, staring, she could see as well as feel that Bo's lips had not moved to speak but had only opened, inviting contact.

It was the darkness. It was the utter aloneness of this place. She had met this man just twenty-four hours ago. He was a stranger, despite the whispers of intimacy all around them.

Eva didn't remove Bo's questing hand. She didn't dare touch it. It had reached her knee, lifted the flowered skirt so lightly she'd felt nothing until he hesitated and let his hand rest heavily on her skin.

"Eva." His human voice, so real after the ghostly whispers, jarred her somewhat out of the trance the walk through the hallway had induced.

Eva put one hand down on the sleeping bag and mattress to help her find her way to her feet. She would have to search for the sandal once she was standing. But now she had dropped the flashlight. Its light was suddenly muffled against the pile of the sleeping bag. The darkness around them was almost absolute.

Eva's other arm continued to hug the notebook, Bo's project, between her breasts. She opened her mouth to breathe, to calm her agitation, to steady herself.

Bo's hand flew from her knee to the back of her head to hold her still as his tongue found her skin in the darkness, searching, and his lips sought response. Her cry of surprise, the deep breath she'd meant for herself, both were caught and shared between them in the sudden seal his mouth made against her own.

Bo's other hand slid under Eva's gathered gypsy blouse.

It moved along her waist, molded itself to the rise of her back to curve again over her shoulder, this time plunging forward to her breast. His movement was rough. He knocked the three-ring binder from between them.

She felt his body jerk, unseen, against her as he used his knee and then his foot to shove the heavy collection of his hard work away from where they lay.

No, Eva thought but could not say. There was no space, for her mouth was clasped by his own, and then there was no need, for the hand that had come between them to her breast now dove to lift her skirt between her legs, circled to the base of her spine, and caught her up close against him.

Bo rolled her to her back and lifted her to him, holding on. Eva's hands had gone against Bo's chest, pushing at him in her surprise. As he lifted her against the heat rising between them, the heat pressing apart her legs, her arms went around his neck to hold on. *We have to stop!* Had she said anything?

She must have resisted, said something to make him let her go. For suddenly Bo released her mouth, freed it from his own, faced her in such darkness that she could barely make out the outline of his cheeks, his head. *Say something to me!*

As she stared, yearning, gathering reason enough to force herself away from him, she felt his hand move deliberately down her back to the rise of her buttocks, knead, wait, linger, and squeeze again. *I wish he would speak. Persuade me. No, I hope he won't. Am I afraid?*

He pulled her closer, into the heat of his own body. With the full length of his body on hers, he slipped both of his hands lower, down along her thighs. *He wants me to know that he wants this. He wants to make me want him. Can't he tell? I do want him.*

Bo's lips touched her neck in the darkness. He licked and nipped. Into the damp trail he had just made, now he whispered against her skin, "Will you, Eva? Give yourself to me. Now. Now. Now."

When she didn't dare answer, thought she should say no but wondered how bad it would be if she said yes, couldn't decide, Bo's hands slipped under her spread legs. He pulled her tighter against him, harder, so she couldn't mistake what he meant to have, and opened her to the smooth rocking motion of his hips. It was this rhythm that he emphasized with his breathless, "Now. Now, baby. Let me in. Now."

The last word was a gasp before silence.

Bo gave up speaking. His lips pressed in an open circle at the tender bend where Eva's throat dipped to her collarbone. Eva felt his tongue slip between his lips against her skin again. She waited to bear the lick, the nip, that had excited her before. But this time Bo drew hard on her skin, sucked and sighed as he rocked with her.

He was ready to make love. She could feel the burning bundle even through his jeans, a thickening mound that had already filled the greedy gap between her spread legs. He continued to move, to maneuver, to touch everything all at once, pressing a pleasurable response from her, even here, even now, even at the edge of her fear. *He wants me to make the decision. I'm safe, this way. I won't.*

Bo broke the sucking seal made by his lips to whisper, "Let me," his voice breathless, and then he lowered his mouth along her neck again, his lips and tongue tickling a damp line that tingled from the small bones just under her ear to the fragile jutting just above her breast.

"Eva, tell me yes. Tell me now." His voice grew harsh. "Let me have you. Let me love you. Tell me yes." His mouth closed again on hers.

The warmth. The building heat. The taste of him, clean and smooth and moist. *Breathe. Think. Try to say no, try to say not now,* Eva urged herself, for she feared that if she yielded, she couldn't survive this. She would care too much, yearn too much. Need him too much. *I'm afraid. I don't do things like this. I don't feel things like this.*

Eva held on to him as she resisted him. *How can I?*

That urgency filled and burned the whole of her responsive, opening legs. Only his jeans kept the hunger in her from swallowing him in.

Maybe just a little more. "Yes," she whispered, and he lifted himself away.

She cried out and reached through the darkness for him. And as his lips sealed hers and his tongue returned to warm her mouth and his arms to gather her in, somehow the barriers between them slid away and the naked heat and power of him rocked into her, a little, away, more, more, and now all.

She could take no more. Yearning broke in spasms inside her that gushed a wet pathway, sucking in all he had to offer. Her body swallowed him in, reached, swallowed again and again. She could not get enough of his overwhelming surges into her.

Eva heard herself gasp as the heat between them washed away in waves of relief and release. Weakness shuddered through her between each straining peak of ecstasy. *What is this? I think I've heard of this kind of thing. Maybe I've lost my mind. I love this man.*

Eva heard herself moan. *Did I make that sound?* She wrapped her legs more firmly around his working thighs. She heard herself cry out, trying to take in the last of the anguish, trying to taste the last of the hot sweetness as it receded.

When it was gone, and she could see and think again in the bright blackness, Eva pressed herself more tightly to Bo. She trembled a little in his arms. *Don't look at me,* she prayed. *Don't say my name. Don't let me go. What have I done? What heaven is in this man's arms!*

Could Bo read her mind? Silently, lightly, his hand hovered above her belly. He lifted the gypsy blouse away from the sweat-wet skin, and Bo's lips lowered to her belly.

He began to kiss her skin gently, increasing the range of his kisses as she stroked the fine tight curls cut so close to his beautifully shaped head. Bo's hand moved imperceptibly from her blouse to her knees, slid between them and under the ridiculous flowered skirt now plastered to her thighs. Again, the filmy moist material lifted away.

97

Bo began to kiss her legs. This was a different experience for Eva, and she lifted and parted her knees to ease the straining desire growing where her new thong panties, her skirt, and Bo's stroking fingers all came together.

She had not planned for the suddenness with which Bo's tongue would find that aching point of want that she could no longer bear to squeeze between her shut legs.

She could not see him, but suddenly it seemed that again he was everywhere, and his head was down in the area of her lap, and that incredible warmth and tugging at the very pinpoint of her excruciating pleasure would soon drive her out of her mind.

She seized his head and held it close to the gush of ecstasy that threw her hips forward. Bo clung to her, murmured as he licked and stroked, finger and mouth extracting emotions Eva had not known she could feel. Who was this wild woman using her body to act out like an ecstatic animal?

When the rage subsided, Eva's taut legs and flattened tummy relaxed. She collapsed into the comforting depths of the mattress and waited for her world to stop spinning.

In jerks, the dizziness halted. Bo had climbed back up to lie beside her. She realized he held her in his arms.

Don't speak to me. Don't make me speak for this stranger who possesses me.

Bo said, nuzzling the tender tight skin behind her ear, "What is it you're afraid of, Eva? Me? How can I convince you that you don't need to be afraid of me?"

From somewhere came the now familiar echoes. *Can't you tell when you in love? How stupid is you, gal?* And to her amazement, she laughed. Companionably, Bo chuckled with her.

Eva said, "I've never done anything like this. I don't know what to think about myself."

"I know what to think. That you're too beautiful, too sensual, not to have done anything like this. What do you mean? Making love in the dark?" Again, his hand began its quest. "Making love in a cave?"

Eva said, "Making love with a stranger."

"Wolves and doves and eagles meet and mate for life, on sight alone. It's instinct. It's the oldest learning capacity we humans have." He was whispering. Despite the academic words and tone, his message struck a deep and melancholy chord in Eva.

"I've never believed in love at first sight for rational people. I can't say I've ever believed much in love. Except for love between family members," she amended guiltily, her mind hazily returning to Anastasia.

Bo teased, "And how do we get families, baby?"

"Bo, have you, I mean are you, well . . . married?"

"No." Simply. Firmly.

"Have you been?"

"No."

"Why not, Bo?"

"I was waiting."

"For?"

"Love," Bo said simply. "At first sight. That thing you don't believe in. That's the only kind that I do believe in, Eva. Isn't that ironic?"

It took her a moment to say, "That can't be reasonable, Bo. You're an educated man, a professor at a prestigious college. You know that people have to learn trust. They have to decide to make commitments over time."

Bo said carefully, his hand stroking her leg, her tummy, her breast, "Because I'm reasonable, Eva, I know that love is learned over a young lifetime. That's where family comes in. If you've had a loving family growing up, you know all there is about what you can love. If you're in touch with your emotions, you will sense that potential when you meet that person."

"Is there only one chance to love, for each person, in your philosophy, Bo?"

Bo was thoughtful. They had turned to face each other and now talked within inches of each other's whispering lips. It took no effort for Bo to move just enough to kiss Eva's mouth before he answered. "In my philosophy, I would hope that each person only needs one chance."

Bo lay back and drew Eva onto his chest. "I once kept birds for company. Two at a time, always a couple. I would catch one and take it outside in its cage. When it drew a mate, attracted a bird who would come and hover around its cage, I would trap that one, and that's how I would make my wild pairs. It was uncanny, but they would live and die as if they were one being.

"But once, I bought a pair of parakeets. I didn't think their bond would be so strong, since I chose

100

them both and they had no say in the matter. But then the female died before her time."

Bo's voice caught. After a while, Eva thought he would not go on. But as she said, "Never mind, Bo," he said, "Never mind how she died, but it was suddenly."

Bo took a deep breath. "I want you to know about this, Eva. When I took the female's body from the cage, the male was frantic. He flew out while the cage door was open and pecked at my hand to get her away from me. I was the one who had worked half the summer to make enough money to buy her for him, but he wanted to protect her from me. As if I was the threat. Of course, he was a bird and he couldn't understand my role as caretaker. But he had never done anything like that before."

Bo looked at Eva in the dark. "Can you understand? He was a bird, an animal we think is driven only by instinct, but like many bereaved people, he refused to believe that his mate was dead until he'd flown all around this room, looking for her. Only when I let him get to her body did he calm down. And I caught him and got him back inside his cage. I would have let him go, but I was afraid of his frenzy.

"As it was, as soon as he was alone again in the cage, he beat himself against the bars. I did everything I could to calm him down again. I covered the cage. I sat by him and whistled to him for hours. All I needed was to leave him just long enough to go find him a new mate. I was going to ask my parents for money to buy another one. So you see, I do believe in a second chance at love. Many chances, in fact." He smiled at her. Even

101

through the murkiness, Eva could see that his smile was lopsided.

Eva reached for Bo's hand. She wondered if he realized what part of his story had distressed her the most. Where were his parents? Why had he dealt with this tragedy alone here in this dungeon, at so young an age that he had to work half the summer to earn enough money for a parakeet?

Bo squeezed Eva's hand in his. "I finally left him to bury her. When I got back and the cage was quiet, I already knew what I'd find before I even took off the cover. He was dead in the bottom of the cage, just that fast. I've never kept birds since. But I learned some of my most valuable lessons from that last pair. I learned to trust what I believe is true."

Eva didn't want to risk the banal things she was afraid she might say, avoiding the question that plagued her. *Why were you alone here for so long, so young?* Bo's pain was palpable. She leaned forward, felt for his cheek, and kissed it.

Bo said, "Love is our first instinct, and it is true."

"Why did you keep birds?"

"For companionship. I was a pretty lonely kid."

"Why were you lonely, Bo?"

"Can't you tell? I'm different."

Perhaps this was not an unusual self-assessment, Eva thought. But Bo said it ponderously, expectantly, as if Eva's response to this statement would be more crucial than she might realize.

"Tell me about that. What makes you think you're different, Bo, and how did that make you a lonely child?" Eva had seen nothing in Bo to warrant his being ostracized as a child. Whatever was different about him must have been known by reputation instead of by observation. Was he bookish? Shy? Awkward in sports?

Unwillingly, Eva thought of the myths in Baby Joy's writings. Would they have been known to children when Bo was a boy?

"I was a solitary child, Eva."

"An only child?"

"That, too. Only and lonely."

"Weren't there children in this huge extended family of yours that you could play with?" Eva thought of her envy of Bo's family and sense of ancestry that had her crying into the dawn.

"Sometimes," Bo said. "When I could trust myself."

"Bo, trust yourself? What on earth can you mean?" Eva felt a twinge of real alarm. Alone, smothered in the blanket of pitch dark created by stone all around, below her feet and edging toward her from the walls, what was she now discovering about the man to whom she'd yielded up her sensuality?

Bo selected his words with obvious caution. "What frightens you about coming down the stone corridor, Eva? It used to soothe me. There were years, when I was a child, that the trek down the stone corridor was all that I had to make me feel that I was normal, that there were those in the past who would have understood me. That I was, basically, all right."

His low voice mesmerized. Eva felt herself slip into a suspended state, not dreaming, but not quite in control of her thoughts.

"To come down the stone corridor, Eva, for me, is to go into a state between the worlds. There are no realities except the ones in my mind. What I feel to be true is all that exists. By the time I come to this room, which has always been my favorite room, I'm outside time and place, in touch with worlds beyond this one."

"Are there such worlds?" Eva asked.

She could hear Bo's mild laughter, feel him touch her. For reassurance?

"Our minds are greater than our bodies. Our heavens, Eva, and our hells are more powerful incentives than the moment we're living in. That's all I mean. Those other worlds and the people I encounter in them are real, no matter how fantastic, when I'm in here. I understand them, when I'm in here. That's why, when I decided to bring Baby Joy's work to the academic world, to transcribe it and publish it, I brought it down here. The moisture could damage it, if I don't work fast enough. But in here, I'm sure that I can trust the people who speak to me."

Eva started. Dared she ask? "Bo, do you hear voices in the stone corridor? In here?"

She couldn't see his face, of course, but Eva regretted her exposing candor as soon as she asked the questions. A person who heard voices was mentally unstable. Of course, when she entered the hypnotic world of the stone tunnel, she, like Bo, was only immersed in her own subconscious. Perhaps she should amend her slip and disavow hearing the ghostly echoes right away.

Bo said, "I wouldn't say I hear voices. No. I'd say I feel convictions. I understand. I trust myself to think in ways that I wouldn't, in a room with wooden walls and windows to let in sunlight. When I read about our ancestors who were trapped in this room, imprisoned in this room, murdered in here, or who sought shelter in here, Eva, I'm there with them. You heard me say this stone corridor and this room suspend me outside time and place? It's not that I'm nowhere. I'm everywhere. I'm alive in Baby Joy's time."

"Do you think Baby Joy wrote her stories in here? She was hiding, as you said, from the Reconstruction raiders, the patrollers who became the Ku Klux Klan. Maybe that's why her stories are so unbelievable."

"Why are they unbelievable, Eva? By whose standards?"

Eva sighed throatily. "Come on, Bo. By our twenty-first millennium standards. Aren't they? A catwoman? Werewolves? Women with wings? I have trouble seeing academic value in such fantasies, Bo."

His silence lengthened until Eva felt he would not respond. She began to picture herself as she must appear, her Gypsy clothes rumpled and sweaty, her sandals lost among the mossy stones, having just given herself to a stranger. And what was she thinking? She had to find out where her daughter had been all this time. Perhaps Anastasia had returned.

Eva sat up. Bo touched her arm. "I have to go," she said.

"Just hear this, Eva. Back on the continent, in Africa, there were beliefs about shapeshifters. Have you heard of those?"

Eva hesitated. *What is the easiest, surest way to get out of this? I don't want this conversation to go any further down this road.* "Not about Africans, but about Native American shamans, yes," she conceded.

Bo seemed to sense her resistance but persisted. "It's a spiritual theory, honey. There are accounts by European and American colonizers and travelers who describe shapeshifting as a spiritual exercise. The person lies down in his home, and his spirit goes into an animal or actually shapes a creature, almost like an illusion that others can see and interact with. Even hurt. Some of these spirit creatures can kill or be shot, and the person whose spirit inhabits them or shaped them can be wounded or killed, in this way."

Eva said a little shakily, "That's not quite how Hollywood shows it. But of course, I guess Hollywood is working with European shapeshifters. Is that what vampires and werewolves would be?"

"Good question, baby. Werewolves, certainly, would be shapeshifters, to some extent. The concept of control is lost on them, though, isn't it?" His voice lowered even more, became suggestive, tentative. "Werewolves are at the mercy of their emotions, aren't they?"

Eva shook her head, though he couldn't see her in the dark. "I thought they were at the mercy of the moon. When it's full, they change."

Bo said-and was there reproach in his voice?-"I imagine shapeshifters, even werewolves, would find the full moon as lovely to look at as the rest of us do. Hollywood dramatizes the effect of the moon on wolf shifters. The helplessness adds drama." His voice softened again as he cajoled her. "But if it's an emotional change, wouldn't that be drama, too?"

Eva sighed, letting her frustration show. "Bo, perhaps. What can I say? I really don't understand this."

Bo reached for her. His hand moved from her arm to draw her into an embrace closed by his other arm. He held her close and still to whisper, "What if strong emotion threw a person into bestial change?"

He's frightening me, Eva thought. *It's not the darkness. It's not these stones that seem to be creeping in on me. It's Bo. His changes of mood. His impossibly confusing hints at-what?-something unreal. Always something too far beyond belief. No wonder he has such faith in the worth of Baby Joy's writings. He believes in any nonsense.*

"I think I understand what you're saying, Bo. But wouldn't a person of African descent, an African enslaved in America-or an African American person, after Emancipation and citizenship-wouldn't that kind of person change into an African animal? What did the colonizers and travelers to the African continent encounter? Shapeshifters who became European animals? I bet not. Shapeshifters who threw their spirits into African animals, right? Leopards and elephants and lions?"

To Eva's amazement, Bo tightened his hold on her and richly kissed her neck. "Exactly!" he said, as if she had just agreed to support his research. Didn't he hear her resistance in her voice? In her questions?

Bo was excited now. "Do you see what happened with coming to the Americas, even against their will? They had to use the forms that existed here, just like the herbs they used to cure themselves and the changes in their religious practices. They had to reshape their physical and spiritual practices, based on what was available and what was forced on them, here in their foreign, hostile prison of a new world."

"So they threw their spirits into the animals available to them here?"

"Or shaped their spirits to reflect the qualities they needed," Bo said, "based on the animals their spirits found here."

Eva shivered a little. It was damp and cold, and she wanted to get away from Bo. Away from these encroaching stones and from his world of impossibilities. She heard the pleading whine in her question, "But you don't believe in this, do you, Bo? These are academic arguments you're making, aren't they?"

And she felt her dread when Bo answered only, "What we've just discussed proves the validity of this shapeshifting theory, Eva. It proves that Baby Joy's stories have credibility."

Is he insane? Or just out of touch with reality?

"I have to go," Eva said, breaking Bo's embrace so she could rise from the depths of the bed. "I need to find out what's happened to Anastasia."

What have I done? Let this madman toy with my feelings and body, and then use that awful compromise to make me swallow his ridiculous project? What a fool I've been. It's the vulnerability. I'm new to this place, that's all. I'm worried about bringing Charley and Anastasia all the way out here. I've got to get hold of myself.

Eva yanked at her skirt and jerked her blouse into place, as well as she could judge, in the darkness. *Do I smell like sweat? Like the mildew of that hideous mattress?*

Like lovemaking? Oh, how humiliating!

"Let me walk you to the end of the tunnel," Bo said and took her hand. When had he risen from the creaking box spring? Why had she not heard the rustling of the sleeping bag, the brush of his steps across the stones?

Eva pulled back. "I need to find the flashlight," she demurred and flung herself onto the sleeping bag. *Where is it? If I find it, I can light my own way out. I don't have to be alone with him anymore. I don't want to be alone with him anymore.*

Bo said, "Here, darling," and pulled her by her waist toward him. She felt the hard cylinder of the flashlight press into her hand. With relief, she flicked on the beam.

She was startled at the seriousness-no-the sadness shadowed on Bo's face, in the edges of the light.

Unsettled-*What did I say? Is it my leaving that's disturbed him so badly?*-Eva relented. "Thank you, Bo. I'd be grateful if you'd walk with me."

He didn't try again to take her hand. But as they reached the seemingly endless black tube that stretched to the kitchen, to normalcy, and to light, he said, "The solitude and the silence of these stone rooms are soothing, Eva. In here, there is freedom to be whatever fate has made of you."

"I don't believe in fate, Bo."

"I wish you would let yourself feel it. Roar, scream, weep, and no one knows. Even you, yourself, don't quite know what you've done in here, once you leave." Eva reached for his hand.

He stopped and lifted her hand away from him, back toward herself, to form a bend in her arm. Into this crook, he slid the heavy notebook to rest against her chest. "Some of Baby Joy's writings," he said. "Journal entries describing how she wrote, what the writing did to her, but also some of the stories."

He took his hands away.

Eva watched him move, light-footed like a prowler, down the barely lit pathway ahead of her. Would the shame of what she'd done with this man catch up with her at the corridor's end? Right now, watching him glide ahead, she felt exultant. Wanted.

Loved?

He turned to her and regarded her, a sinewy shadow whose bulk was silhouetted against the glow of the cave's mildew. He waited for her, watched her, but said nothing more to her.

Eva hesitated to approach or pass between him and the stones.

If I love him, why am I so afraid?

CHAPTER SEVEN
TEARS AND TERROR

My angel rends my heart. Why has she returned like this? Everyone is gone. She is too late.

She says it is my duty, what only I can do, and therefore I must. I am the first who can write.

They flow to me down burning streams, those other people's memories. I will go mad. Perhaps I have already.

The words would not leave Eva's mind. Throughout the dinner-or "supper" as her companions called it-Eva's mind and eyes wandered to the notebook she still clutched in one arm.

Evidently the entire day had gotten away from her. Now she could think back to the Tea Party Cafe that morning and how much time it must have taken for Bo to exasperate her with his credulous faith in Baby Joy's tales of historical horror. Eva recalled the waitress's anxious impatience, her weary sigh each time Eva and Bo staved her off with another purchase.

They must have been at that table well through the lunch-or "dinner"-hour. Where had Eva left those four bags of expensive pastries?

To say nothing of the surrealistic afternoon and evening in Bo's stone labyrinth. In Bo's arms. Eva blushed even now at the intensity of the memory of his lean, long body pressed to her own, demanding response, demanding entry. Had all that really happened? How long was she in there with him? *It feels like I went down that stone corridor lifetimes ago.* And what did their passionate coming together mean to the two of them, to Bo as well as to Eva, now?

And where, *where*, could Anastasia have been all this time? Eva could understand if Anastasia had lost track of time, exploring, and hadn't realized how late it was. But surely, wherever she was, she could see that the sun would soon set.

Unaware of the time, Eva herself had meant to run all the way to her room, lock herself into the dust and darkness and brood alone, undisturbed. But when she burst into the swept and almost orderly kitchen, bustling with plumbers' assistants and the gaggle of teen young women coming together to eat and flirt, Eva had been compelled to stop.

Cornered and benched, expected to eat and be "sociable," Eva got up and located the four bags of Tea Party pastries on a shelf damp with newly washed museum-quality cutlery, bowls, and ladles. She carried her offering for the community feast only a little sullenly, on top of Bo's massive notebook, to the table.

It was hard to believe that this was only the first time that day that the young people had shared a break and a meal, to judge from the advanced stages of romantic play-acting that African American youth so enjoyed. Most of them were far too wrapped up in coyly lowered lids and rakish swaggers to notice whatever Eva did, so long as she observed the proprieties and sat with them. Discreetly unwilling to supervise their flirtations, Eva retreated to her own thoughts.

Eva was childishly proud of her flight through the emotional maze of the stone corridor. She had, after all, negotiated its treachery both ways,

112

descending and arising. She felt she might have conquered something crucially destructive in herself. Still aching with shame and actual soreness where Bo's teeth and sucking had hurt her, Eva still reeled with shock over her encounter with Bo. Who was that passionate woman he had drawn from her, proven existed in her?

Eva decided to attribute her uncharacteristic wantonness to the subconscious releases of the maze. Like drugs. Like hypnosis. At least she had survived it. Now, must she forget it all, leave it behind in the dark with Bo?

She carried no token, no prize but one notebook, a fraction of the labor produced by Bo's solitary sojourn in that dungeon of tears and terror.

So, right there at the table, surrounded by festive laborers, Eva stole that first, untimely glance at the lonely woman's words. She was not thinking, in the least, of Baby Joy when she flipped open Bo's notebook. She only wanted to savor her victory over the labyrinth.

But the first page Eva encountered after the charts and contents brought her elation crashing about her. Eva stared, stunned, at Bo's transcription of Baby Joy's first words. "My angel rends my heart."

Who was Joy's angel? Was this a lover? A child? A friend? It seemed clear, as Eva thought about those first few lines, that it was this angelic demon of a person who had insisted Baby Joy write down her hellish stories about her ancestors.

Looking at the words on the pages, Eva rapidly changed her mind about the purpose of Baby Joy's fantasies. They were not triumphant tales of magical victory over enslavers. They were symbolic autobiographies of how slavery-and the treachery and savagery needed to defeat it or escape it-had warped people into monstrosities, unrecognizable to themselves.

"How horrible," Eva finally heard herself murmur aloud.

"What you say, baby?" the plumber asked with a smile. He stood above her and to one side, having come close to select a sandwich from the pooled fare on the plank table.

Had someone gone to that gas-station-of-all-trades to pick up this motley selection of finger food? Or was this what was left uneaten, broiling in the kitchen shadows, from the housecleaners' earlier shared meal?

The plumber's pick was evidently a vintage egg salad sandwich, to judge from the smell that rose about him with each heavy bite. He stood munching and watching Eva with so benign a grin that she suspected she must have drawn attention to herself, talking out loud to no one in particular.

She rose to the challenge of the normalcy the plumber now offered. "Oh, I'm just thinking out loud. Has everyone got something to eat? Because I'd like to offer my part of the potluck and then, maybe, go look for my daughter. I'm getting pretty worried."

Within seconds, Eva realized she had dropped a bomb.

Dimly, she recalled that they had been discussing cranking up one of the pick-ups or old four-doors scattered across the tough grass out back to blast a local radio station that tended to play rap and new rhythm and blues for a couple of hours on weekday evenings. Having worked all day, the young people now wanted to party.

Their spontaneity reminded Eva of the neighborhood parties she so missed in the South Central ghetto and Watts projects. At a moment's notice, people were apt to drop the day's sweat and grind, emote with their bodies in pantomimed, controlled abandon, and fantasize, becoming heroines and cads in their hastily improvised dramas. Eva hadn't meant to disrupt that for these uncomplaining youth.

Eva only meant to excuse herself and wander outside, shouting Anastasia's name. But she said her disturbing words just as Portia, resplendent in cuffed and creased blue jeans and a pink man's shirt, entered through the back kitchen door carrying a picnic basket.

"Good evening, all," Portia called as soon as her blue and pink flowered bandana appeared in the doorway, overlapping Eva's effort to excuse herself.

Perhaps the others were fooled. But Eva noticed immediately that Portia's radiance was already clouded.

"What's that you say, baby doll?" Portia asked Eva too casually after greetings had been exchanged. "I'm sorry I couldn't spend the day with the young womens I found to help you all clean up. Just too much work to catch up on, my own self. But what about Anastasia? That's your girl, right, Eva? You know she got them blue eyes from our side of the family?"

Despite the banter, Eva was startled by the look of genuine anxiety that she was sure she had seen distort Portia's porcelain facade before the usual placidity could again descend.

Or had she imagined it? Already, Portia was opening the basket on the center of the table and dispensing hefty roast beef, lettuce, and tomato sandwiches to all who did not protest that they were either vegan or too full to eat for another week.

"Uh, oh." The plumber, a gentleman to the last, offered an appropriately aged sparring partner to Portia, in case she wanted to join the group flirt and have a little fun. "What you bringing in here now, girl? I swear you must done left that man nothing at home to eat but the wrappings off the butter."

His assistants laughed, but the teen girls noticed Portia's aloof response and sobered.

Portia's next words confirmed Eva's suspicion that all was worse than Portia intended to let it appear to be. "Charley, where is that nephew of mines? He ain't helped go look for that girl? He know she don't know her way around here."

Unreasonably, Eva felt that Bo was maligned. Eva defended him. "Aunt Portia, Bo's asleep." What a social gaffe! In this old-fashioned company, the first question would be how on earth Eva knew something so intimate about Bo as that he was sleeping.

The assembled tableful of youthful and experienced faces all turned to her. Eva felt herself blush beneath the gaudy outfit in which Bo had decked her, probably for just such a moment of public humiliation.

"He stayed up all night putting together his project to show me," she stumbled on, "and then. . . ."

116

Eva ceased speaking as the memory of their gasping, clutching, shameless revelry in the darkness and the damp of the dungeon defeated her cool recital of their academic interests. Her head dropped, and she noticed the notebook. She held it up in her defense. "It's a bit disturbing," she finished truthfully enough.

"Well," Portia responded supportively, "it ain't like you need nothing like that to worry about at a time like this. Ruth Bethany, go get that lazy boy for me, your Uncle Bo, you hear? Tell him I got something I need him to look into. And where your mama at, do you think?"

The lovely young woman who had whisked Eva and Charley's underthings from the front porch earlier that day answered, "Aunt Portia, she home today. Aunt Eva, he in *there*?" indicating with a jerk of her head the doorway to the stone corridor.

At Eva's nod, Ruth Bethany rose from the bench squaring her shoulders for a descent into the tunnel that, Eva suspected, the teen found as daunting as she did.

"Good." Portia had already turned to the astonished Charley. "Baby, I think I seen you with one of them portable phones yesterday. Let me use it. I got to call my husband. He'll know what to do. You open up that thing and get it going for me." Portia meant business. And apparently, everyone but Eva and Charley knew why.

Before Portia had finished punching in Ham's work number, Bo was in the doorway from the dungeon. Ruth Bethany's courageous posture relaxed as she fell back from the doorway to let him enter.

Eva wondered if her heart had hammered itself to a dead stop. *Will he look at me? Will his look say something to me about what we've done? What we've become to each other?*

"Bo, you heard your aunt calling for you?" Ruth Bethany asked.

Apparently, Bo had little patience for niceties just now. "Hello, Aunt Portia. Hello, everyone."

"Hey, Bo," went up all around.

"What's this I hear, Aunt Portia?"

Portia said almost brusquely, "Eva's baby girl done took off. Seem like all day, to hear it from Eva. Why you ain't out there looking for her? You know perfectly well that. . . ." And then, no doubt about it in Eva's mind this time, Portia's eyes shifted to Eva, and she fell silent.

Charley must have noticed the odd look, too. She piped up helpfully, "That there are snakes out there, Aunt Portia?"

Eva could have kicked her cousin for bailing Portia out of the need to explain what was so threatening outside. In fact, Portia's response to Charley's suggestion of snakes was so enthusiastic that one would have been led to suspect that the demure Southern lady secretly practiced serpent worship. "Yes, honey," Portia gushed at Charley, and her glowing smile added the "good girl" her mouth was apparently reluctant to say. "It's snakes around here something awful," Portia confided happily. "Oh, ain't it just, Bo?" she enthused.

But Bo seemed to have abandoned his aunt to her charade in favor of finding a weapon. He was now throwing historical clutter around on the

118

freshly washed kitchen shelves. *Is he angry?* Eva asked herself. *Why?*

Bo turned to the plumber, sober and thoughtful now that he was through chewing. "You got a crowbar or something I can use, Mr. Jackson?"

Only now did Eva realize that she had not been frightened enough by her daughter's disappearance. She thought of herself with disgust, swooning in the dark in the arms of a strange man when her daughter was . . . where? Doing what?

And why were the others, who were not all overly protective mothers, as she often accused herself of being, even more worried than she? *Because I'm wrapped up in myself, and I've neglected my daughter all these years, and what happened today is no different,* Eva berated herself.

Whatever her adventure had been with Bo, it was clearly forgotten by him. His look was disinterested to the point of rebuff as it passed over Eva to light on Portia. "Tell Uncle Ham he'll know where I'm going, Aunt Portia. Tell him I'll head out and meet him there."

The plumber was clearly a past master at keeping women from worrying. He re-joined companionably, as if they were contemplating a fishing trip, "Me and my boys is right behind you, Bo."

When Charley asked, "So, will you run water in for the toilet tomorrow?" no one answered. The nimble and sinewy assistants had already slid out from the benches around the table and briefly blocked the reddening light coming in at the door on their way out.

The teen women sighed, eyed each other, and began to say things such as, "Well, I guess it's back to work." Except for Ruth Bethany, who said pointedly, "Aunt Portia, you want us to look around here?"

Portia said, "Ruthie, that's a good idea. Now you all young womens will come back to have dessert with the mens when they return, won't you? Take and see can you find you some flashlights. Stay in a group. Don't nobody wander off alone."

Eva felt her throat tighten at this casual comment. Dark. Danger. Stay in a group. And her Anastasia, a stranger from a distant city, was out there all alone. Charley came around the table to take Eva's free hand. Only then did Charley say, "Aunt Portia, I don't mean to be rude. But don't you think it's time someone told Anastasia's mother and aunt what on earth has all of you so worried?"

Aunt Portia was as cool as an evening breeze. "Why, Charley, whatever can you mean? You don't see it getting dark outside? If that gal ain't found her way home in the broad daylight, you sure you want her wandering around in the dark? Anyhow, you know me. I ain't got time to stand around here jawing, Charley. You don't neither, the way I see it. You do your best to comfort that girl's mama while the rest of us try to see can we help hunt that little gal down."

And she, too, along with the clutch of curvy teen workers, vanished through the glow at the door.

"Oh, Charley," Eva said. "What's happening?"

"Come with me," Charley said. "You still got the plumber's flashlight? I'm not too sure we'll need it."

Eva assumed she'd left it on Bo's sleeping bag when she fled her shame about their encounter. But it was on the table. Leaving it, the two women slipped through the kitchen door to face the wreck of the plantation's old quarters.

Before them in the gloaming were the scattered remnants of huts, shacks, sheds, really, that spotted the scraggly land between the big house and the fallow cotton fields. Among the rubble of the sheds in which the enslaved had lived were the circular stone pits for long-ago cooking fires that Eva had tried to investigate - was it just that day?-and the weedy patches of the people's out-of-control former gardens.

Off to one side was a stone well. Opposing it were more splintery sheds that housed tools and latrines and the pump where they had first washed their hands after their encounter with the outhouse. Was all that just last night?

Closest to the house was a sturdier brick building that must have been the historic kitchen Bo described. It was this that Charley and Eva sat to face as the pick-ups and cars filled with searchers and circled off to the dirt road that met the U before their house.

"What is it?" Eva asked Charley as the noise of forced jollity, the last giggles, and the revving engines faded to sibilant silence. She noticed that her voice quavered despite her best efforts to sound calm.

What was out there with her Anastasia? Crickets? Cicadas? The snakes grown to mythically threatening proportions, with Charley's use of them to represent all that was ominous and unexpected?

"I don't know, Eva," Charley said. "I'm waiting to see."

"What are you waiting to see?"

"I don't quite know, Eva. Hush."

They sat on what would probably be considered the back porch, though it was too skimpy for comfortable use. Like the front porch, it was wooden, insect-ridden, and rotted from decades of disrepair.

Eva's scalp crawled. "Charley,"-*Am I whimpering?*-"why aren't we out looking?"

"Eva, we are. Just wait."

Eva felt tears sting her eyes. This was not what she had wanted for her daughter and her cousin. And she had a premonition now, out here hoping for a sight of or word about Anastasia, that the situation could only deteriorate.

The rustic facade was shredding all about them and would soon fall away. Even if-no, *when*-they found Anastasia, they were destined to learn that the beauty of their venture into the Deep South had been of their own imagining.

Real life was turning out to be too much like Bo's recital of Baby Joy's stories. There was always something lurking. There was always some hidden but necessary truth, some unrecognizable reality, that Eva did not want her little family to be a part of any longer.

How could she explain this to Charley?

Randomly, fighting desperation, Eva thought of the gruesome pictures of her ancestry that Bo had conjured on the front porch the night before and, more vividly still, in the cafe. She thought of the writhing, moaning fool she had made of herself in Bo's dungeon and closed her eyes to blot out the image.

They would find Anastasia, and they would leave this ill-fated foray into history.

"Charley," Eva said, "I want you to tell me what this fiasco has cost you so far. And I'll demand it and a solid bit of profit out of that Uncle Ham character. He or Bo can buy this wreck off of us, or they can sell it for us. I'll bring up the probable worth of the stained glass window. That should tilt the price in our favor. We'll find Anastasia tonight and be out of here by tomorrow morning."

"Eva," Charley said. "If you don't hush. . . ."

But her threat died down as the steady hum of an expensive car drew closer, became louder.

Charley had risen, open-mouthed, by the time Uncle Ham's blue Cadillac swerved into the backyard. He spilled from the car, huffing and overwrought. Apparently he had not gotten Portia's message right.

Charley shouted to him, "Uncle Ham, Aunt Portia said for you to meet up with them someplace else. Bo said you would know where it was. You're not supposed to be here."

Eva gaped at her screeching cousin. "Charley, why are you screaming at the man?" she demanded of her cousin's backside in the gathering dark. "And since when are you so cozy? 'Uncle Ham!' I told you that we're through playing family. We're out of

123

this madhouse in the morning. Just as soon as we find Anastasia."

Uncle Ham stumbled to a stop. He weaved and focused on Charley. Was he drunk?

"Oh, my God. Charley, look." Eva rose and tugged at her cousin's arm. "He's got a gun."

It was true. All along Ham's dangling right arm ran the dark stiff lines of a rifle.

Charley barked with authority, "Ham, what are you doing with that thing? Get it out of here."

Ham raised the rifle, not to sight through it, but to examine it, as though he weren't quite sure himself how it came to be attached to his arm. He started to explain, still waving the rifle in mid-air.

Charley shut him down. "I'm not playing with you, Uncle Ham. Get that thing off my cousin's property, or I promise you I'll have the police out here in a hot minute. You're not shooting anything around *this* house. Not in your condition."

Ham lowered the rifle. The movement caused him to stagger. He turned and looked almost helplessly toward Charley again in the near dark.

Charley said with less ferocity but continued force, "I told you, Uncle Ham. Aunt Portia said for you to meet up with Bo. I'm sure he thought you would know where to find him."

Ham muttered, "I know. I do know."

His voice was raspy and grated in the smooth darkness. But Eva was relieved to hear him speak. His silence, weaving in the gathering shadows with his arm and the rifle intertwined, had unnerved her.

It occurred to Eva that she had never liked Ham. But now she would be grateful to whoever might help find her daughter.

124

"Uncle Ham," she called, imitating the rich sweetness he must have grown accustomed to responding to in Aunt Portia's voice, "please help find Anastasia."

"Well, I'm trying," he whined defensively. But at least he followed this by turning back to make his way to his car. He slid inside, still attached to the rifle, and somehow got the car to pull smoothly around to the front of the house.

But then the engine shut off again. The two women heard and turned to look at each other. Uncle Ham had not driven away. They turned toward the unseen front of the house. And they waited.

"Did you hear the car door, Charley?" Eva asked.

"I don't know," Charley whispered. And then again, "Hush."

But Eva didn't hush. Not yet. She must warn Charley first.

For, silently, like a hunter stalking prey, Uncle Ham was coming back around the house. Eva was sure of it. "Charley," she whispered, "he didn't go."

Charley's head whipped around, not to face the edge of the house around which Eva was sure Ham would soon reappear, but to sight the brick kitchen separated from the main house by a curving series of flagstones barely visible among the weedy wildflowers along the way.

Eva clutched Charley's arm with full force now, sure that something-wildly, she tried but couldn't think *what*-had just gone terribly wrong. "Charley," she said again more urgently.

Then Eva was shocked into silence. For, watching with Charley the solid wooden door of the kitchen, she realized it had just eased open.

Standing against the blackness of the windowless interior, Anastasia stared at them with an intensity that was almost despair.

"Anastasia," Eva cried aloud and started forward.

She released Charley's arm. Now Charley, in her turn, caught at Eva. "Wait," Charley urged her.

And only now did Eva see the thin young man close behind Anastasia's shoulder.

His skin, rather light golden in color like Anastasia's own, set him off from the darkness beyond him in the brick kitchen. His hair, like hers, was caught in a bundle of tangled locks. But whereas Anastasia's dreads glowed with the sheen of expensive hair dressings, this young man's welter of hair seemed pomaded with drying mud.

In fact, as Eva gaped, it occurred to her that everything about him was savagely unkempt. Even his eyes, bright in the darkness-blue like Anastasia's, perhaps?-were distended and wild.

"Anastasia!" Eva called again, as if in warning.

Anastasia, desperate, wrung out by some new, trying experience, responded to the alarm in her mother's face and voice. It could only have been Anastasia's concern for her mother and her own exhaustion that deflected her from what Eva would soon learn had been a day-long vigil, an intense concentration of purpose and method.

Anastasia started forward to reassure her mother. The young man behind her-*her captor? kidnapper? homeless friend?*-followed.

126

It was Charley who tried to warn them. She had not forgotten Ham. She pushed past Eva, her hands outstretched toward the young people, shouting, "No. Ham is here. Go back!"

Eva turned, only then remembering the drunken hunter. Ham had cleared the edge of the big house and pounded forward. His feet hit the ground toes forward, legs wide apart, as if to brace himself at an instant's notice.

To take a shot?

Eva couldn't fathom this. She couldn't quite keep up with what was happening.

She turned back to her daughter. Anastasia appeared to be caught between the wild young man at her back and the raging older one coming up fast at her side.

Eva screamed, "Anastasia, run!"

Eva leapt forward, her only thought to enfold her daughter in her arms and carry her, like an infant, to safety. She heard Charley, too, begin to run, but couldn't follow in her mind where Charley was going.

What Eva could see was that Anastasia, eyes focused solely on her mother's eyes, had sprinted away from the young man at her back, thoughtlessly doing as her mother commanded.

Briefly alone, the young man turned to face Uncle Ham. And it was in that seconds' worth of hopelessness that transformed his face so sorrowfully that, even in the darkness, it wrenched at her, that Eva began to understand.

This strange young man was not after Anastasia. He had not trapped Anastasia in the kitchen.

Anastasia had waited all day to rescue this stranger.

Anastasia, released from her mother's eye contact, slowed and turned toward the young man she had left behind. She seemed to call his name, for he let go of his transfixed contemplation of Ham and reached for her.

Anastasia, a sprinter, slowed and turned back to take his hand.

Finally, Eva could hear, could think, and realized that Charley was shrieking at Ham, "Don't shoot! You bloody stinking drunk old fool, don't shoot!"

Ham fired.

Eva and Anastasia had almost reached each other before the younger woman turned back to help her friend. Eva's hand went forward to grab at her daughter's and tug her to safety, into her mother's arms, until whatever must happen next was over.

But there wasn't enough time.

As Anastasia turned to let the young man catch up with her, to take his hand and run together, three fat splotches like pressed roses blossomed on the white eyelet camisole across Anastasia's chest. Eva could see the splotches against the white fabric even in the dark.

Eva threw herself forward, straining, flying, to reach her daughter.

As they fell together, she heard the dry thunder, the single crack of air around what must have been a burning bullet. It was only then that she understood that Ham had fired his rifle and someone had been shot.

But who?

Beneath her, Eva pressed herself to her daughter, wrapped her arms around her. She tried to turn and threaten Ham. "Back off! Get out of here. You'd better get out of here. Charley, call the police."

She heard herself scream the words, felt her face distort, unable to release the pull of horror at the corners of her mouth that wanted to just go on screaming or start sobbing. And only because she had turned to face her daughter's attacker did Eva see that Charley had reached him. Charley slammed her hand upright against the barrel of the rifle so that Ham's next shot blazed like a signal into the sky.

"Stupid black bitch," he grunted and shoved at Charley, trying to get her away so he could aim for another shot.

And he turned his head just a little to glare at the place where Anastasia stood no longer.

It was not, evidently, Anastasia that Ham had been trying to shoot. Eva saw his look, the hatred in it, and the glee, as he watched his real target.

Eva looked up from where she still held Anastasia as the young man her daughter had been trying to save stumbled. He had stopped when Ham first fired, apparently unsure, himself, who had been shot when he saw the blood sprout on Anastasia.

Now, spared the second hit, his body seemed to overcome the resistance of his mind. Eva watched, sickened by the weight of her sympathy for him, as the young man's hands flew from his own spotless chest to the dark flush spreading across his belly.

He stumbled forward as though he would keep running. Or possibly kneel to inquire about

Anastasia. Like a penitent, he sank to his knees at Eva's side. His sea-green eyes implored, but his mouth moved without a sound.

As Eva rose to her knees to extend to him an arm, to let him into the circle of safety she had created for her daughter but that only he, it seemed, needed, she heard Anastasia scream.

The young man fell across her daughter's lap. He jerked as if in sleep and then lay without moving.

CHAPTER EIGHT
SOJOURNING SPIRIT

How do I call an angel? Do such as you answer prayer? Or is that the work of gods, like slavery?

I told you I must lose my mind. I walk the halls of my mother's home in dread. I sit trembling to a soup of forest herbs, like Mother Magdalen's own. I hope to calm my nerves, to rest my sojourning spirit. I take the air among the roses and contemplate your statue. I remember what you were to my childhood and cherish such memories.

Suddenly, hallways, soup, and statue are no more. There is no more warning than the instant when I hear the screams. They are usually my own.

Then blood, again my own, shines on my hands, flows from cavities that were my breasts, spews from my mouth roped in bile and vomit, and my body is not my own but something whipped to ribbons, strung by thongs and dashed with salt in boiling water, hanging helpless.

I am raped, I am castrated, I am eviscerated nightly, daily, hourly. What is time to me? How many times have I held my own entrails in my hands, grabbed them from the hounds at my feet and stuffed them again into the ragged flesh between my ribs? Why? No one should live with what I know of dying.

And yet, I live. As I die beneath my enemies' gaze, ripped wide, my life more theirs than mine even as I lose it, I know that I will wake again in gardens, hallways, sitting quietly at table, my face

131

in a bowl of soup. Maybe even in my bed, to faint and sleep away the nightmares my life has become.

Too soon, again comes the torment.

In this lucid thought between the terrors, Angel, tell me. Do you, who wanted this of me, ever look back to see what your desire has created? Or am I, as you have left me since my childhood, quite alone?

You have forsaken me.

CHAPTER NINE
FEARFUL TRUTHS

When I come to myself, the voices echo still.

I must write till sorrow eases, till I drain myself of pain, till this new voice leaves me some little peace. I chew nibs for my pen. I burn the ink and cut the sheets of paper. By shadow, by candlelight, I write until the voices, like my eyesight, fade. Then I collapse.

I am their voice, condemned to speak their stories. "I be afraid. I be hunted. I be killed tomorrow morning. I hope it quick." Will their voices, their accursed memories, ever let me be?

All those people I loved and thought I knew, and those who came before, whose lives were the legends of my childhood. Can it be true that they suffered so? Those who raised me, fed and bathed me, taught me to work beside them in the gardens and the fields. I was comforted by the daily sight of their smiles, their faces shaped by worry, the swollen ridges of their scars, all my life. How could I not have guessed their fearful truths, their haunting secrets?

Throughout that night, Eva learned to question how one perceives reality. By morning, she understood that sanity was more a matter of function than of thought or emotion. Perhaps, she reasoned later, it was the night's lesson on the power of perception that saved her sanity in the face of all that happened next.

Eva and Anastasia managed to drag the bleeding young man into the outdoor kitchen while

Charley fought off Uncle Ham. The young man, "Tansy," Anastasia called him, had hidden there all day with her, awaiting a chance to flee to the safety of the new heiress's protection.

Eva was devastated by Anastasia's rapid, breathless recital.

"Mommy, you just don't know. He's the real heir. That's why Uncle Ham shot him. They've all been trying to get rid of him. All his life. He's never had anybody to protect him."

But try as she might, Eva could not wrap her mind around Anastasia's story. Surely it was too dramatic, too romantic, to be remotely true.

According to what he'd told Anastasia, Tansy was an orphaned boy raised by a distant aunt like a wild thing in the woods. Eva could believe the story of incompetence. An aging distant relative suddenly left to care for a small boy treated him with helpless neglect. Attempting to be his guardian kept her almost comfortably in his decrepit mansion, feeding and clothing both of their bodies on his meager interests.

Anastasia wiped angry tears in the deepening darkness. "Every day Tansy's middle-class relatives expected his body to be found in the woods." Killed by beasts? Shot by hunters? Wasted, maybe, by malnutrition and disease?

Instead of dying of neglect, Tansy grew to a kind of primordial manhood. Anastasia described a creature hiding in the forest to watch his civilized hunters drive up in shiny cars to check for signs of his decaying corpse or, at least, for increased senility in his guardian.

"Anastasia, he sounds like a fairy tale," Eva complained as they tried to settle him comfortably on the dirt floor. Both the wooden table and plank bench in the antique outdoor kitchen proved too high to lift him onto, even when he roused from his swoon and tried to help them.

"But there's more." Anastasia's voice had the high, persistent tone of a soprano maintaining a glass-shattering note. Anastasia was determined to be heard. Eva knew that, if they had not been forced to shut and bar the kitchen door against the starlight, for fear of Ham's determination to kill the helpless young man, she would see Anastasia's ocean-blue eyes round with shock and fixed like hypnotic orbs upon her own.

Eva could tell that her daughter had rehearsed this speech all day. Anastasia flung at her mother the most improbable parts first and then grounded every fantastic detail in materialism, greed, and cruelty. "Tansy thinks they let his great-aunt live to such an old age because they were sure she'd kill him off, somehow, with her neglect."

"A child knew that he was neglected? Where did he get such a sophisticated understanding of the law?" Eva heard herself avoiding the horrendous part of what Anastasia had just said, "They let his great-aunt live." Was Anastasia saying these picnic basket-toting relations had contemplated killing the old woman who lived in Tansy's mansion before Eva's intrepid little band came to these fecund backwoods and swamps from Los Angeles?

Anastasia would not be baited. "Tansy once had parents, Mommy. He knew what his life was like before they died. Haven't you wondered about the death of your own parents?"

This blow struck Eva so swiftly that she could not respond. Stunned by the onrush of unwanted memories, she shushed Anastasia as well as she could by insisting they must see to Tansy's wound before he bled to death.

Eva left Anastasia alone in the dark with the dying young man only long enough to peer through the star-speckled blackness outside in search of Charley. "Charley," she hissed into the spreading night. "Charley, are you all right? Has that fool shot you, too? Charley, answer me!"

For the longest, it seemed there was nothing. And then, as Eva's eyes adjusted to the layers of descending pitch, she heard her cousin's rapid step.

Charley came around the house, limping. "I couldn't get that damn rifle away from the maniac," Charley called out before she reached the kitchen. "We'd best get out of here to the nearest police station before he gets back with all his country cousins."

"You can't be serious," Eva said.

"Don't matter if I'm serious or not, Eva. *He's* serious. We have done landed in a mess of trouble, as the old folks say."

Eva wanted Charley to come into the kitchen so they could all be bolted safely inside before Ham-and anyone who might support his pursuit of this wounded creature-could return.

But Charley would have none of it. "Eva, I don't need to come in and figure out what to do. I already know what to do. We got to get that boy to a hospital, and I don't know where one is. And neither do you. So we best just load him in my car and get out of here while the getting is good."

But Charley, silhouetted in the dark with one long hand planted on a slender hip, had somehow in the last three days lost her power to intimidate her younger cousin.

Eva said simply, "No, Charley. You're not supposed to move a wounded person, and we've already dragged him across the ground a good three yards. We'll lock ourselves in the outdoor kitchen after you call on your cell phone for an ambulance."

Charley sighed. "Aunt Portia kept my cell phone after she used it to call Ham. I can sneak into the house kitchen to look, but I'm pretty sure it won't be there."

Eva didn't want to ask why Charley didn't seem to think Aunt Portia might have unthinkingly dropped the phone on the kitchen table after using it. The implication of sinister intent to isolate and murder, even on Aunt Portia's part, was overwhelming, given the ebbing life of the youth in the darkness with her daughter.

"All right, Charley. Will you go in the house kitchen and look for it, though, before we give up on it?"

Eva would not have blamed Charley if she had declined to risk trapping herself alone in the house with anyone who might have returned from the search for Anastasia. But, to Eva's relief, Charley was game.

"Don't let anybody in here, no matter what they say, until you hear my voice," Charley instructed before she slipped nimbly into the surrounding dark.

Could this really be happening? This was the question that drew Eva up short every time a decision had to be made over the next twenty minutes. There sat her daughter, rocking on her knees, her mourning silhouette sliding in and out of blackness like an ancient maiden about to keen over the loss of her betrothed. And there lay a strong young stranger, soaking his rags in his fresh bright blood.

Eva watched at the opened door, afraid to leave her post for fear of invasion by long-lost family and friends now intent on murder.

Charley at last limped back into sight burdened with supplies from the house, suddenly a dangerous place, off limits. Now, what to do?

Assiduous argument among the three embattled women ended with both Charley and Anastasia's slamming the dusty Jag over the driveway's pebbles, on their way to bring back both an ambulance and protection from the mayhem at the plantation. Eva, the now disputable heiress of the place and its intrigues, would stay behind the bolted door to protect the young man from further violence. Silently, Eva admitted to herself that all she now offered him was a peaceful death.

It was Eva's idea that only she should stay. But her mind refused to believe that her protection of Tansy as heir to the property would be necessary. Things like this didn't really happen, did they?

Eva bolted herself unwillingly into the semidarkness with the shooting victim.

Charley had brought the bag of Tea Party Cafe pastries, the plumber's flashlight, and Bo's notebook. Eva had been briefly shocked at the banality of the pastries and then, on second thought, she had insisted Anastasia take them on the mad car ride. "You can't have possibly eaten anything all day," Eva argued when Anastasia resisted.

"But Tansy hasn't eaten all day, either!"

Eva pointed out mercilessly that a young man shot somewhere in the solar plexus was in no condition to eat. "You won't do Tansy any good fainting in the car from shock and hunger when Charley needs you to help spot a police car or a fire station." Eva hated the motherly bluntness even as she used it. What on earth would Anastasia think of life, of the world she lived in, after an experience like this?

Perhaps, Eva persuaded herself as she settled into the lonely vigil, once they'd had time to sit and sort out all the different stories that were bound to be in circulation about this young man and why Ham shot him, they would be able once again to believe that Anastasia had inherited a reasonable world. Until then, Eva determined to blank her mind by concentrating on Anastasia's young friend.

Eva hoped he would not die. She tried to remember if she had ever been around a human being who lay dying. Her mind approached her parents and lurched away.

Eva came away from the flash of memory stunned and numb and began to talk to the young man, to ease his mind in case he was conscious.

He didn't seem to be. Charley had managed to lug in cleaning rags swirled in soapy water, by way of disinfectant, slopped over one arm to avoid contamination by Bo's dust-covered notebook. Eva had plopped the sodden mass into her lap. She now picked them apart and, one by one, wrung them out around the wound as well as she could in the unsteady light of the rolling flashlight. This would have to do for washing the area. Next, she pressed the wad to the wound, hoping to staunch the flow of blood. She was worried that Tansy didn't even scream in response to this barbaric treatment.

Eva doubted that her efforts could do any good. Wouldn't he die of internal bleeding long before her daughter and cousin returned with help?

All alone here with a suspicious stranger. Suddenly, Eva couldn't stand the thought. This young man, Tansy, like Eva, was apparently orphaned. But he had had no Charley, no visiting uncles full of hope and promise, to keep him going.

Anastasia said he had spent his life hunted. Anastasia tended to be insightful about private things.

Eva began to talk to Tansy. Whoever he was, and why ever Ham had shot him, he deserved to die among friends. Apparently, he had liked and trusted Anastasia. But in such turbulent circumstances, Eva decided that the two of them couldn't possibly have shared the kind of trivial, intimate information that made people feel they knew each other. So she began telling Tansy about her daughter.

Eva hoped her voice was comforting. If there were mercy in an unjust world, the nursery-rhyme cadences of Anastasia's babyhood would reassert themselves in Eva's voice and soothe Tansy into memories of his own early childhood.

"Tansy is an unusual name," Eva began. "Is it a nickname? I doubt that Anastasia told you about her own list of nicknames."

Eva sighed. Now they were no longer strangers in the face of approaching death, but distant relations opening their lives to each other. "When Anastasia was very little, I started calling her 'Anna.' I remember thinking it sounded sweet and old-fashioned. But as soon as she got to day-care at the university where I was studying-I was on my bachelor's degree, at the time-the teachers started calling her 'Annie,' which I just couldn't bear. So I insisted they say the whole name, Anastasia. I still remember being called out of class the first day everyone switched. My poor baby was crying because she thought no one at the day-care liked her anymore."

Eva fell silent, remembering how it hurt to learn that it was she who had caused a school full of people to hurt her daughter. "So we left the college that day to go to a park and feed the ducks and talk about the beauty of her full name, Anastasia. But it wasn't until after we'd played on the toys together, the teeter-totter, and the seesaw, and especially the roundabout, that she was happy again and ready to forgive me for costing her all her friends."

Dimly, Eva thought that perhaps it was unfair to make the helpless young man hear about her daughter's social metamorphoses. But this was the route her thoughts about her daughter now took, and for the life of either of them, Eva couldn't seem to redirect herself.

"The next nickname was a nightmare. I had Anastasia in a public elementary school and discovered that jealous girls were calling her 'Nasty.' This was because the poor girl had so many boys ready to fight over her that some of the other

141

girls said she must have done 'nasty' things to have all those boys 'liking' her. The awful part is that 'Nasty' is pulled right out of the second syllable of 'Anastasia.' You know. 'Nast.'"

Eva had discovered this name in crumpled notes at the bottom of her daughter's backpack, the paper still damp and the ink and pencil streaked by Anastasia's tears. Even as she slammed her way into the principal's office, Eva, a part-time community college lecturer by then, recognized the community claiming implied by the offensive nickname. For the first time ever, she now admitted to this dying young man that the notes and the name probably had much to do with her decision to go on to graduate school. How do African Americans communicate their radically non-European social stories?

Eva had swallowed her pride and asked Charley to pay to put Anastasia into a snooty private junior high school, hoping a change of community would soften Anastasia's youthful years.

But the plan backfired. Anastasia adapted too well. While Eva studied literature, linguistics, and budding cultural theories about formerly enslaved African societies, Anastasia now dubbed herself "Stacey" and became part of an upper-middle-class elite who had never known poverty, ghettoes, or projects. This gave Anastasia entree into all the best campouts and slumber parties.

Eva discovered Anastasia's distress over this youthful bout of social climbing when they traveled to a women's conference in Ethiopia. Anastasia sat in their sparse, vermin-infested hotel room and wept in her mother's arms over the superficiality of her self-protection back in America.

Eva shook her head over this memory. "Anastasia started high school-still private, but back in the Watts area-as 'Asia' in solidarity with the women of India and the drought-afflicted Sahel belt. Until someone pointed out that adoption of the nickname Asia implied that she was ashamed of her African ancestry. So after this trek through the ups and downs implied by breaking her name into sections, my daughter started college as what I consider a whole person, at last. As Anastasia."

But the posters of elegant, starving bodies continued to grace Anastasia's bedroom walls until Charley sold their suburban villa to come to the Deep South. Almost idly, Eva wondered where those posters might be now. Packed away? Stored? Shared with commiserating friends?

Coming here had been done in such a rush, Eva couldn't be sure of any of their former belongings. Like their former lives. Suddenly, irrevocably tossed aside.

Just like that purely academic trip to Ethiopia that changed their lives forever, it struck Eva that, after these few days of driving South and invading their own historic ruin, she and her daughter would never again be the same people. What was gone? Their innocence? Their naive idealism?

Eva couldn't tell what it was that jolted her into awareness of the young man's rattling breath. She lifted her hands from the blood-sodden lump of cleaning cloths on Tansy's stomach and barely stopped herself from crying out in horror. Blood and life seeped from him as she prattled on.

143

She must get help. He could only have minutes left. Seconds. There must be someone, something, that could help. "Wait here," she said stupidly. "I hate to leave you, but I'll only be at the door."

Eva slipped in spreading blood as she scrambled for the door and then couldn't grip the heavy bolt in her sticky hands. Only the grimmest gritting of her teeth kept her from sobbing aloud as she hammered at the rusted bar with her bloody palms.

Eva couldn't tell why the bolt finally slid. She threw her body against the weight of the ancient door and screamed as it creaked wide, "Help! Somebody. Anybody. He's dying!"

No one answered. It seemed incredible to Eva that she heard no response but the trill of crickets and the call of night birds, undisturbed.

Eva fought down a scream. She had thrown her fists to her mouth to keep from releasing the panic that would make it impossible to think. Something bitter and salty assailed her tongue. Had she swallowed his blood?

Eva retched, choked, coughed. She spit a mouthful of the metallic taste that she hoped had come from the rusted bolt onto the dusty ground. She called more weakly, "Please. Somebody. Come help him."

Her throat closed. She didn't try to call out again.

Eva left the door open and went back to the still body on the floor. He shouldn't die alone. This little she could do for him.

No longer worried about moving him, Eva knelt and lifted the young man's head onto her knees. The thick tendrils of hair cascaded in bunches over her thighs and wadded under the bulge of his head. His unusual face was no longer handsome. The high cheekbones were suddenly stark. The sunken cheeks seemed skeletal. His mouth was slack and his eyes oddly sealed.

Sadness struck Eva like a blow. For an instant, she was sure she would never again be able to breathe. When had she last inhaled? At the door?

Then, gasping, her first breaths wrenched free in sobs.

It was a long while before Eva could bring herself to stop crying. When she did, it was another long while before she could force her hands from her face to touch what she was sure was the cadaver on her lap. Her first grief-stricken effort was to wipe the wet pool of her tears from the young man's head and face.

His clammy warmth surprised her. Of course, Eva thought to herself, it takes time for a dead body to cool. She wiped at his forehead again, more gently. Definitely, there was warmth still there. Was he alive?

Eva's fingers trailed ever so lightly down to the young man's throat. Faintly, so barely there that she accused herself of hallucination, Eva felt at his throat the faintest pulse.

She pressed harder. Yes, the blood still beat in his neck, rushing feebly to feed his brain. She must keep talking to him, assuring him to the end that he was not abandoned. After all, companionship was all she could give, but who would want to die alone?

But there was nothing Eva felt confident to say. She knew nothing that he valued, and her small talk about Anastasia had brought them both to the point of devastation. She could not afford to escape his plight again in reminiscences about her daughter.

Could she talk about love? The meaning of life? At a time like this, when he surely saw and felt more about the life he was losing than she could possibly address? Perhaps something about afterlife? Assure him of peace? Of a God?

It was at this point that Eva reached for Bo's notebook. These were plantation stories. While she worried about what to say, Tansy was losing precious seconds of human contact. The goal was that he should not feel alone. And after all, if this had in fact been his plantation, then these stories might be of some slight interest to him.

The point was to keep him in contact.

Eva dragged over the notebook and opened it on the floor near his head. She laid the heavy flashlight on the open pages so that her hands were free to smooth his hair and touch his shoulders, reassuring him that he was not alone. Then she began to read to him.

The stories were confusing. Baby Joy wrote as though possessed. If Bo's transcriptions were at all accurate, Joy's voice and choice of words changed completely with each character's autobiography. Baby Joy seemed to speak for generations of women, descending through times of increasing peril, at the plantation.

But as Eva read, what began to strike her and carry her away from the terror of the moment and

146

the handsome young man's incipient death, was the stories' unreality.

What, if anything, was real? The stories, though told as memories, were all fairy tales.

Eva knew of this kind of thing. Many cultures throughout the world took a dim view of history that did not recognize and interweave myth, legend, and religion. But Eva had never encountered anything like this.

These stories stolidly presented fact and the wildest myths at the same instant. It started with a child who could fly. She grew to womanhood in slavery and had to decide whether or not to abandon her own enslaved child. Then there was the story of a flock of flying women who drove off patrollers, interrupting their reign of terror that cleared the roads between plantations.

It was only as she began to read of a small family huddling right here in the outdoor kitchen, listening to the hungry snuffling of a woman who had become a bloodthirsty cat right outside the bolted door, that Eva paused.

Fascination gave way to fear. What was real?

Here Eva knelt, her legs numb, with death on her lap and the door wide open. She yearned for an end to the suspense, however it might come. If Charley and Anastasia brought an ambulance, or if Ham returned and finished his bloody work, would tonight ever seem real to her? How would Eva ever resolve this experience in her mind?

Was this what Baby Joy had done? Whether or not she was possessed by the spirits of her dead ancestors, as she seemed to think she was, had she rendered the horror and hope of their stories by bringing the dreamlike, nightmare quality into real life?

Eva continued to read.

The long-ago night, shrouded in mind-crippling disbelief, had passed, and when morning brought sunshine and relief from the prowling monster, the mother of the enslaved family denied that it had ever existed. The harassed cook and mother, Miss Vivian, allowed no one to talk about it.

Survival, Eva thought. But had the denial helped the little embattled family to survive?

And just like that, Eva remembered. Unbidden, unwanted, Eva remembered that Charley's parents had gone South, "to take care of family business," as her own parents had explained to her. It had not been important to Eva at the time, who was still a child and only wanted the teen-aged Charley to herself on any pretext.

Soon, Eva had feared, Charley would go the way of all African American high school graduate girls. Everyone talked about it. Charley would marry, get a cute little Spanish stucco house in Inglewood, and Eva's best friend and babysitter would be gone forever.

But it was not Charley who was gone. Word came that Charley's parents had met with a tragic accident. And then uncles came from the South.

And then Eva's parents, too, were gone.

The memory, stark and unexplained, ripped back into Eva's consciousness, destroying all illusory realities that she had constructed in the decades that carried her further from childhood and that crippling series of traumas. She sat silent against the onslaught of the unsought memory.

As the shock passed, Eva realized she was too exhausted, too astonished to read aloud any more. She could not bear to check for the young man's pulse.

She flicked off the flashlight and, in the graying dark, began to sing to him.

These were lullabies she recalled, she couldn't tell why, suddenly from her own mother. They were like spirituals, haunting, pitched on sorrowful keys, and their words lingered and repeated, gathering meaning with the voice's cadences.

Images flashed in Eva's mind. Her mother's face, smiling, and her father's eyes, twinkling a bit in California sunshine as he lifted her into his arms for a hug. She remembered a sharp cry of reproach, a tender voice cooing her out of a sulk, the sudden clear smell of her mother's fried chicken carried on a platter to the family's picnic on the front lawn. What was the occasion? Just a Sunday afternoon?

Yes, and there was her mother's Sunday cake in the center of the picnic blanket. Chocolate.

As suddenly as the memories flooded Eva's mind, they receded. Eva watched as they disappeared.

It was like losing her parents a second time. She grasped at the trailing feelings of familiarity, of nostalgia. One moment, Eva saw her mother's sunny smile. The next, she saw Tansy pitching to her feet, shot and shocked by the impact of the killing bullet.

The memories wouldn't remain clear.

Then, the stone angel in the rose garden interrupted her memories to spread its wings in an arc of light and reassurance. Its chiseled lips parted to speak.

Surely, it would comfort her. Eva leaned into the reverie to listen.

Light flooded her mind and soothed her. Perhaps she lost consciousness. Later, she believed she must have passed out and slept, still cramped and kneeling, from sheer exhaustion.

When Eva opened her eyes, she was rested and alert. Eva's first realization was that the door to the kitchen was still wide open. She thought that she had better work her way out from under the young man's head to close it, in case Uncle Ham returned before Charley and Anastasia could bring help.

But her legs had no feeling. She could not move. Eva steeled herself to look at where the young man's head weighed her down. Would she see him dead in bright sunlight?

But he was not there.

Where she knelt, she saw a cake of mud and blood, and the open notebook, and the extinguished flashlight. But the young man, the wad of bloody cloths, and any trace of his body having been dragged across the ground, were not there.

Except for the evidence of his wound, it was as if he and the night's vigil had never been.

CHAPTER TEN
FEAR AND LONELINESS

Eva's shouts brought no one running. She dragged herself to the open doorway and, clasping the rough doorframe, pulled herself to her numbed feet, calling out all the while.

"Charley! Anastasia! Where are you? He's gone. Something's happened to him."

Eva's first steps along the stone path landed her again on all fours, crawling as she cried out. "Anastasia! Charley!" Her legs were in terrible pain, recovering feeling in stabs and pinpricks, and it occurred to her that she could not drag them along much further without screaming. She sat up on a smooth stone and looked frantically around. "He's gone. Where are you?"

Suddenly, as if in answer, Ruth Bethany's vaguely familiar head appeared in the opened back doorway of the main house. Her look of amazement would have been comical if Eva had not been terror-struck. "Mama," the teen called to someone in the house behind her. "Aunt Portia, look. I've found her. It's Cousin Eva, crawling on the ground."

A rush of cooing copper-skinned women fairly stampeded past Ruth Bethany to get to Eva, who recoiled, shrieking in panic. "Where is my daughter? Where is my cousin? What have you done with that boy? Where is Tansy? Don't touch me!"

Dimly, Eva could tell that she made no sense to these people. Her racing mind assured her that this was their fault, not her own. She knew what she meant, and if they had been as cautious and aware as she had had to be since arriving at this mansion of nightmares several lifetimes ago, they would know what she meant, too.

Eva turned on the women, snarling. "Where is my daughter? What happened to that boy she left with me?"

The women didn't bother to try to answer Eva but turned this way and that, consulting each other as they took turns reaching gingerly toward her, as if trying to see who might touch her first while upsetting her the least. "Baby, don't nobody know where your daughter at. We done heard from the police your baby and that Charley gal was in to the station, telling some kind of wild tale, but they ain't come back yet. Baby, let's get you in the house."

Someone, perhaps it was Portia, decided to take a firmer tack, of the kind for which African American women were well known. "Eva, you probably got every right to be upset, baby. But you can't sit out here on the ground screaming. Ain't nothing going get better this a way. Now you have got to come on in the house and let us take care of you. You tell me what you scared of, and I'll take care of it. That's a promise."

Eva turned to Portia with despair contorting her face so badly her words were distorted. "Aunt Portia, don't you know your husband tried to kill that boy? Anastasia left him with me, and now I've lost him."

Portia's blank slate of shock, closely followed by distress, could not have been faked. Eva knew that, whatever Ham was up to, Portia had not expected it.

It was clearly a struggle, but Eva watched Portia suppress the questions that flooded her mind. The first thing Portia said was, "Sound like we got a lot to talk about. But that don't change how we got to get you in this house. Eva, can you walk, baby?"

Gentle, insistent hands seized Eva on multiple body parts and hauled her to her feet. When she slumped, unable to stand, the hands slid around her, and arms held her up. Huddling in a mass, the women lugged Eva between them into the back of the house.

There, a chorus of cries brought men running. The sight of the very same men who had set out hunting for Anastasia-or was it really for Tansy?-just the night before set Eva leaping backwards, struggling to get out of the women's grasp.

"No, now. None of that." Women's voices shushed and calmed her like a frightened animal.

"What's wrong with her?" one of the men asked, leaping backward himself. He was probably, Eva's mind scrambled to identify, one of the plumber's assistants.

"She done had a scare. Now, if you all mens can't help none, get out the way."

Eva was aware that she must seem hysterical to these people. But it was only, she assured herself, because they did not know the urgency of the situation. They needed to listen to her. They needed to go find Tansy. They needed to stop someone, probably Ham, from whatever he was doing to Tansy at this very moment. They needed to go find Charley and Anastasia.

They would not listen. Instead, the women recruited the startled men to lift Eva helplessly from her feet and carry her, calling out all the way, up the main staircase to the darkness of her bedroom.

When she was dropped and her arms pinned to her chest on the dusty feather mattress of her bed, Eva was dismayed to hear, "Olivia, you brought that kit?" And, incredibly, a hypodermic needle flashed briefly between Eva's eyes and the limited light that straggled in at the dust-coated bedroom window. "No," she shouted and rolled to both sides, trying to escape.

But Eva's protestations were useless. There was the prick of the needle, and it seemed that in seconds, Eva's emotions had cartwheeled away from any realization of the disaster that only she knew enough to try to avert. She did not forget that Tansy was dying and had been stolen from her care. But fighting about it seemed suddenly pointless in the greater scheme of things.

Wherever he was, she would persuade Anastasia to believe that Tansy was in the arms of angels. *After all, once you've watched death claim your parents, only your own children can ever cause you quite so much pain again. But Anastasia's too young to know that kind of truth, just yet.* In the wake of the hypodermic needle, Eva realized immediately that she felt deeply philosophical about the tragedy she had just witnessed.

"Find Anastasia," Eva whispered to the woman so like Portia, but not quite Portia, who leaned in close to her as her eyes and mind closed down.

Eva was aware as she slept off the drug that people about her thought she was out of her mind. She made a noncommittal mental note to explain herself more calmly, if she ever woke again. She had very little faith that she would wake. Hazily, Eva found it odd that the thought of eternal sleep did not cause her much alarm. She wondered vaguely if this was what dying felt like.

She doubted it. The young man she had held on her lap only last night had appeared calm, but she had sensed he was terribly afraid. And terribly sad.

Eva was not afraid that she was dying. But she did wish she could have remained awake, to break the news about Tansy to Anastasia, whenever her daughter and cousin returned from their fruitless search for help. Eva had no doubt that Anastasia and Charley would have to be back soon. What had Portia said? That they had been seen by the local police.

"You had no business to give it to her, Aunt Olivia," Eva heard a man's voice say quite sternly. "You're not a doctor, and the administration of a drug was unauthorized. She didn't agree to it."

"Then let her sue me," a woman's voice snapped back. "I was afraid she would hurt herself. In fact, I thought she already had hurt herself. We couldn't do nothing for her if we couldn't even get her to stop kicking and screaming. Wash off all that blood and see where it was coming from."

The voice sounded like Portia's, but not quite. Eva struggled to open her eyes. This man sounded familiar and, in that familiarity, faintly comforting. He might know something about her daughter and cousin. Eva should call out to him, let him know that she was aware and thinking, and that he could speak to her, speak for her, and find Charley and Anastasia.

Eva mumbled, shamed to hear that her words were slurred and indistinct. Her eyes remained shut.

"What did she say?" the man asked. "She's trying to come to."

A cool, damp cloth pattered across her forehead and down one cheek. The breeze that trailed it refreshed her. "She's coming around. Don't crowd her, now, Bo. Give her some air."

"Should I go get her daughter and her cousin? She'll want to see them, as soon as she comes to."

"Bo, let them sleep. All these poor city womens is done wore theyself out with all this whooping and hollering. And the rest of us needs a break, too, you ask me. Let the whole lot of them get some rest, and we'll sort it all out tomorrow. You going back to that cave of yours to get some sleep?"

Whatever the man-Bo, was it?-said, Eva couldn't be bothered to follow. She had heard the important part.

Anastasia and Charley were asleep. That meant that their whereabouts were known, and they were safe. Eva could relax back into the embracing lethargy of the drug.

She let go and succumbed.

Only as she roused, suddenly and fully alert, did it occur to Eva to wonder if Tansy was included in the injunction to Bo to "let them sleep." Eva doubted it. Hadn't there been a statement about "womens"?

Tansy was gone. This was the thought that brought Eva up with a start, looking wildly around her.

She was in the dust-coated hovel that she had claimed as her bedroom. A soft light, odd in quality and color, glowed on a nearby table. It was a camp light, two long fluorescent tubes caught in a plastic brace that stood on a fragile antique table, casting light up onto the room's darkened window. Beside the table and the glowing light dozed a man.

Bo. He looked solid, refreshingly at ease as he slumped in the fragile Queen Anne chair beside the tea table, his head bowed over his flat belly, his long legs stretched toward Eva's enveloping bed. Eva's heart leapt toward him, startling her. What had brought on all this tenderness?

Then memories flashed through her mind. Running through the stone corridor. Sitting together in the rose and willow bower to gaze at the bright statue of an angel. Kisses, embraces that mined veins of aloneness and dismay.

"Bo," Eva said weakly.

The name was said as a question. The question was meant to ask what was going on, what had happened to herself, her daughter, her cousin in this place? Why were they here, and why had no one warned them away? Was it too late to leave and reclaim normalcy, in their unappreciated former lives?

Bo stirred, mumbling in his sleep, but he did not awaken. He lifted his head, his eyes still tightly closed, and then nodded into sleep again.

Eva determined to get herself out of the bed and down the hallway to search for her daughter.

Her struggles woke Bo. He leapt from his chair and dropped to his knees at the bedside, gently restraining her. "What is it, Eva?"

"My daughter." Her throat was dry and her whisper hoarse. Was it from the hypodermic? "I have to go see if she's here. If she's all right."

"She's here and she's fine. She's asleep, right now. It's the middle of the night."

"And Charley?"

"Asleep, too."

"I have to talk to them. They don't know I've lost him."

"Lost who, baby?"

The endearment brought tears stinging into Eva's eyes. "That boy. He was dying on my lap. And then he was gone."

Bo's voice was gentleness itself. "Eva, you have to try to make sense, honey. What boy?"

Was it possible that Bo really didn't know, hadn't heard the one thing that Eva felt she had repeated at every opportunity, until she had said nothing else coherent? "Bo, Anastasia brought him to me. Tansy. And Ham shot him. And now he's gone."

Bo's face was in so much darkness with his back to the camp light that Eva could not be sure of his expression. But his stillness spoke volumes. Eva accused, "You don't think I'm making any sense."

"It sounds like a dream."

"Didn't Anastasia and Charley say anything about him? Ask about him?"

"I didn't talk to them. Things have been kind of confused around here."

How could he not have talked to her daughter and her cousin, and yet presented himself by her side? Outrage flared in Eva and then subsided into frustration. Was this emotional roller coaster an aftereffect of the hypodermic? Or of the shock?

For, surely, Eva remembered holding a dying young man.

"Bo, it was a nightmare."

"I believe you, baby." That endearment again. How soothing it was, after all the chaos and despair. "Can't you sleep anymore? I think if you make it through the night, Eva, it'll do you good."

"Sleep through the night? Bo, there's a dead boy out there somewhere. And it's my fault." Eva caught at Bo's tee shirt. His hands clutched her wrists in such a way that she could no longer pull herself along the bedclothes.

"Eva, you're not making any sense."

"Don't say that. Didn't Anastasia ask about him when she got back? I know she did."

"Eva, we need to talk."

"Well, talk, then. I'm listening. And while you're talking, tell me about Anastasia. What did she say? Did she ask about Tansy? What did everybody tell her?"

Eva's throat was clearly burning. It was thirst, no matter what had induced it. She licked at her lips with a thick, dry tongue.

"Eva, you're thirsty and hungry, and you've been through hell. I'll get you something to drink. Just stay still. I'll be right back." Bo rose. He went to the table with his lithe back to her before he said, "I'm sorry, but I have to take the light. I won't be a minute."

Eva was left in the dark with her worried thoughts.

159

What was going on? Were Anastasia and Charley really back? Were they safe, and how could it be that they had said nothing about Tansy?

Eva seemed to wait an eternity in the blackness for Bo to return with something to drink. The silence of the house encroached on her small safe space in this room, away from all that had happened. What could have become of Tansy? What could have become of Bo?

Eva could bear to wait no longer. She eased herself to the edge of the high bed, dragging herself through layers, she was sure, of undisturbed dust. She got her legs over the edge of the bed and was relieved to find that she could now stand on them.

There was much to be explained. What had been said to Anastasia and Charley when they returned from their search for help for Tansy? That Eva had been knocked out with an unauthorized sedative? Who had done it, and why? To shut down her screams about Tansy?

A mixture of panic and disbelief drove Eva to the bedroom door, despite her revulsion for creeping through the house's thick darkness.

But it was not dark.

A splash of riotous color splattered the threshold of the bedroom's pitch. Of course. The stained glass window.

Eva leaned against the doorframe and looked to the creation at the end of the hall. Its colors swam about in the blackness, merged, scattered again, and resolved themselves into icons of struggle and triumph as Eva watched, open-mouthed.

"Have you ever seen anything like it?" Bo asked from close behind her.

"No. Have you?"

"I grew up with it. Only as an adult did I realize how magnificent it is. And how unique. I had to learn to appreciate it."

"How did you learn that?"

"By visiting the great cathedrals of Europe and realizing that they surpass it in artistry but not in genius."

"Who made it?" Eva wondered if her questions were banal in the face of the life and death issues she should be trying to resolve. But the unreality of the last days had caught up with her, and she could not at the moment sustain a sense of urgency.

If the boy had died in the previous night, what could her inquiries do for him now?

Perhaps, in the morning, she could find Charley and get to the police. Uncle Ham should be arrested.

The magical kaleidoscope at the end of the hall splintered into sparks of ice and fire and melded into the portrait of a young man on his knees, his hands in the air and spatters of blood in a crimson halo about him.

Eva gasped and stumbled toward the glass, losing her grip on the doorframe.

Bo's hand shot out to steady her and pull her back. "Come away, Eva," he urged. "Don't look at it anymore."

Eva turned to him in the dark. "But, Bo, did you see? It changed, right in front of my eyes. Did you see?"

Bo turned her so that, to face him, she must place her back to the hallway and its seemingly enchanted glass. "Eva, I've seen many things in this house, since I was a child. Come on. Come away and lie back down."

"Bo, am I hallucinating? What was in that hypodermic?"

"Sleep," Bo said firmly, "and nothing else. Come here and let me hold you."

Perhaps it was fatigue, but Eva suspected it was fear and loneliness. Whatever the urge, she watched wordlessly as Bo went ahead of her with his soft light to the table and turned to hold out to her a plastic bottle of bright juice. It tasted like tropical fruits, perhaps passionfruit and mango. She drank half the tantalizing bottle down before she thought to offer it to Bo. Against the light, she could just make out the gentle shaking of his head.

"It's for you," and, when she insisted she'd had enough, he placed it on the table.

He went ahead of her to the bed. Eva let herself move quietly into his arms, her head against the beating of his heart, without questions in her own mind of what she was doing or why.

Sunlight would bring worry enough.

But sunlight brought the joy of seeing Anastasia safe and buoyant as ever. "Mommy, do you know what happened to Tansy?"

Eva roused herself from the triple drug of the traces of the hypodermic, the rhythms of Bo's heartbeat, and the warmth between his arms. "Anastasia! You're safe."

Anastasia, gentle as ever, let herself be thoroughly hugged before she insisted again, "Mommy, what happened to Tansy? We're hearing the strangest stories."

162

Eva sat back onto the bed from which she had bounded, startling Bo but not waking him. He had collapsed sideways into the lumps of mattress and pillows and continued to doze.

Eva pulled at her daughter to sit beside her. "Where have you been?" Eva tugged at her daughter's hands. "I'll tell you everything I know about Tansy, but first tell me what's happened to you and Charley. I was frantic."

"Mommy, nothing. We tried to get help. We found a police station and told them everything that had happened, how I met Tansy in the woods and hid him in the outdoor kitchen all day, and how Uncle Ham shot him. But they wouldn't do anything." Disgust and disbelief molded Anastasia's golden features. "They wouldn't arrest anyone. One of our cousins is an officer on the force. He came out and talked to us and told us we didn't want to spread stories like that, damaging people's reputations, but he could understand, being new around here, that we wouldn't know what to believe."

"What to believe," Eva echoed. "How is there any question of what to believe when it's a matter of what you've seen with your own eyes?"

"Mommy, everybody's acting like we made it all up."

"Made it all up?" Eva made a firm resolve to stop parroting her daughter's incredulity. "But of course we didn't. We all three saw the shooting, and there's proof that it happened. The blood is still there."

"The blood?" Anastasia seemed, in the murky blend of dirty sunlight through the bedroom's

163

window and the feeble ejections of the fluorescent camp light, to have gone pale.

"Anastasia, honey, don't conclude the worst. I don't know what happened. I held Tansy's head on my lap. I was singing to him in the dark. He'd lost so much blood, and he'd been in shock so long. I turned off the flashlight, so he could have some peace, in the darkness. And then I must have dozed off. I'd been up all night, talking to him, and reading to him, and singing."

"Mommy, you must have been worn out."

"And then when I woke up in the morning, or came to, he just wasn't there." Even as she said the words, Eva sensed the returning chill of unreality. How could a dying-*Or dead?*-young man simply disappear?

It was a while before Anastasia said carefully, "Do you think he got away, somehow, Mommy?"

Eva shook her head. "Honey, no. I think someone came in and took him away."

"But who? And why would everyone deny it now to the police?"

"Is that what they're doing? Covering it all up?"

"Yes, Mommy." Anastasia, youthful and trusting, looked horribly aged by worry for a moment. "Do you think that's part of getting rid of him so they can take over his property?"

"But, Anastasia, what good would getting rid of him do? All it means is that I get his property. How do our relatives-I guess that's who you mean by 'they'-benefit from my inheritance?"

"Didn't they try to convince you to sell it? Cheaply? Probably to one of them, disguised as some kind of developer," Anastasia mused aloud.

164

Eva wondered with an unhappy pang about the destruction of her daughter's innocence. From what experiences or entertainments had she learned such a jaded view of human nature?

Eva said, "But I've refused to sell."

They were both silent. Eva wondered if her daughter, like she, was questioning if the three of them were now in as much danger as Tansy had been all his life.

"We have to get out of here," Eva said.

"No, Mommy. We have to stay."

"Anastasia, what are you saying? On the one hand, you think our long-lost Southern relatives may have done away with Tansy and his body-excuse my flippancy, sweetheart-to get their hands on his property. Then it only stands to reason that we, as the next inheritors, are in terrible danger." Eva heard the strident note in her voice and struggled to speak calmly.

Couldn't Anastasia see the peril that threatened them? "Honey, if anything happens to me, you're next in line to inherit this place. Then Charley, as my next of kin after you. We have to get out of here, or if we stay, give them what they want, so they won't hurt us. Even if this wreck were a palace, it wouldn't be worth losing the only people I love, Anastasia."

"Mommy, you're not going to lose anybody besides Tansy. We raised such a stink that the local police are going to be hounded by exposure, if they don't investigate. Aunt Charley shouted all over the police station about private investigators and the FBI, and that was before we got back here and heard that nobody knew anything about Tansy, and you were sedated. The police have been here once, already."

"When was that, honey?"

"While you were knocked out. Boy, did Aunt Charley let Aunt Olivia have it, for doping you up."

"Aunt Olivia?"

"Aunt Portia's sister."

Eva heard the note of reserve in Anastasia's voice. Eva said in sympathy, "The place is crawling with Southern ladies so sweet butter wouldn't melt in their mouths, isn't it, honey?"

"Not any more. The police threw everybody out except us and Bo."

Eva started. "Why did they leave Bo?"

Anastasia said delicately, "Because Aunt Portia swore you gave him permission to stay and take care of us the other night."

The other night? When was that? Eva wondered. *How many eons ago?* In another lifetime, before she'd ever held a young man, dying.

Anastasia went on even more quietly, "And because you'd been calling for him in your sleep."

Eva was so startled by this that she gave a little jump. "Calling for him?" When Anastasia didn't answer, Eva insisted, "Bo? I was calling for him? That can't be. I was worried about you and Charley."

Anastasia said softly, "When I went up to check on you, I heard it, myself."

Eva flushed with shame. "Honey, I don't know what to say." All this death and terror, and her daughter must have stood by her drugged mother's bedside thinking that Eva cared only for a strange cousin who'd shared with her a casual encounter in

166

a dark dungeon. How wrong. How hurtful. What had she exposed, in her drugged ravings? How much did everyone now know?

How humiliating. Eva struggled for something to say that would reassure her daughter of her place of importance in her mother's heart.

But it was Anastasia who spoke first. "I asked the police to let Bo stay, too, Mommy. You never have anyone to turn to, when you're scared. You have to keep from frightening me, and you have to keep from upsetting Aunt Charley. I thought that your calling for Bo must have meant that you were really scared, and you'd found somebody to turn to just in time."

Eva put her face in her hands.

Behind her, Bo said tenderly, "Anastasia, thank you for letting me stay."

Anastasia looked at him from an emotional distance that, lowering her hands from her face, Eva couldn't quite tell was mistrustful or, simply, noncommittal. "Mommy, I hope I did the right thing."

"Thank you, honey. Bo, do you think you can tell us something straightforward about Tansy? Please don't say none of this ever happened, because my daughter knows she spent the day with him, and I know I spent the night on his death-watch. Who is he, and do you know what's happened to him?"

Bo sat up and eased himself off the bed. He went to the little tea table by the grimy window and slipped the twist cap off the bottle of tropical juice. He sighed and took a deep drink.

He put down the bottle, recapped it, and stood with his back to the women for what seemed a long while. He seemed troubled and in deep thought.

Eva watched how the curve of his back slid in a moderate S against the light struggling in from outdoors. She was shamed by a sudden urge to have the right to go to Bo, to slide her hand along that curve and ask him to hold her against the awe of this terrible unknown world opening all around them.

Eva had just resolved to withdraw Anastasia's question, to say, "Never mind, Bo. We don't want to know any secrets about Tansy, or anything else. Whatever it is that causes that much worry, we don't need to be burdened by it," when Bo spoke.

"I'll tell you everything I know about Tansy," he said, turning at last to face Eva and her daughter. "But you have to hear it all the way through before you ask any questions. And when I'm done, you have to promise to tell me where my work stands with you, Eva."

"Your work?" Eva was surprised and put off. "What does your work have to do with anything, Bo?"

Bo said in the darkness, "I found my notebook in the outdoor kitchen, after the women brought you in here, Eva, and I found the blood on it. At first, I was a madman, thinking that someone had hurt one of you. I knew Uncle Ham didn't want you to stay here, at first, but I never would have expected anything like-" Bo caught himself "-like what I was afraid happened, until I saw what I thought was the evidence of foul play. I thought that was why you'd gone ballistic, Eva. I thought they might have gone after you and gotten Anastasia, or something equally tragic."

Anastasia pounced. "So you knew your family was potentially dangerous about this inheritance business, Bo, and you didn't say anything to warn my mother?"

Bo shook his head. "No. I didn't know anything of the kind. And I still don't. It's just what I had to assume, when I heard the screaming, and I already knew you'd disappeared. Then I went into the outdoor kitchen and found the blood, some of it on the notebook. It looked obvious. That's why I stayed by your mother, even after I heard from Aunt Portia what had supposedly gone on. I didn't want to risk-"

Anastasia finished for him. "You didn't want to risk that your first suspicion would turn out to be true, and that your family would do away with us to get this property."

Bo groaned. "Look, it's been a trying few days. I can be excused for melodramatic thinking."

Eva spoke up. "Is that all it was? Melodrama? What of the blood you yourself found, Bo, on the notebook? It wasn't mine." She held her arms out, the filthy peasant blouse sleeves pulling away from her smooth skin. "It wasn't Anastasia's or Charley's, as I'm sure you saw when they returned."

"Yes, I saw, Eva. I still can't explain the blood."

Anastasia said angrily, "It was Tansy's! How hard is that to credit?"

Bo said wearily, "Anastasia, hear me out. It's impossible to credit that the blood is Tansy's."

Anastasia shot back, "Why is that impossible, Bo? Because your relatives would never shoot the disinherited heir?"

Bo wouldn't look at either of them. "Tansy isn't an heir. Not really. Not anymore, if he ever was. Look, let me start over." He turned a pleading look on Eva.

Eva said coldly, "Why isn't Tansy the heir anymore, Bo? Was something done to disinherit him?"

Bo looked as if he'd given up. "Tansy can't be disinherited, Eva. Anastasia, Tansy simply isn't real. He's just a story. He doesn't exist."

CHAPTER ELEVEN
BRIDE'S DEATH IN WATER

Anastasia refused to follow Bo to the downstairs kitchen or anywhere else. She insisted on staying there in the gloomy darkness of her mother's room to hear Tansy's story.

Bo wanted them to have coffee, hot chocolate, breakfast. He wanted Anastasia to relax enough to laugh or cry. She would have none of that.

Anastasia listened to Bo's disturbing story with an intensity that tore at Eva. Eva would have spared her this if she had ever thought that such an experience might be possible. A boyfriend shot down just outside the reach of her protective arms or, outrageously, rumored to be the stuff of superstition?

Tansy's story left Eva, herself, reeling from the impact of the improbable upon her very material concept of the world.

Bo adopted lecture mode. "Tansy is an idea. You could say he represents our past. Our family's collective past, and our community's historical past. Tansy is the history of slavery and rape and being hunted down at the plantation. His story seems to have come into being when our five-times-great-aunt, Baby Joy, started writing her biographies of our ancestors' lives."

Eva couldn't tell why, but now she bristled.

Oblivious-or determined-Bo persevered. "Maybe Tansy was Baby Joy's nephew, as his story suggests. Or maybe he was her illegitimate child. Lynch and rape raids increased, you know, after the

171

Civil War and the emancipation of those who had been enslaved."

Eva, also a professor, challenged Bo. "Did you say Tansy's story 'came into being'? What does that mean? Did Baby Joy write it? I had the impression she only wrote women's stories."

Bo raised his hands as if in surrender, placating Eva. "You're right. She did write women's stories. I mean that, as well as I can trace Tansy's story, he seems to have become a local legend around the time of the Civil War."

"How did you find that out?"

"I looked into archives about local news and folklore. I questioned old people who had heard tales from older people when they were little."

"So your sources could be limited or mistaken," Eva pointed out. "If there is a Tansy story, maybe Emancipation is not when it started. Maybe that's only as far back as you can trace it."

"And if there is a Tansy story, that doesn't mean there isn't a Tansy," Anastasia said hotly. Eva saw that her daughter was trembling, probably with trauma as well as outrage. Bo's story did seem offensively ridiculous.

Eva put her arms around her daughter.

Bo reminded the women, "You said you'd let me tell the whole story before you started asking questions. Let me tell you everything I know or suspect. Then, if you still have questions, I'll do my best to answer them. Fair?"

Anastasia leaned into her mother's arms, as she had done as a small child, hearing a story.

According to Bo, if Tansy was a story that had grown up with Emancipation, Bo took Tansy to be the grinding shame of the history of slavery. Tansy represented everyone's fears of degradation. Tansy was the symbol of helplessness in the face of increased persecution.

Freedom had further brutalized the already animal status forced upon the Africans of America. Captive, they had been beasts of burden. Freed, they were wild game hunted for sport or captured anew to be beaten back into servility.

"Tansy is a wild herb," Bo pointed out. "The story has it that Tansy, the youth, was the product of a young girl's rape. She tried to get rid of him by drinking an infusion of wild tansy, which is a natural abortion-inducing agent. Enslaved women knew a lot about abortion-inducing agents," Bo, the historian, could not resist explaining. "Abortion was one of the most common forms of rebellion against enslavement."

"But the herb didn't abort the baby, in this story," Eva summarized.

"That's right. For some reason, probably a moral about inevitability, the baby conceived in rape and shame is born, despite its mother's efforts. And in a very African throwback, an act of commemoration that serves as an historical lesson, she names the baby for her anguish about carrying it: Tansy."

Anastasia, still in her mother's arms, sighed deeply but said nothing.

Eva, the literary scholar, said, "So you're saying that Tansy as a fairy-tale hero symbolizes the shame of a history of slavery that everyone wants to forget, to abort, but can't. He persists, like the unwanted history persists, and is born into the new age of supposed Emancipation."

"Yes." Now Bo was eager. "But he's the wild bastard, the unrecognized heir who no one wants. He lives in the woods, the source and repository of everything unknown to the rational mind, in West African lore. The realm of the untamed spirit world."

"The unconscious?"

"Maybe," Bo conceded. "All cultural translations aren't so simple. All I know, as an historian, is that Tansy springs up with a very significant African religious past, just when his newly emancipated African community in America is about to undergo some serious trials."

"Are you going to tell us Tansy's African religious meaning?" Anastasia wanted to know.

"Yes. That's next."

Eva pointed out, "He did say no questions, honey."

Anastasia retorted, "But he takes too long. This isn't a college lecture hall. He's in your house, Mommy, telling you that the attempted murder we both witnessed never happened."

"I apologize for testing your patience. I wanted to be thorough. Now I'll be brief. Tansy is a distortion of the name of a sacrificial prince from an ancient West African religion. This religion developed a secret society empowering women. The extraordinary coincidence about Tansy, Eva and Anastasia, is that he is a fish and a prince of peace and prosperity for his community, much like the historically later figure of the Christ. Tansy's West

174

African name is Tan Zay. I'm sure you can hear the similarity."

"That's an extraordinary carryover," Eva said. "How many decades would Tan Zay's name and qualities have had to lie dormant in an enslaved community in the American South, before they resurrected in Tansy?"

Bo shrugged. "Baby-I'm sorry, Eva-it's hard to tell."

Anastasia looked away. Eva held her tighter.

Bo plowed on. "But it wouldn't have been the first time that ancestral memory manifests itself after uncounted generations. There are lots of Tan Zay stories everywhere in the world where enslaved Africans needed hope for survival. My favorite is from Haiti. There, he's Tay Zan, his powerful name further hidden by inversion of the sounds."

Anastasia gasped and sat up from her mother's embrace. "I've read some of those stories. Tay Zan always has a bride, and her family kills him."

Bo said quietly, "And his blood appears on her breast."

The three of them looked, suddenly and unwillingly, at the brown drops stiff on Anastasia's white camisole top.

Anastasia said defensively, "But he comes from the water, from a river or well, and his bride drowns herself there, combing her hair and singing that they will always be together." She flung at Bo contemptuously, "I don't comb my hair. My hair is in dreadlocks." And she raised a thick lock triumphantly at him, as though this destroyed his theories.

Bo almost smiled. "The comb and the long hair on a woman who becomes a mermaid have long ancestral histories in West African religious myth. The importance isn't actually in combing one's hair. It's in the empowerment of the community of the sacrificial fish-prince and his mermaid bride."

"Sacrifice?" Finally, Eva re-joined the conversation. "You mean, not only does the fish-prince die, but so does his bride?"

Bo became grave. "In the folk traditions, yes. The meaning of the bride's death in water, Eva, singing and combing her hair, is that she becomes like the African mermaid goddesses, a powerful source of protection and prosperity for her community."

Anastasia said, "So the fish-prince takes a human bride who becomes a mermaid and a goddess?"

"Something like that."

"And Tan Zay takes his mermaid bride with him into death?"

"Yes, Eva. At least, in formerly enslaved communities, the story is told in such a way that both the fish-prince and his bride are both sacrificed, like the Christian Christ."

Eva said, "Then it's simple. I've got to get Anastasia out of here."

Anastasia tried to push away. Her mother held on. "But, Mommy, wait! Does the bride die in the original African story?"

Bo said, "Not as far as I'm able to research it, no. You have to understand, this story is the basis of a secret society of shapeshifters and other powerful women and men. It isn't all that easy to look into."

"Shapeshifters, Bo? Do you mean werewolves and things like that? Are you telling me that traditional African religions are nothing but a bunch of pagan superstitions?"

Bo said, "Are they pagan for embracing a system of beliefs different from those of Christianity? I'm telling you what I believe I know. I'll have to leave it up to you to make value judgments, if you want them."

Anastasia slid from her mother's arms and rose to face Bo. "So what happens to the sacrificed fish-prince, Dr. Wolfson? Does he return to life, like Christ?"

Bo hesitated. "In the original West African religious tradition we're referring to, he becomes a powerful voice his bride carries on her head."

Eva caught her breath. "You mean she goes crazy, like Baby Joy, always hearing other people's voices telling her their stories?"

Bo said quickly, "That's not what I mean, no. Actually, the fish-prince dies to become the voice of the sounding leopard, a voice of power and authority over his people." Bo's words did not soothe Eva.

She insisted again, "I told you, I'd better get Anastasia out of here."

"Mommy, there's nothing to be afraid of. The whole story is impossible to carry out, here in the Deep South. There are no leopards," Anastasia reasoned.

While this conclusion made great and reassuring sense to her daughter, Eva was unmoved by it. Shapeshifters. Sacrifice. Death. It sounded like the most B-movie voodoo talk she had ever

177

heard. If this was the substance of Bo's research, he needed to find another vocation.

Eva told him so.

Bo was silent a moment before he said quietly, "I guess I did ask you to tell me your thoughts about my work, Eva."

"I think that your mumbo-jumbo is a disservice to African Americans. We have spent a few hundred years fighting great odds to establish ourselves as respectable members of society," Eva pronounced.

She despised the whiny plea for approval from one's historical tormentors even as she uttered it. But accurately describing her political views was not Eva's goal. Eva flung the insincere words at Bo, daring him to respond.

Desperate for him to respond.

Bo could not know how deeply disturbing his Tansy story was today, the morning after the mysterious disappearance of the dying young man. Eva was haunted now, in gray morning light, by her memory of the youth's startled, sea-green eyes, fixed on her own earth-colored ones in amazement and distress as he went down in a shower of blood at her feet.

"Mommy, that's nonsense," Anastasia interjected. "How can an old traditional religious story make African Americans less respectable? Who's going to judge us? Who has a history that's more respectable? The ones who tolerated slavery and supported lynching?" Distracted, Anastasia began to pace. "If I've understood this story correctly, the young man comes back, resurrected."

Eva glared at Bo as if to say, *Now look what you've done*. What she said to her daughter was,

178

"Oh, come on, honey. It's just a myth. A fairy tale. It doesn't happen. It can't happen."

Anastasia turned to face her mother. "It's happened so far. Look at it. Back in Baby Joy's time, and again now. Tansy is created, and Baby Joy writes those stories you've been talking about with Bo. He returns, and you, Mommy, play the bride and read him those stories as he's dying, sacrificed again. It was you who carried the voice of the sounding leopard."

Eva was dumbfounded. "Anastasia, it's just a story. It's a myth about a religion that probably died hundreds of years ago. *There is no voice of the sounding leopard.*"

Anastasia confronted Bo. "I'm right, aren't I, Dr. Wolfson?"

Bo opened his mouth to reply. Eva snapped at him, "Don't you dare take her questions seriously! You're just telling horror stories to frighten us out of this house. You should be ashamed."

Bo's face lost its look of scholarly interest and intensity. In the semi-dark, his face was washed first by surprise and then by wariness.

Eva went on. "You want the house, and your greedy uncle wants the property. You claim you have an interest in that crazy old woman's writings, but that was just to dupe me into paying attention to them. She was out of her mind. And while her rantings are very touching, they're nothing but nonsense."

Bo said, "Eva."

She cut him off. "No more! Stop this. Can't you see what you're doing to my daughter? She's just had a terrible shock, and you're filling her head and

179

her heart with this fantasy about resurrecting lovers and Christlike shapeshifters and-" To Eva's horror, her voice caught on a sob. She turned away from Bo, determined to shut down the emotional explosion.

He called her name softly, no doubt to comfort her.

Eva whirled on Bo. "That young man was dying in my arms. On my lap. Against my body. Dying!"

Eva's hands went up, reaching for Bo. She realized that they were shaking. She clenched her fists and thrust them down at her sides. She leaned toward Bo as if to hide her trembling hands behind her. "This ridiculous story you're telling is offensive. Outrageous. Unnecessary. If you're doing this to make me sell the house cheaply, there was no need. I would have sold it for pennies the second I saw it. I hated it."

Bo's hands went out toward Eva, fingers spread, reaching through darkness. Anastasia had stopped pacing and now hurried over, as if to come between Bo and her mother.

Bo stopped in mid-stride. "You've known since the first evening that I wanted to buy the house to protect my work with Baby Joy's writings. But I've respected your claim and presented my work to you. This story I'm telling you now isn't even included in Baby Joy's stories. It's just my own effort to explain-"

"Explain what? Your uncle's violence? Your family's greed? Their murder of an innocent young man? Community sacrifice! Nonsense, Bo. Do you hear me? Offensive, ridiculous nonsense."

Bo backed away from Eva and stood staring at her. He seemed, by the rise and fall of the shadows outlining his ribcage against the deeper darkness, to be breathing heavily. "If I've offended you, I apologize."

Eva forced her voice to a firmness she did not feel. "I want you to get out of this house until we can leave it. That will be in a few days."

"No, Mommy!"

Eva turned dully toward her daughter. "Honey, I have to get you out of here. This man is playing mind games."

Anastasia pleaded, "His Tansy story is the first thing I've heard since we got here that makes sense."

"Oh, honey. You're in shock. We're both in shock, and he's playing us for fools."

"Mommy, you forget. I'm the one who spent the day with Tansy. I'm the one who heard him talk about his life. I've never liked or trusted Bo Wolfson until this minute."

"You never trusted him?" Eva was dismayed. How alone her daughter must have felt. "Why didn't you tell me, Anastasia?"

Anastasia hedged. "I didn't exactly distrust Bo, either. I felt like he was deliberately hiding something. Whatever it was, it seemed to be very important to him."

Eva turned, suddenly quieted, to study Bo. Outrage and fear still had her heart hammering in her chest.

Eva was convinced that her daughter was endangered by the story that this strange man, Bo Wolfson, had just told. Only, Eva could not tell if, as Anastasia thought, he believed the story and told it to share information.

What if he simply wanted to frighten and intimidate his listeners? Eva could not believe that Bo thought his story had any value other than to scare her and her daughter out of their new home.

But what was the secret Anastasia sensed in him? "Bo, my daughter is seldom wrong about such intuitive things. Is she right about you? Are you hiding something from me?"

Bo licked his lips and did not reply.

Eva pursued. "After that outlandish fairy tale about Tansy, what more could you possibly have to hide?"

Bo crossed his arms over his chest.

Anastasia came near her mother. "Mommy, I have a feeling it's not important at this time, whatever it is."

Eva raised her head, countering Bo's apparent arrogance. "If it's not important now, it will never be. We're leaving as soon as I can work things out with Charley."

From behind her, Charley said, "Then we're not leaving, Eva."

Eva whirled to face her cousin. "Charley! You're all right," she said, as though Charley's safety had ever been in doubt.

Charley came into the dark room. "Yes, Eva. I'm all right. But I don't think you are. Maybe it's time to tell this man to take his flimsy stories and cut out of your house, cousin."

"I was just doing that."

Charley reached for her cousin, shaking her head. "No, Eva. That's not what I heard. What I heard was you telling him that his shoddy fairy tales had scared you out of your inheritance."

Eva was silenced.

Charley finished hugging her cousin and let her go. "Bo, maybe you asked to stay because you had some research work to do. I don't know because I haven't seen you do any. But one thing I know. That boy was real, and wrestling that rifle out of your uncle's hands was real, and arguing all night with that policeman cousin of yours was real."

Charley paused. When Bo said nothing in reply, Charley continued very deliberately. "All I know is, if you are willing to go to such lengths to get Eva out of here, to tell such farfetched hogwash instead of whatever is the truth of the matter, I don't trust you."

Anastasia said, "Aunt Charley, I don't trust him either. Not completely. But the stories he just told about Tansy and Tay Zan and the folktales, those are accurate."

"Thank you, baby. Accurate, perhaps, but not true. And they don't have a thing to do with why Uncle Ham shot Tansy and is going to get away with it."

Anastasia was incredulous. "Is he going to get away with it?"

Charley said, "That's why they hid the body, sweetheart."

A small cry escaped Anastasia. Eva threw her arms around her daughter again. "Honey," she said to the suddenly shivering young woman, "I'm sorry."

Charley said, "The best I can figure about why this academic idiot is standing here spinning campfire scary stories to get us to pack up and leave, is they must have hidden the body around here, Eva, on your property. And they want you out of here as fast as possible."

Eva looked up at Bo. She had been furious with him. She, like Charley and Anastasia, had not fully trusted him. But she would never have thought him capable of this. "Bo, is this true? Did you help hide Tansy's body? Or do you know where it's hidden? Are you trying to get me out of here so it won't be discovered?"

Bo remained quiet. Eva felt a surge of hurt and fury rise against his silence. How dare he take her trust, her openness, her willingness to listen to his petty and insignificant research, and respond with this stony silence when confronted with the suspiciousness of the circumstances?

Petulantly, fighting tears, Eva spat at Bo, "I trusted you."

This was not wholly accurate in detail, though it was true in essence. Eva did not say it with any expectation of a response from Bo.

But now he spoke. "Eva, you were right to trust me. I want you to keep on trusting me. I've been honest with you. There is no one known around here as Tansy. How do I prove a nonexistence? Can I take you to look at court records? Talk to the attorney for the estate? That's my own father, Eva. I'm in a no-win situation, trying to persuade you to believe me."

Charley snorted with contempt. "His father has legal control of the estate? Well, I better get a private investigator in here quick."

184

Eva felt tears again. She had been moved by Bo's brief speech and wanted to return to her growing faith in him. She wanted this escalating nightmare to turn out never to have been. She wanted Anastasia to be safe returning to her ancestral country home. She wanted normalcy and peace.

Bo said, "Eva, what can I do to show you that I'm honest with you? To show you that you can trust me?"

"You can tell me what it is you're hiding."

Bo was caught off guard. "What?"

Eva repeated, "I told you Anastasia isn't wrong about people's issues. She's uncannily observant. Intuitive. Insightful. If she says you're hiding something, experience tells me she's right. What is it you're hiding, Bo?"

She persisted. "Is Charley right, Bo? Are you trying to get rid of me so you can help cover up wherever Tansy's body has been hidden? Are you involved in his murder?"

In her arms, Eva's daughter protested faintly. "Mommy."

Bo said, "Eva. No. I'm not involved in his murder. I don't think he was murdered. I don't think he exists."

Eva made a sound of disgust and tried to turn her back to him, still holding Anastasia. Bo's hand shot out in the dark and pulled her around again to face him. "Your daughter's right," he said simply. "I am hiding something. Don't ask me to tell you what it is. It can't hurt you, Eva."

"Then why are you hiding it from me?"

185

"I wasn't hiding it from *you*. I hide it from everyone. It's not about anyone but me."

Eva was jarred by the intensity of his voice. Was he gay? Saddled with a prison record? Tested HIV positive?

But they were strangers, after all. Bo needn't feel any obligation to tell her his personal secrets.

And yet, "What is it?" Eva asked. Almost begging.

Charley and Anastasia remained silent, focused on Bo, apparently willing him to come through for Eva. *Doubting him?* Eva wondered.

Bo seemed to struggle with the choices before him. Tell Eva his great secret? In exchange for what? Permission to stay? First refusal to buy the house and property, if she left?

"Is there anything I can do to convince you to stay, Eva, and not give up on the property?"

Charley taunted, "And not to give up on you, right, Bo?"

Bo repeated, "And not to give up on me."

"Mommy, ask him to take us to Tansy."

Bo stiffened. Eva looked at him. "Will you do it, Bo? Take us to Tansy?"

"If I can. Give me until tonight. Promise me you won't leave before tomorrow morning."

Charley laughed. "That's easy." It was true that not leaving was a promise easily given. Filth, fatigue, and hunger made travel unappealing if not impossible.

When Eva had made the unnecessary promise, Bo reached to shake her hand. "By tonight," he said and went soundlessly from the room.

The first thing the women did was to go together into the downstairs kitchen to wash up at the pump. Apparently, even while they were sedated and sleeping upstairs, the plumbers and cleaning teens had continued their work until ousted from the premises by the police. The little pantry next to the kitchen now sported an indoor toilet that flushed with a great rush of cold well water that swept everything before it into a septic tank.

Charley locked herself into the new water closet first while Eva and Anastasia plied the pump in the kitchen, running water into the larger tin tub that someone had brought them for baths.

"So," Anastasia asked conversationally as the cool well water filled the tub, "will this room become the bathroom-literally, I mean-and the outdoor kitchen become the cooking place?"

Given their experience with Tansy, Eva found the question disturbing and did not at first reply. Finally, Eva ventured, "Honey, I'm not sure I ever want to set foot in that place again."

"You won't have to, Mommy, if Charley and I do the cooking." Eva searched her daughter's face. How could she be chatting so casually about cooking in the outdoor kitchen when her new friend had just been murdered there?

Eva did not trust herself to reply again. Instead, she peeled off her grimy gypsy costume at last and dropped it into a swirl of deliciously soapy water in the aged copper basin she had used for laundry only-what?-two days before.

Had anyone brought in all the handwashed clothes from the front porch rails? Had she or Charley located the underclothes delicately hidden

187

for them by Ruth Bethany? And, as pleasantly surprised as they were to find no plumbers and cleaning team hanging about today, what would they do about all the work that still needed to be done if they were to remain at the plantation house for even a few more days?

Charley said, "I wonder if your promise to Bo not to leave precludes my driving down to that gas station superstore to find us some food. I sure could use a cup of coffee."

Eva said, "Why don't you take Anastasia and go? I'll wash the clothes and lay them on the railing to dry. That way, if Bo's around and notices the car leaving, it shouldn't take him long to see me on the porch and realize I've kept my promise and stayed."

Curiously, Eva wondered how her challenge to Bo had become a test of her own ability to keep a pledge. Trapped by her own effort to entrap, she thought. Idly, as though there was a future to their relationship, Eva wondered what African moral Bo might call up to verify her impression of having been tricked by a trickster.

Enjoying the hot sunshine on her face, Eva carried the first basin of washed clothing from the back door to the front porch. Stretching out the skirt, blouse, and skimpy underthings he had bought her, Eva went over the screaming scene in her bedroom.

She must have been maddened by the sedative and the shock. It was the only excuse she could give herself for such an explosive loss of self-control.

But, she argued with herself, hadn't Bo's own peace-making promise to locate Tansy proven the lie of everything he'd said about Tansy not existing?

This thought struck Eva like a wet piece of clothing in the face. Surely, if Bo located Tansy now, she must never, never trust him again.

As this realization crystallized in her mind, Eva returned to the house's back door. She was in time to see a figure working its way toward her from the woods.

Though he was still far away, the distinctive, slender figure was Bo's. When he realized he had Eva's attention, he raised one hand in a sweeping wave.

Eva's heart leapt. Could he have found Tansy already?

Through her mind flashed the image of Tansy on her lap, dying. She could not, would not go with Bo to see Tansy's body. Eva watched Bo coming on, loping toward her slowly across the weedy fallow cotton field. She was relieved that Anastasia was not with her to hear Bo's news.

She stood transfixed outside the back door, the empty copper basin propped against her hip by one outstretched arm, like a washerwoman. She watched and willed this oncoming shape outlined by sun and shadow against the trees not to be Bo, not to come on, not to reach her.

Before he was close, Bo called out, "It's not going to work, Eva," and she went lightheaded with relief.

"Why not?" she called back, just for good form. It wouldn't do to appear to be cowardly.

Bo didn't speak again until he'd reached her. As he came up the half-buried stone walkway that led to the back kitchen door, he asked almost lightly, "Where are the others? Out shopping?"

Eva ignored the effort at casualness. "What's happened, Bo?"

Bo shook his head and came so close to her that he had to remove the basin from her hip and hand and set it on the ground. He straightened and took her fingers in his own. "Eva, I'm not going to find him," he said softly. "I've circled the property, and the tracks from the kitchen don't pick up anywhere. It's the strangest thing I've ever seen."

"Are there tracks from the kitchen?"

"Well, not tracks. But as you know, there's that pack of blood on the ground."

Eva said impatiently, "Only a dog could follow a blood trail."

Bo turned quietly, firmly away from her. He said nothing. He stared out beyond the outdoor kitchen, as if looking past the fields and into the encroaching woods.

Into-what had he called it?-what was hidden from the rational mind. It occurred to Eva, watching the muscular curves of his shoulders slide to slender, powerful hips, that the forest world that surrounded them was not fearful to Bo. Did he, perhaps, know it as well as Tansy had?

Two fantasy creatures battling for a wood-and-stone house that both of them wanted to claim, their only obstacles three disoriented women who understood absolutely nothing of the ancient, mystical world in which they battled.

Eva watched Bo, shut out by his intense concentration, and felt suddenly, irrationally afraid.

CHAPTER TWELVE
WHAT WE WANT

Eva was jarred by her realization that she had no idea when or where Charley had bought the fragile china plates, expensively discolored by obvious antiquity. A little ashamed, Eva wondered if she should ask.

Instead, as if she'd read the meaning of her cousin's thoughtful gaze, Charley spared Eva and explained, unasked. "The cleaning crew came up with these from some recesses of 'stored things' that I think we should explore."

"They are strangely lovely." Eva turned the eggshell-darkened porcelain. The china was so fine the dessert plate in her hand was almost transparent, allowing her to sense the outline of her fingers on the sunny side. Tiny hand-painted rose buds bled across the border, twisted helplessly in intricate vines. "Is there a whole set?"

"No doubt," Charley said.

"Should we be eating off of it, then?"

The question was not so much for herself as to demonstrate, finally, an interest in something that Charley might gain from this mad dash to the buried Old South. Antiques were a flourishing business these days. Perhaps Charley could recoup some of her losses, if the house contained a few mint-condition antiques. Charley would know big city sales contacts.

Charley interrupted Eva's unvoiced thoughts. "Don't even think about it." Charley softened the sharp comment with a smile. "I brought the plates out to our humble picnic just to show you that there's as much that's priceless about your inheritance as there is terrifying, Eva. Cheer up, little one."

The endearment, which Charley had adopted when she suddenly took over the role of Eva's parents-a big child raising a smaller one-brought Eva a twinge of tenderness and pain. Eva swallowed the familiar bittersweet mix. How would she ever get on with the business at hand?

Eva had put it off as long as possible. When her daughter and cousin had returned with their "spoils," as Charley called the spicy, motley collection of bright and steamy gas station food, Eva could not stand to be trapped in the house to eat. Nor could she bear the front porch, with its hope-filled memories of their first day at their ancestral home.

Eva had led Charley and Anastasia to the willow and rose bower. She sat on the stone bench and waved a hand to invite them to sit with her in contemplation of the willows, the wild and tangled rose vines that clambered up splintered trellises, and the angel poised as if to spread her wings in flight.

Eva would have been hard pressed to explain what she thought she would get out of bringing her loved ones here. Would the angel dissolve reality again and stir softly for them, too? Would its wings sparkle? Spread? Beat and lift the lovely being into the air above them?

Eva wished she had not read Baby Joy's stories, had not held Tansy as he lay dying. Did not suspect Bo of innumerable impossibilities, murderous and metaphysical.

192

"I will not insist that Bo tell me his secret," Eva said at last to her daughter and cousin. "Try to understand. I don't want to know what it is."

Charley was quick to re-join. "But what if it has to do with our safety, Eva?"

"Aunt Charley, I don't think it does. Not at this point, anyway."

Charley said, probably more sharply than she intended to, "Child, your sixth sense is a truly wonderful thing, but some of us like things to be concrete. How can you know Bo's secret won't compromise our safety? Even if you suspect what Bo's secret is, you can't know all possible developments that could come from our not knowing it. After all, there must be a reason the man is keeping whatever it is a secret."

"It just has to do with being different, I think, Aunt Charley. I can't explain."

Charley said, "Nor should you have to. He's the one with all the murderers in the family. He should be doing the explaining."

Eva shook her head. "Charley, Bo's family is our family. If Bo has murderers, so do we."

"So they're family now, Eva? I thought you didn't trust them."

Eva was, at last, too weary of the topic to care about winning one more argument. "I'm just saying that maybe walking away won't work."

Anastasia's soft voice was thoughtful. "Maybe what we try to leave behind will haunt us," and Eva was struck by the fleeting memory of her parents that she had had while holding Tansy. How often, how intensely would this memory resurface, increasing its nuances of feeling each time?

Was this what happened to the African Americans who fled the persecution and pain of the South? They left behind something precious they had not known needed them, was an inescapable part of them. An intense and helpless offspring of-what?-their own suffering.

"Fanciful," Eva muttered aloud. Immediately, she remembered saying that to herself, about her thoughts, the moment she'd stepped from the car and seen the house for the first time face to face.

But, come to think of it, why had her parents come back to this plantation, so long ago? Following Charley's parents, who had died on this trek back into the past. Why had both their parents come back here? And why had all four of their parents died here?

Could it possibly be true that Eva had never asked this question of anyone?

"What's fanciful?" Charley asked.

Eva snapped out of her reverie. She looked at her cousin and felt as if a ray of light, perhaps reflected from a wing of the glittering angel, filled her own mind with brief clarity. She must ask Bo if he knew why their parents had returned here, and why they had died here.

Could she trust Charley and Anastasia with knowing what she meant to find out?

No, of course not. They would be agog, hiding their anxiety and waiting behind windows and doors while she talked with Bo to find out what he had to say.

And ultimately, Eva suspected, both Charley and Anastasia would decide that Bo was guilty of committing whatever fatalities he described. Best to throw them off, for the time being. Get back to their current obsession. What did she think of this secret of Bo's her daughter and cousin were so determined to uncover?

Eva said, inspired, "Charley, what if Bo's secret is only private?"

Anastasia sighed, the patience of youth trapped among hard-headed elders. "Mommy, that's just what I've been trying to say. At least for the time being, that's all I think it is."

Charley said, "Somebody needs to tell me what you two are talking about."

What if Bo's secret was as simple as the reasonable fear that he had no academic future, based as it was on publishing Baby Joy's historical horror stories?

Worse still, and more inexplicable to bring up in front of Anastasia and Charley, what if Bo's secret was a previous relationship? A marriage? Not knowing about that foray into experimental intimacy, wouldn't they wonder why that was a secret?

Eva thought-and hoped she'd become too tanned during the blistering drive south for her blush to be visible-of her brief, soul-searching encounter with Bo. How could he say the simplest thing about himself to her, knowing that she faced him aligned with her daughter and cousin, waiting to know his secret, his insecurity, his vulnerable issue?

Wouldn't disclosing a marriage to all three of them cause Eva embarrassment? Confusion? *Hurt.*

A child.

Tansy. What if Tansy was not a mystery but was Bo's own unclaimed offspring?

Eva felt her throat tighten. But how could such a secret be harmless? Why would Bo have disclaimed all knowledge of Tansy's existence, if he knew or suspected that this hunted being was his own son?

Eva suddenly gasped for breath. "This has to stop. The secrecy. The wondering. I'll ask Bo to speak with me privately. If he will tell me what this secret is, so be it. If not, we'll have to decide what to do, without knowing what he's keeping from me. From us, I mean."

Anastasia's hand snaked around the grease-stained paper bags of deep-fried sweet potatoes, breaded crawdad rolls, fried okra, and the yawning isolation that separated the women momentarily from each other. She touched her mother. "Mommy, you don't have to confront Cousin Bo now. It can wait. You've had enough."

Charley added, "I meant to protect you, little one, not scare you worse. Leave it. But we're not getting out of here." She dipped a work-scratched hand into bags at random and began scooping bright steaming strips of food onto the fragile porcelain each woman held.

"Not leaving?" Eva asked. Was this what her subterfuge had brought into the conversation? When had this decision been made?

Anastasia explained with unnerving calm, "Not till we've found Tansy and can take him away, too."

Eva must have groaned.

Anastasia said defensively, "Mommy, we can't just leave him to more danger from these people."

Eva said, "Honey, you're going to have to face-
"

"That we don't know anything about what's happened to Tansy," Charley intercepted. Eva started to object. But Charley quelled her with a glance. *Not now. Please.*

Eva's arm went around Anastasia's small, brave shoulders. "And if we never find him again, Anastasia? We have to plan for all possibilities, honey."

Charley insisted, "Cut it out, Eva. It will take time to know all that. In the meantime, we have a lot of work to do to make this house liveable and saleable, if it comes to that."

"If it comes to what?"

"Selling it," Charley said simply and bit a long bright strip of grease-dripping sweet potato. She licked her long fingers with drama. "Ooh, where have these been all my life? You think loving a certain kind of food is in the genes?"

"So we'll get to work, like you always say, Aunt Charley," Anastasia said brightly and shrugged out from under her mother's arm.

End of discussion, Eva thought. Since when had these two become conspirators? Eva turned a curious gaze toward her cousin, just beyond the slope of Anastasia's slender shoulders.

"Is that what I always say?" Charley quipped. "Well, I must not have known what I was talking about, 'cause I ain't never seen work like what's waiting for us now."

Anastasia laughed, a fairy sound in the lowering light of the afternoon.

Charley turned back to Eva. "Cousin, this isn't even what we were supposed to talk about. Is it, Anastasia?"

Anastasia happily shook her head no, her mouth stuffed to bulging with several gas station concoctions Eva preferred not to figure out.

Charley's tone became cajoling. "Eva, honey, me and Anastasia promised ourselves we were only going to talk about enjoyable things over dinner. One topic: what do we want to do?"

"That's easy, Charley, but I'm not sure it's going to be enjoyable. We have to get back to Los Angeles as fast as we can and see if we can get our lives back together."

Charley clicked her tongue. Anastasia giggled through her mouthful, still smiling. "Wrong answer, little one. I didn't say what do we think we *have* to do. I said, we're going to talk about what we *want* to do." She waited for this to sink in. "Strange concept, huh, Eva?"

Now it was Eva's turn to sigh. Didn't these two understand anything about their predicament? Surely neither of them had more reason than she, Eva, to pretend that this escape to the South could work. But even she was ready to admit it was a bust. Time to pull up stakes for the real world of city, stress, and opportunity.

What was here for them? *Mystery. Baby Joy's madness. Tansy's murder.* And maybe danger for the three of them, but how could they know? Whom could they trust to tell them enough to piece a whole picture of their situation together?

But Anastasia's eyes shone with anticipation. What harm was there in going along for just one dinner conversation?

Eva swallowed her frustration. "Show me how to play this game. Okay, what do you two want?"

Clearly, they'd been at this together for a while. Charley leapt in to get them started. "A retreat and roundtable for professional women," she fairly squealed. Anastasia made groaning noises and rolled her eyes in what, Eva realized, were expressions of excitement.

Charley was beaming. "I figured it all out. Everything I've been talking about-" *When was she talking about anything?* Eva asked herself, stunned "-comes together if we just call it a retreat and think-tank-no, roundtable-for professional women."

Eva hazarded, "Charley, what comes together?"

Charley bounced in place on the stone bench, clutching her plate. Eva watched Charley's pounding bottom, dumbfounded by this display of youthful enthusiasm.

Anastasia must have finished working on her collection of comestibles, for she bellowed gaily, "All of it, Mommy."

Then Anastasia dropped her antique plate joyfully into her lap, where, by the grace of a kind fate, it stayed put, and began to tick off possibilities on her elegant fingers. "The bed and breakfast idea-right, Aunt Charley?-and the roundtable-sessions-at-the-dinner-table idea-I like that one best, Mommy-and the community garden idea, and the guest-community-gift-and-barter shop idea! A retreat for those who need a haven and a workshop for those who want information and connections. How to rebuild the Gulf for women who can pool their resources to help each other do it! Seasons with these hardworking women, and getting our privacy back when we want it. And, someday, tours of our work, like our community garden, skill center, and barter shop."

Anastasia gave up and waved both hands with abandon. "Oh, it all works, Aunt Charley. It's perfect."

Eva opened her mouth to ask a question but could think of nowhere to start.

Looking away from her mother and aunt, Anastasia grew abruptly sober. "I'll offer day care for toddlers and children." Then she hushed and inserted more exotic strips of fried local wildlife into her mouth, chewing as she ruminated on such a possibility.

Eva was speechless.

On the one hand, she was relieved to learn that Charley was not worried, evidently, about financial loss due to this venture. On the other hand, her cousin's timing, for an investment broker who had somehow weathered the crash of '08, seemed disastrous. *We're just about to abandon this and get out of here. What's Charley thinking, putting plans like that into Anastasia's head? Isn't the loss of Tansy enough for her to cope with when we go?*

Eva said, "Anastasia," but was again cut off by Charley, smiling full force like an excited little girl. "Excuse me for not telling you sooner. I know you've been worried that I wouldn't get anything out of my investment, restoring the house and grounds and all. But the house didn't cost us a penny-"

"It cost you your job, Charley."

"-so we have to expect to lay out something. Don't dramatize, Eva. At least, not about this. I'm excited about this." Charley's look pleaded, *Can't you tell? Don't you care? Can't you let me be the dreamer, for once?*

Charley added with great emphasis, "Eva, I *can't* run out of money. The more I invest in this project, the more I'll make. I promise you. Professional women or their employers can pay for their stay, and anyway, I need good uses for what I've made of my life."

Eva could understand the desperation of this message, if not what it meant to Charley. Hearing Charley express her own dissatisfaction with success struck a sympathetic chord and quelled her protests about this indulgence in what seemed useless daydreaming.

Eva brought herself up short. She had been invited into something Charley and Anastasia must have started sharing some time during the string of recent crises. They had just shared their survival fantasies with her, and she was blowing it. Eva could see that. What she couldn't see was why she was the only person who seemed to remember they were talking about settling down in the middle of a murder scene.

Eva tried again. "Charley, we have to think of what's happened here," but this time it was Anastasia who would not let her go on.

"Mommy, we don't know what's happened here. But we do know what we'll face if we turn around and try to go right back to L.A. I know what I'll face. A semester I can't get back in school, and I'll just be working full time with everybody asking me what went wrong, thinking I flunked out of college in my second year. And what if Tansy-I know you don't want to hear this, Mommy, but you said explore all the possibilities-what if Tansy, *for whatever reason*, is alive and wonders what happened to me? I can't even write to him."

Eva's shoulders sagged under this burden of probabilities. Just this morning, it had seemed so obvious that they must go. Now, the two women whom she loved and wished to protect had suddenly, illogically, devoted themselves to magical plans to make a go of staying.

No, more than that. To make it crucial that they stay.

What could she say?

Charley prompted Eva, "So come on, cousin. What would you want to do?"

Eva had pledged herself to join the fun, but she'd made a mess of it so far. Why was she so resistant? *Play along.*

Eva said slowly, thinking, "I'd want to see the house restored. I want lights and running water."

"Showers," Anastasia squealed.

Eva smiled. "And clean floors and well-lit hallways. Don't you two wonder what that stained glass window looks like when you can really see it?"

"*Your* turn," Charley insisted. "*We'll* talk about what *we* want."

Eva smiled. "All right." She borrowed Anastasia's finger technique. "Electricity all over the house, even in Bo's dungeon."

Charley shivered dramatically. "Cousin, you're obsessed with that place."

202

Anastasia laughed. Eva plowed on, bending backward another finger with the pressure of her determination to count. "Running water in three full bathrooms and a working kitchen. With a stove. And a microwave. And music blaring from a CD player at all hours of the day and night. I am *starved* for tunes."

This was fun. Eva relaxed and looked at her small family. The other two women beamed upon her. This felt good. How far did she dare to take this game? "And I'd enroll Anastasia at Cooper College, so she can finish getting her degree."

Silence. Judiciously, Eva fed her trembling smile a bright orange strip. "Mm," she said with true surprise. "Sweet and kind of spicy. What is this thing?"

Anastasia looked distracted. "That's the deep-fried sweet potato. A degree in what, Mommy?"

Eva was trumped. "Oh. In what? Well, honey, I don't really know. What would you like to major in?"

Anastasia wasn't making it that easy. "What does Cooper College offer?"

Eva looked with despair at Charley. "I thought we were just wishing. I really don't know what the college offers, except-" as inspiration struck "-you know, it started as a teacher's college. That's why it's named Cooper, for Anna Julia Cooper. She was born enslaved but was liberated and able to learn to read by the time Emancipation and Reconstruction came about. She was such a quick study that she started school at age six and was teaching adults by age ten. She was a far-seeing woman who wrote a book about how African American families and communities, and American society as a whole, would have to restructure themselves if the nation was going to not only survive the legacy of enslavement but even prosper, in a moral as well as financial sense."

To Eva's amazement, Anastasia looked intrigued. Her plate forgotten, Eva's daughter pulled her braids tightly back from her face, a gesture she often used to indicate unwillingness to be distracted from whatever had caught her interest.

Anastasia released the wild tangle and it spread again across her shoulder blades, fanning from cheek to cheek and out into the wet summer air like a sparkling halo. "So, do you think it's still a teacher's college, Mommy? Remember I just said I might run a day care for Aunt Charley's professional women guests? Do you think a degree in education would help?"

Anastasia sat up straighter, staring ahead. "I'll open a preschool in the detached kitchen."

Eva was aghast. "Where Tansy was just-"

"Visiting!" Charley finished for her and glared pointedly at Eva.

Anastasia dreamed on. "I'll call it Anna's Academy and teach reading readiness. Do you remember, Mommy and Aunt Charley, that I was called Anna in nursery school?"

Charley beamed. Eva cringed. Evidently, Anastasia didn't remember that episode in exactly the same way that her mother did.

Charley gushed, as though she, too, had forgotten all those nursery school tears. "So you'd be naming the school for both yourself and your new role model, right, Anastasia? What a fulfilling scheme, honey. I see great promise here."

Anastasia ruminated. "And what for the older kids who might come?" She brightened. "I have it. Test-taking skills. So they won't fear standardized testing. We'll learn to make test-taking a self-challenging game."

Charley said matter-of-factly, "Of course, older kids can often use reading improvement, too, you know."

Anastasia pondered this point with due solemnity.

Eva sighed. Oddly enough, she now felt reluctant to pursue these thoughts. Her upbeat idea about getting Anastasia back into college had more to do with assuaging her own guilt for pulling her out of the University of California system than with getting her into a profession as demanding and, often, unrewarding as teaching. Was Anastasia, the idealist, up to the disappointments of being licensed to teach in one of the poorest states in the Union?

"Honey," Eva started, "this is Mississippi, you know. I'm not sure teaching here is quite the thing for a city girl like you."

Charley intercepted. "Wishes meet reality," she said with triumph. "That's where we start. Cooper's a private college, isn't it? Historically African American? I just bet we can get Anastasia in, with her sky-high SAT scores, and with me paying her tuition cash-on-the-counter, before school starts in the fall." Charley mimed slapping a bundle down with the open palm of her hand. "Let's get on it." And she reached into a cotton drawstring pants pocket to fish around for her cell phone.

"Hold on," Eva pleaded. "Who are you calling?"

"Information." Charley tossed a tendril of some brown-and-white fried animal into her thoughtful mouth. She chewed.

Eva reached for the phone. "Wait. Let's not do it that way." Charley and Anastasia regarded her. "Why don't we wait until I talk to Bo. Remember, he teaches there."

On cue, Bo's dusty Volvo hummed into hearing range. Anastasia actually clapped with anticipation. "This is working," she pronounced.

"Good sign," Charley agreed.

"Since when do you, a businesswoman, believe in signs?" Eva wanted to know. She glowered at her enthusing cousin. How had she missed the signs of this growing hysteria?

It took Bo no time to find the women in the rose and willow bower and invite himself to dinner. "Thought you'd have finished long ago," he opined as he stretched his sinewy, jean-covered legs out on the far side of Eva.

He had sat too close to her on her side of the bench. In fact, Eva was sure that his choice of squeezing in beside her instead of taking the obvious roomy space next to Charley was a dead giveaway of their one, ill-advised experience of intimacy.

To cover her embarrassment, Eva let Anastasia leap right into the topic at hand. "Cousin Bo, we're wondering what I can major in at Cooper College, starting this fall. Is it too late for me to get in as an education major? Cooper does still offer education, doesn't it?"

They'd run out of fragile porcelain plates, which Bo said he wouldn't have felt comfortable touching, anyway. He scooped a sample of everything into the palm of one hand and picked up chunks of fried okra and chicken livers, and broken strips of onion rings, licking grease from his fingers as he talked.

In no time, he'd persuaded Anastasia to enter Cooper College as an African American Studies major, to assure herself of after-the-deadline acceptance, and then to add an education minor or double major at the beginning of her second semester.

"African American Studies has just come back into its own at Cooper," he explained, "and is hungry for promising students. Top students have been going into the tried-and-true, job-guaranteed-upon-graduation majors for too long. You'll be a godsend, and a shoo-in. You can start the education classes you need right away, even before you enroll as an education minor."

"Double major," Anastasia corrected him. "Might as well get two degrees, while I'm at it." And in an aside to her mother and aunt, "I agree with the thinking that an educator needs to major in a subject besides educational theories. I've decided I want to be an expert in some area of African American Studies."

Charley and Bo beamed upon her. Bo continued advising. "Your two years at UC will come in handy for your general education requirements at Cooper. This will work out beautifully."

"Splendid," from Charley. "Eva, I'm so glad you brought it up."

Eva smiled as tepidly as weak tea. What had she been thinking when she mentioned college?

At last, the sun was sinking, and the four of them began to slap mosquitoes from arms and ankles. So happy were Charley and Anastasia with the thought that coming to the plantation would not interrupt her young future, but help assure it, that they were still tossing around plans for contacting electricians and plumbers not related to anyone in their extended family as they gathered plates and sacks to go inside.

Bo lingered below the stone angel with Eva. "Why so glum? Wasn't this what you wanted? For your move here not to have compromised your cousin and daughter's lives?"

In the blushing fall of blackness, speckled by fireflies and humming with the music of nightbirds and cicadas, Eva closed her eyes against her sudden, aching wish that she could slip into Bo's arms and be held against her feelings of uncertainty.

How lonely to stand in the dark with someone so desired, body and tastes so intimately known, and be unable to touch him.

"Bo, I wanted them to be all right, here, yes. But that was when I still hoped it was safe and reasonable to stay here."

She felt his breath whisper against her ear more than she heard it. "And you don't hope that anymore?"

"I no longer think it's possible." She looked up toward him. "Do you know what happened to my parents and to Charley's when they came down here? Or were you too little to understand what went on?"

Eva had left him an out to assure that Bo wouldn't lie or evade. She watched him, thinking, *Maybe I don't want to know. Maybe he was too young to know. He was only a child, wasn't he?*

But Bo said, "I know what happened, Eva. I'm just not sure it's the best thing for us to talk about right now."

Eva felt suddenly dizzy and slumped back down onto the stone bench. *All these years.* Why had she never thought about the fact that she and Charley didn't really know what had happened to their parents? What had they always said, when asked? "An accident." Vague. *Innocuous.*

L.A. African Americans grew up with the stories of lynch, rape, denial of health care, and learned to inherit their forebears' fear of the Deep South. Eva and Charley's parents had nostalgically, foolishly gone "home," and the Deep South had somehow "got" them.

Uninformed. Why had no one made sure they understood?

But here she was, alone in the night with someone who knew. Was she brave enough to insist that he tell her? *Right now?*

Eva looked toward Bo, where he stood above her, and realized that, any minute, he would come sit beside her, take her hands, look into her eyes.

And he would tell her. *Ready or not.*

Eva felt anger rise to meet his tenderness. Was this what it took to make him reach out to her?

Always, her own pain? Couldn't he ever, just once, reach out because he cared?

Or even because he needed her, just once, as deeply, as personally, as she was always finding out that she needed him?

Spitefully, Eva struck out at Bo's desire to be gentle. She sliced into his concern for her with the other question she had meant to ask him tonight. "Never mind about my parents, Bo," she said suddenly. "I have another question. Is Tansy your child? I was just wondering. Is that your secret?"

Even in the semidarkness, Eva could see Bo's hurt and anger. When his lips parted to speak, Eva instinctively drew back, as if from a challenge.

"Yes," Bo said very deliberately. "Tansy is my child."

210

CHAPTER THIRTEEN
I WANT TO TAKE CARE OF YOU

Eva felt that cold wave pass through her insides that signaled shock. For some reason, the words did not bring to her the image of a young boy unloved and abandoned, as she had feared, had hoped not to learn was Bo's fault.

Instead, she saw another woman, a deeply loved woman-for surely Bo would have a child no other way-who took what Eva so wanted and who, then, must have left Bo anyway, dissatisfied.

Eva stared at Bo, who had not waited for her, had not cared that she existed and would one day find him, negligent and lying about his son.

Bo spoke on into her astonishment until Eva began to hear his words. "And he's your son, Eva. And he's your dead parents' son. He's Charley's dead parents' son, and he's all of Charley's unborn babies. My God, Eva. Tansy is all of our progeny and all of our ancestors. What do I have to tell you, baby, to make you stop fighting me about this?"

Eva whispered, wishing she could rise to face him at eye level, "You have to say something more reasonable than that, Bo. I can't understand that. And I think what you've just said to me is horrible."

At that, Bo did drop down onto the bench beside her. He slid forward until he was almost on one knee and twisted to face Eva, seizing her still fingers.

She searched his face, wondering at her own numbness. Had that reference to her dead parents thrown her into shock? Or was it the way he'd tossed her question about her parents and Tansy together? *That was cruel of him,* Eva thought.

Or was it the sharp image of his previous life, without her, that had hurt her so badly? *How silly,* Eva scolded herself mentally. *I've had a husband. I've had lovers. Why would I think Bo's life should have been more celibate than mine?*

Bo raised Eva's fingers to the pillow of his lips, the heat of moist breath. "Eva, let's not. Please. No more, honey."

Eva tried to swim out of the fog of her hurt and withdrawal to focus on Bo. He dropped her fingers and seized her face. Now he was on his knees.

He held her face and looked with such intensity into her eyes that Eva became fearful. What must he do, what would he say to break this tension, end this standoff?

He stared, inches from her eyes, her skin. Eva thought that he would have to kiss her just to rise and walk away.

"Eva, I can't do this. I *can't.*" Bo let go of her cheeks from between his palms, pushing her a little away from him.

And that was how he rose and ran to the house without embracing her, after all.

When Eva could rise, she made her way to lean against the comfort of the stone angel, under its uplifted wings. She thought, for no reason she could fathom, of Baby Joy's winged African women, enslaved and flying to freedom. It was an old African American myth, that some people could fly. But hadn't Bo told her, during their long talk in the Tea Party Cafe, that an African myth held that flying women were witches?

Eva couldn't help wondering, gazing into the moonlit calm of the angel's lowered eyes, if the flying women escaping slavery would have been considered angels or witches. Maybe that was a question she should have asked Bo, instead of the ones about her parents and Tansy.

When Eva made it to the kitchen, she expected a knockdown drag-out with Bo. It had to come. *It might as well come now.*

Bo had done none of the things he had promised just that morning. He had not found Tansy. He had told her no secrets, neither his own nor about the deaths of her and Charley's parents.

Eva dreaded not only throwing him out but missing him, afterward.

She emerged from anxiety into a kitchen lit with kerosene and candles and raucous with laughter. Anastasia and Charley had spread their collection of desserts onto the worktable top in ancient, awful clay bowls. A battery-powered radio spat static and early Sixties rhythm and blues. Bobby Blue Bland rasped in his sweet, gut-deep baritone:

I want to take care of you.

Let me take care of you.

Eva sank onto a splintered bench end nearest to the outside door. Anastasia pushed a magazine and a bowl filled with chocolate and sugared confections across to her.

"Aunt Charley found it," she explained. "An article about a women's retreat."

Even Bo was smiling. He turned eyes so beseeching upon Eva that, in the shadows between

213

flickers of candlelight, she wondered if he really meant to ask, *How can I reach you?*

She swallowed past the lump in her throat and dropped her head to study the glossy photos of the magazine article.

Anastasia prattled on. "Of course, Aunt Charley's retreat will be unique. It will start small, just us and a cook and maybe a group of maids to take turns coming in once a day. We'll develop our services as we find out what our particular clientele prefers."

Eva wished she could chuckle over Anastasia's peculiar mix of sophisticated jargon and childish excitement. She raised her head and smiled.

Under the bare table, Bo slipped his hand over hers and squeezed. The touch, the secrecy, the urgency, brought tears to her eyes.

Now the radio scratched out a forties recording of Elmore James's "Catfish Blues."

Listen to that, Eva thought. *He's singing about being a fish who can climb out of the water to make love to a woman.* Eva reached with her free hand to turn up the volume.

Well, I feel like a catfish

Swimming on down in the stream.

"Do you hear that?" Eva asked everyone. "A blues song about a man who's a fish and loves a woman. How long have African Americans been singing about this?" *How real are Bo's awful theories? And all these strange goings-on? Do people really have these beliefs? And how did I miss seeing them, all these years?*

Bo said, "There are a lot of blues catfish love songs, Eva. Blues mermen songs, I guess you could call them."

"You know what I want?" Anastasia interrupted.

Charley quipped, "Everything your mama and I bring up."

Anastasia twinkled. "That, too. You know what else I want?"

"Tell us," Eva managed to say.

"Days to go by that all seem the same. You know what I mean, Mommy? Aunt Charley?"

Charley said gently, "You mean routine, don't you, little cakes?"

"Probably. I want the days to pass without seeming like each one is a week. Or a year. Like the few days since we got here. It seems like each one was-not long, but-*demanding*. I can't take too many more days like that."

Charley shook her head. "None of us can. I tell you what. Now that we've got a plan, what you're talking about-it's called *normalcy*, by the way-starts tomorrow."

Charley rose and stepped backward over the bench to leave the table. "So, my dears, the sooner to bed, the sooner to rise, the sooner we'll all get started turning those wishes into our new lives. Did that rhyme?" Charley rambled as she went around the firelit kitchen dimming the kerosene lamps and snuffing most of the candles.

Anastasia followed Charley from the room, tossing back over her shoulder goodnight calls to Bo and kisses for her mother.

Eva and Bo continued to sit. The heat of the heavy, closed room, its damp air thickened by the lingering scent of kerosene and the smoke of the candle wicks, was suffocating. Now from the radio crackled Sam Cook's "Bring It On Home":

You know I'll always be your slave

Till I'm buried, buried in my grave.

Oh, honey, bring it to me.

Bring your sweet loving.

Bring it on home to me.

Bo's fingers interlaced themselves slowly, carefully between each of Eva's and squeezed tighter. "Can't we stop fighting each other? This isn't what I want. Is it what you want, Eva?"

"Is it your turn now to play the 'What I Want' game?" *Can't I ever stop smart-mouthing him? What's wrong with me?*

"I guess it is. Are you going to ask me?"

"What?"

"What I want."

Eva looked at him in the remaining candlelight from a twisted candelabra on the heavy wooden table where they sat. The grotesque antique must have been beautiful once. What had happened to it?

She remembered Bo's tales of the battles the freed Africans fought in this house, the house and farm implements used as weapons of war, as barricades to prop the huge doors against the banging mobs.

Eva didn't want to think of this now. She and Bo were alone. What was it about this house, about being in this place, that brought out from her so much raw need, such explosive emotion?

216

Charley and Anastasia had abandoned them as if there were no volatile silences, no sidelong glances about to erupt into tearing, screaming accusations in the tinderbox of this sultry Southern kitchen.

Eva said, rising, "I think I'll just go to bed."

Bo beat her to her feet, his hand still entwined in hers. He reached for her other hand as he stepped over the bench and pulled her to him. "You guessed it, Eva. That's exactly what I want."

He had the presence of mind to reach forward and flick off the radio before he tugged Eva with him toward the dungeon door.

Eva pulled back. "I can't do this," were the first words she could say. Had she heard him right?

"Yes, you can," he said. "Look. I'm going to show you." Tugging, cajoling, Bo got a flashlight from one of the dark wooden shelves by the dungeon door and flicked it on. "You need to understand this house, that's all," he said. "Let's start with this door."

Had he deliberately misunderstood what Eva meant? She had meant that she could not go to him, go with him, lie down with him and make love. Surely that was what he'd just offered her.

But, whatever his ultimate goal, Bo meant to teach her not to fear his stone tunnel. He flashed the brave little circle of light onto the kitchen side of the door. "Do you see that, Eva? See the sliding bolt?"

Eva stared at it obediently.

"That bolt indicates that the door was originally shut from this side, the house side. Do you know why?"

217

"No, and I don't want to think about it."

Bo tugged her into the space between his arm and his side. He bent slightly toward her and placed the warm cushion of his lips against her forehead. "Yes, you do, Eva. A mind like yours has to think. Give it healthy thoughts. That's nothing but the lock people used to close up this house when they left it. This stone tunnel was probably the first part of this house ever built. There was probably a time that this stone tunnel was the whole house."

Eva looked at Bo skeptically. "What do you mean?"

Bo hugged her more tightly, jollying a smile out of her. "See? Knowledge fights fear. The British subjects who came to this area in the mid- to late seventeen hundreds were under siege more from each other than from anyone else," he said. "That's not a history we get in the textbooks, but it's true, and we need to be aware of it."

By now Bo had eased Eva forward against his flat stomach, pressed too close to him to avoid feeling the rise and fall of his chest as he breathed and talked, the tightening of his stomach with each movement. His arms encircled her waist lazily, his wrists crossed below the small of her back.

Now, as he talked, Eva stared into the irises, read the playful smile that flicked at his lips and vanished. "The shelters they built for themselves, before English law moved in and made their homesteads safe from each other, had to blend into the wilderness, as much to fool each other as any other enemies. So they lived in caves, in stone huts, or in hollowed-out trees." He bent his head to kiss the hollow at the base of her throat. "This stone

218

tunnel was probably the first shelter built by the family that eventually built this wooden house. But unlike most families, they didn't build the mansion apart from the first shelter. They probably never thought they'd ever be safe from their neighbors. Look at this."

Now Bo released Eva and pulled her around to the other side of the door. She whimpered a little as they entered the tunnel.

"I don't want to do this, Bo." She yanked back, to get away.

He hushed her like a child, pulling her into the round between his arms and his body again. "Shh. Don't scare yourself. Listen, Eva. Don't pull away. Just do this. Look at this and let me tell you about it. If you're still not ready to come with me after that, we'll do whatever you want."

Eva began to hear the rhythmic words, and she ceased to struggle. She allowed Bo to edge her to the dungeon side of the heavy door.

Bo shone his light. The little white circle seemed a pinpoint against the stony vastness. It took time for Eva to realize that, on the dungeon side of the door, there was also a sliding bolt.

"Is that what you want me to see, Bo? All right. I see it. Why is it there?"

Bo chuckled as though she were a particularly bright student. "Good girl. That's there because, when this was the planter's house, this is how the family got locked in safely at night. Being inside the dungeon meant being safe, Eva."

His face had become still, sober. He looked intently into her eyes. "Are you listening to me? The safety was on this side of the door. The danger, all the marauding pirates, the pickpockets, the debtors and prostitutes let loose out of English prisons, all that danger was out there, outside this tunnel. Outside this door."

Eva swallowed. Should she tell him anything about what this tunnel meant to her? Could he be trusted to understand? "But when I'm in here, I hear voices. I feel as if I'm going mad."

"What do the voices say?" Was he faking his profound sympathy for her?

"It doesn't make sense. It all sounds sad." Eva licked her lips. Her tongue was dry and stuck to the skin. "They say sad things about running and hiding, and about loss. Some of them I think are people I might know. Maybe even my parents. It scares me to think so. But the others." She shook her head. "I don't know why I would hear any of them. But they're all disturbing."

"Ancestral memory. There's your thesis for your dissertation."

Eva pulled from him. "Now you're making fun of me." She headed for the other side of the threshold. *Why did I trust him? Why did I think he would care? I must be a fool.*

"Never." He yanked her back to him with such force that he lost his grip on the flashlight. It clattered to the stone flags, rolled, but did not go out.

Light splattered weakly across their feet. Eva would have bent to retrieve the flashlight, but she was loath to reach through the darkness for it.

"Honey," Bo soothed, "look at me. Only at me." His fingers raised her chin and held her face steady near his. "How far can you go, baby? Tell me. I won't push you any further than you can go."

"I can't go any further than this," Eva insisted.

In the darkness, she realized that Bo's breath was now upon her own lips. *How close has he come?*

Bo's voice, low and deep, said, "Can you go this far?" The softness of his mouth had followed breath to rest upon her lips, inhale her words as they were spoken, eat the moist air between them as she spoke.

She thought he wanted to know if she could stay where they were, and she meant to say no. She needed to retreat to the brittle wooden box of the plantation kitchen.

But she had no chance. As soon as his question was spoken, as if jealous of the words, or as if the words had another meaning, Bo followed them to her opening mouth to suck them back into his own.

It was a kiss. Dry at the start, and then moistened by soft touches of his lips and tongue, the kiss started as a surprise and became an invasion.

Bo held Eva's head in place with both hands, his own hands free now of the flashlight. She felt his long fingers cup all of the back of her head as he bent into the growing urgency of the kiss, inhaling the words she couldn't say, swallowing back his own breath thick with the tears she had shed in the rose bower, stingy and devouring, pouring himself into the one space she allowed him to enter.

His tongue followed into the vacuum where his words had been consumed. In Eva's head, the images he'd fed her about the sliding bolt to lock out the dangers of the night clicked into place and made sense. *Safe inside here. No one hears. No one can come in.* She eased against him.

Their mouths were lubricated now, wet enough to part without pressure or tugging, and Bo whispered, his lips sweeping against hers as he shaped each sound. "Can you come this far with me, Eva? Can you go further? Tell me."

She meant to say she could, *This far I can manage,* but there was no time. For on the instant that he finished the last word, Bo returned his lips full force to hers, opening a tunnel between their mouths like the tunnel that held their bodies, a mirroring space where his tongue now moved, and where he sucked at her mouth, at her feelings.

"Eva, come with me. Come on." Bo's hand plunged between them, pushing her away from the pleasure of his body. Eva heard herself whimper with shame and desire just as Bo's hand scooped under her thighs to lift her into his arms to be carried.

Bo hefted her sharply into a rough embrace and she realized he was carrying her along down the hallway. "No! No, I can't do this."

"Yes, you can." Bo stopped again along the stones. Now Eva felt her back pressed into the moist wall. The curves of stone fitted her gently, holding her still against Bo's liquid muscles, pressing her, pressing into her, on the other side.

His hands kneaded the undersides of her thighs, working them further and further apart, urging her to let him in. Eva strained and arched her breasts forward against his chest. Bo bent his head to nip a trail of sharp sensations down her throat, along her collarbone, to the fragile swell of her small breast.

The nipple rose to him and was sucked into his hot and lapping mouth.

As tall as he was, Bo drew the nipple and the breast into his mouth while still standing, pressing her into the stone wall. He lifted her again, and this time her legs went around his hips. She sat up and forward, settling onto that hot and urgent wanting between them. Bo held her, called her name, "Eva, let me, let me, let me in," and moved her to meet his rhythm.

Bo's lips were wet and seared the fragile bones along her jaw when he raised his head from her breast. She couldn't see him in such darkness. The flashlight was a pinpoint far away. Every move he made was a surprise.

Eva said, "Yes," and held on tighter.

She needn't have. When Bo moved away from her, she dropped from the wall only as far as the curve of his waiting arms.

She was caught up against his chest. When had he pulled off his tee shirt? Or was that sweat that made it cling like skin?

They moved like swimmers through water, gliding through the thick darkness without pause toward each other, with each other, as he carried her on toward his room. Eva shut her eyes against the blindness.

Bo consumed her as they flowed together. Now she felt teeth at the faint edge of her earlobe, now his tongue full and flat along her neck, drawing the skin into his sucking, nibbling mouth. "I want you," he said as he licked and bit. "I want you so bad."

She had never heard him talk like that. She had never heard his voice so low, his grammar wrong.

She felt carried along by a stranger who was the real man, the man who had been a boy wandering these halls, tortured like his ancestors.

"I want you, too," she said into the darkness.

He swung her when they breached the door of his room. He didn't stumble but went smoothly through the opening and to the far corner, where his sleeping bag and mattress should have been.

Was he an animal, that he could see through blackness? Eva wondered, and then she marveled that the only voice inside her head was her own. How had Bo stilled them? Or had she?

But there was no time to think. Smoothly, she was laid upon the thickness of his sleeping bag against the cool damp stones, and hungrily, almost angrily, his gripping hands, his moaning mouth went for the muscles, the moist and sweating skin, the curves of female fat, the curling hairs, the slippery, parting flesh beneath her clothes.

In the blackness, there was no telling time. How long did they lie together, exhausted, and how often did they wake to touch and find each other near, and come together urgent for another immersion in what they had forbidden themselves, to fall asleep entangled and exhausted again? Eva couldn't tell. Sometimes she feared that the night must have passed. *It must be morning.* It must be the next day. The following evening.

But they could not, would not let each other leave. There was an ancient latrine even further down the corridor, among the stones, and here Bo took her when he woke and had to go. Without light, Eva could not believe her courage as she felt her way behind him, holding his hand and pressing back at the rocks that bulged in the walls. Briefly, whenever she woke alone, she wondered at her courage and at her madness. Surely it was madness that shattered such fear.

She woke to an offering of water at her lips.

"My supply," Bo whispered. "Take a sip."

She pressed her lips to the hard small circle of plastic, opened them, and let the liquid enter her. Again she fell asleep.

She woke to food. "How long have we been in here?" she asked.

"Are you afraid?"

"Not with you."

"Then it doesn't matter. Eat."

They were some kind of hard crackers, probably rye and corn. Rice cakes followed.

Don't rats or mice get into your supplies?"

"I can't tell, in the dark." Bo chuckled, and Eva smiled though she knew he couldn't see it. She felt so heavy. Satiated. *Happy.* She couldn't think when she had felt so loved.

Again, she slept. Would she never wake? What must her daughter think?

It was this thought that finally snapped Eva out of her lethargy. When she woke to it, Bo was asleep beside her.

She sat up, abruptly, fully awake, and looked around her. There was no possible way to know the time in this stone maze. Was it day? *Night?* Could she find her way without Bo's help? Should she wake him?

Somewhere, perhaps, the abandoned flashlight lay at the entry to the kitchen. If she had the courage to get to the door of Bo's chamber, she might see which way to go, if the light still burned. Naked, Eva eased from beside her new lover.

Best not to think of that, she told herself guiltily. Not to think of leaving him to wake without her, to wonder what she felt and why she left.

This was his lair. He knew it, and he was not afraid of the darkness. What if her cousin and daughter had been looking for her?

Eva forced herself to her feet.

It was impossible to think of finding clothes. She would have to find her way out naked as she was and hope to stumble upon scattered clothing, his or hers, along the way. She couldn't think of that, either.

She did not find the door easily. At first, she ran her shins into the glass covers of Baby Joy's writings. Eva cried out and then hushed, waiting to hear something from Bo. The silence in the room had become even more absolute. Surely, he no longer breathed with the ease of a sleeper. *I woke him.*

But if he was awake, Bo chose to say nothing to his fleeing lover. Eva found her way, shins scraped and possibly bleeding, to the hallway door.

She paused and looked back but, of course, through such pitch, she could not see him. Would he know she had not wanted to leave? She hoped so. She called into the stillness, "Bo, I'm sorry. I have to go."

Say "I love you!" she urged herself. *What will it cost you, now?*

Nothing. Perhaps he wasn't awake. In the stillness, there was silence and a decision to be made.

226

Eva slipped into the hallway.

It was true. Faint and far ahead, she could see an almost imaginary point of light, tawny and weak, stretched obliquely across the floor.

She wanted to go back. She was hollow inside, but not quite from fear. *Loss?* But she needed to do the right thing, make sure that her loved ones, her daughter and cousin, hadn't worried about her. Was Bo her loved one, too, after this?

Did she love him? Of that, she had no doubt. Then, why hadn't she said so?

I was ashamed. I was swept off my feet. I didn't know if I could trust him.

I was overwhelmed.

As Eva walked back through the way that had brought her to a resolution of her relationship with Bo, she argued with herself. *If he was awake, he said nothing. How could I speak into that silence?*

And what if he didn't want her to go? *He could have said something to me. I could have explained.*

Would she have? Even as she fought with herself, drawing to the end of the tunnel, Eva wondered at her obsession with protecting herself from this man who had never hurt her.

She paused only briefly to pick up the fallen flashlight and flick it off before crossing the threshold to the kitchen. No one was in sight. The house seemed still and dark with the quiet of the small hours.

Eva found her way up the mumbling, creaking staircase and into her room and her bed without encountering anyone. She hesitated only an instant before slipping under the moth-eaten covers, still nude. If Charley asked, she would say it had been too hot to sleep with anything against her skin.

When Eva finally woke, she thought that she must not have been in the dungeon with Bo for more than one night, after all. Despite the breathless sessions of lovemaking, the sweaty, clingy drowning in a damp blackness like an earthly womb, and the sense that she was reborn when she emerged from her lover's lair to go to her own bed in the gray before dawn, no one else acted as if she'd been gone for very long.

No one rapped at her door. No one poked in a curious head to see if she were up yet.

As Charley and Anastasia got started on their new lifestyle of normalcy, their noise traveled from the hallway, up and down the curving staircase as plans and phone calls were made, workmen and cleaning women showed up, and deals were struck.

Shouldn't I get up? Be a part of all this? But still Eva lingered in bed until the last trace of sleep fled. She was in no hurry to get up, go downstairs, encounter Bo, and discover that, even now, their full-blown lovemaking had not made them a couple in his eyes. Her body still tingled and ached. She wanted to relish the memories.

And yet, even now, Eva remembered with bitterness the afternoon she'd cowered in Bo's arms in his stone room only to have him join the search party in the kitchen without so much as a glance for her.

But that was different, Eva argued with herself now. *Anastasia had disappeared.*

Surely, things should be different now. Their love was acted out. Their resistance was broken

228

down. Anastasia was warned away from Tansy, who, anyway, was dead and gone. *Well, at least gone.*

Eva drowsed for the last time, out of sheer stubborn refusal to waken, and dreamed fleetingly of Tansy running with Anastasia through the woods.

This last dream woke her with a vengeance. Clearly, she was rested-*too* rested for her taste, if she had time to have nightmares about the resurrection of Tansy-and it was time to get up and get involved.

CHAPTER FOURTEEN
CHRYSALIS KITCHEN

There was everything to get involved in. Eva threw on a pair of unwashed jeans and one of her last clean tee shirts pulled from her backpack.

At some time in the last two days, Eva must have found the presence of mind to bundle her bloody new Gypsy skirt and Anastasia's bloody white camisole blouse into the old overgrown latrine. She thought for a moment that, when there was time, she would wash out the Gypsy blouse Bo had given her and slip it in with Anastasia's washed jeans, as an offering to make up for getting rid of her daughter's beloved camisole.

But not today. Eva emerged into the coffee and croissant-scented kitchen just in time to learn what Charley had already set up for the day. Charley and Anastasia were preparing to go pick out wallpaper, paint, parquet, ceramic tiles, and rugs.

"You're leaving without me?" Eva cried in true distress. "But I want to go, too."

Bo's dungeon door was open. Eva's voice must have carried down his tunnel. For, to Eva's relief, Bo soon appeared, rubbing his eyes and smiling shyly. "Is that coffee I smell?" Bo's slanted eyes cast a glance full of shaded meaning at Eva. If the others intercepted the look, they pretended to have seen nothing.

"Yes, that's coffee, and you'd better drink some of it," Charley decreed. "You need to be awake and alert when the electrician arrives. You're the only person here who knows what land is Eva's, and what she has access to, and all that." Charley shook her head ruefully. "I'm just not up to calling in that Uncle Ham of yours. If he shoots somebody else around here, I'm liable to shoot him back, this time. And then everybody'll be in jail."

Bo went meekly to the coffee and paper sacks on the table as Eva slipped into the new bathroom to wash up. When she came out, Anastasia and Charley had disappeared. The blare of the Jag's car horn told her where they'd gone.

Bo looked up from sipping his coffee out of an antique wooden mug, careful of leaks through the splintered cracks. When he saw Eva, he sloshed the mug down onto the table and came quickly around the benches to pull her into his arms. "You left me alone." He pressed a kiss against the ear where the resentful words stung. "Please don't leave me alone like that, Eva, without a word."

Stunned, Eva stiffened in his arms. She was torn. She wanted to defend herself, but at the same time, she wanted to comfort his vulnerability, to be the woman who could soothe the lonely boy speaking to her now.

Or was this the voice of a controlling man?

"I didn't want to go, Bo. I said good-bye, but I didn't want to wake you. I was afraid that, if you asked me to stay, I would. And then my daughter would know about us before I was ready to tell her. Before I knew what to tell her."

Bo lifted his head from the trail of kisses he was blazing down Eva's throat. "Whenever you're ready, Eva, tell your daughter that I love you and I've given my life to you."

Bo watched the effects of this proclamation chase each other across Eva's face. When her surprise resolved into tenderness, Bo added, "And when you're ready, give me your answer. Will you marry me, Eva?"

Eva knew, as soon as she heard the words, that she was incapable of saying anything coherent. Bo was a stranger whose past was almost entirely a mystery to Eva. Worse, Bo was entangled in some as yet unclear way in a murder committed and covered up on Eva's property. How could she consider tying her life to his? *If not your life, then why keep giving him your body and soul?* Eva asked herself.

When Bo's eyes did not break their hold on hers, up so close, so dark, so still, Eva lifted her face to kiss his lips. As she did, she heard Anastasia patter through the foyer toward them.

"I have to go." Eva made good her escape.

Marriage? Was this what she wanted?

Eva had only known Bo for what translated into the thinnest fraction of her life's experiences, deep and troubling though they were. She had been drawn to him though terrified of loving him, and here he was, offering the emotional security of knowing he would be with her for the long haul.

Morality and idealism were served by Bo's offer of marriage. But the modern cynic who could survive an academic environment all the way through to a doctoral dissertation had encountered many philosophies that decried such morals and ideals. If this was a good thing, why did she feel so unnerved by his proposal?

Why did he avoid telling me his secret? Eva asked herself as she ran into the sunshine dappling the porch.

Storm clouds swirled above, throwing shadows between the bright streaks on the wild grass at the edge of the U-shaped drive. Eva thought with amazement that it was an indication of how little time they'd been here that there had not yet been even one summer thunderstorm.

Eva surrendered the front passenger seat of the Jag to her ebullient daughter. Hastily dressed and lacking even a quick swipe of lipstick, Eva floated exultantly through the day's errands, nursing the secrets of her relationship with Bo.

Bo wanted permanency. He offered her stability. He must love her. Of course he did. And she loved him. Why had they not told each other this most important message throughout their passionate, vulnerable night, their quickly whispered reassurances the next day?

They rectified this omission that very night. As the day's storms pummeled the house, opening fissures for drafts and leaks to cheer the visiting hordes of contractors, servicemen and women and all their assistants, Bo roasted corn on the cob and pepper-marinated chicken in the kitchen on a new outdoor grill. When the storms and contractors receded, the weary, hopeful patchwork family gathered to throw out pans and buckets of rainwater and feast by candlelight and radio blues.

"It's good to have a home-cooked meal again." Bo beamed in the face of a compliment from Anastasia.

"You never said you could cook," Charley accused him.

"He didn't want to have to earn his keep," Eva chimed in, as giddily proud of his skills as though she had interviewed and hired him for inclusion among her loved ones.

Bo said, "Does that mean I can stay?" and all eyes turned to Eva.

She realized with a start that nothing had been decided about yesterday's ultimatum that Bo must reveal his secret, find Tansy, or leave. What did Anastasia and Charley want? Eva had no idea, nor did she want to discuss Bo with them right in front of him.

Eva would argue that he should stay, but why was she still intent on hiding what they had become to each other? Eva was too satisfied with her life, for the moment, to risk disturbing its tranquility. She stalled the expectancy all around her at the table with a noncommittal grin.

Only when Charley and Anastasia had surrendered the day and gone up to bed did Eva and Bo wander out into the slightly cooled evening air. They met in the rose bower.

Under the sheltering wings of the angel, they held hands and confessed what each already knew. They loved each other. They had from the day they'd met.

Did they even believe in such things?

"I believe in very little, Bo," Eva admitted. "I don't even believe in the things I want to believe. I don't believe that my parents are in some spirit world looking down on me and my daughter, even though I want to believe that."

"Will you just believe in me, Eva? Believe that I love you and I'll do everything I can to make you feel safe. I know how this place frightens you. I think I can make this move work for you. I think I can make you content, darling."

"I'm sorry, but I don't have faith in abstracts, Bo."

"When it comes to what can't be seen, or what's seen but seems incredible, maybe we're opposites. That's not a bad thing, honey. The world makes sense when you already believe in ideas you haven't even encountered yet."

Eva laughed.

"No, I mean what I said, Eva. Sometimes, when my research or my personal life leads me to understand some ancient, buried concept, I find I already understand it, and I've always believed it. That's reassuring, not frightening. Not impossible. It makes you feel in touch with something greater than what you see around you every day. How do you feel when you look up at stars?"

Bo tilted Eva's chin to raise her head to look above the angel's bowed face to the spreading sky. But the day's clouds lingered, low and thick between them and the pinpoints of heavenly light. "When it's stormy and you can't see the stars, Eva, can you remember how they make you feel? Can you believe in that feeling?"

Eva felt like apologizing. "I don't trust feelings like that, darling."

"Then maybe I'll teach you to have faith in what your life has taught you must be true."

Eva was just about to say that she didn't believe in women being taught by the men in their lives. It

235

sounded so patronizing. But as she lowered her head from contemplating the clouded sky, she found Bo's lips pressed to her own so that she could not speak. Bo's kiss ended the discussion.

They had not resolved how they would spend their nights. They had come all the way from the rose bower around the side of the house and back in through the kitchen doorway before Eva caught herself up short, wondering what to do.

What would Bo expect? That she should lead him up to her room? Follow him down that nightmarish stone corridor to his own chamber?

What would he think of her newly professed love for him if she did neither?

They paused in the kitchen doorway, still holding hands, standing very still. Bo said nothing at all. Moments passed.

At last, Eva spoke. "We made love unprotected last night. I enjoyed it, but you may not know that I'm still very fertile. And I haven't decided if I want another child."

Bo nodded. Eva could see the outline of the movement of his head against the ruddy glow of flames in the darkness. When he still did not speak, Eva did again. "I love you, and I don't want to be confused or worried about what we have and what we're doing. Can you understand that?"

Again Bo nodded.

"Bo, are you ready to tell me whatever your secret is?"

Did she sense his sudden movement, a start of surprise?

If he had been startled, Bo recovered quickly and gathered his calm about him like a cloak. He bent to kiss Eva one last time. "The day's been long enough. I think our love can last a night apart, or however many nights you need. What I have to tell you will still be there, when I can hold you. I'd rather tell you when you're in my arms, Eva."

Was this a standoff? Eva wondered. She had linked her hesitation to make love with Bo again to his keeping a secret from her. He had responded that he would not tell her his secret until she trusted him enough to come to him again and make love.

They parted quietly. Bo had entered the blackness of the stone corridor before Eva extinguished all the kitchen's candles.

Eva dreamed that night, for the first time in her life, that she could fly.

She had not even known she was sleeping. She thought she rose suddenly from bed, her room oddly brightened by some light whose source she could not identify. Had a noise wakened her? Suddenly she was at the kitchen door.

It was open. Bo stood naked on the threshold of the night, looking with yearning toward the woods. He turned back into the house to face her. *Do you believe you love me?*

She wanted to assure him that, yes, most certainly, profoundly, she loved him. But as she stepped forward, he began to run.

And when Eva looked again, she could not find Bo anywhere. There was only the fleet black shadow of a grotesque thing, an ambling dog with a head huge and disfigured, a lion's or wolf's head with the hackles raised, rushing toward the forest that surrounded the house.

The thing disappeared. Eva was not relieved. She searched the outline of the woods for a sight of Bo, safe from the thing that had pursued him from the house. She wanted to call him but did not want to draw the nightmare being back toward her, back between Bo and the safety of the house. Where had her lover gone?

As Eva despaired, she thought she heard her name. Bo was calling her. She must go to him.

But she was motionless with fear of the thing that had gone out into the woods ahead of her. If only she could fly to Bo.

And with the thought, she flew.

Eva spread her arms, as wide as the black overarching sky, willing Bo to come back to her, to be sheltered in her arms. She wanted to hold him now, lie with him and hear this secret that they each feared might separate them. But Bo did not return.

Instead, she realized that the rose bower angel had come to her, and it was not stone, but a being lighter than the air in which it was suspended.

The angel reached for Eva's extended arm and took her fingers in what felt like a tingling, prickling hand made of stars. Eva felt herself rise to follow the angel to her lover.

She was flying. The angel's wings were weighted with layers of gossamer feathers that sparkled in the misted air. They lifted, swept downward, and buoyed Eva and the angel higher, above the oncoming trees. Eva yearned for such wings and turned to look over her shoulders as she slid through the sky. Her own wings were there, not as full and starlit, but speckled brown and black, sleek and swift. Camouflage wings.

238

Eva flew beside the angel. She looked down between the tufted tops of the trees. A black dog bounded along beneath them. *Nothing to fear,* she reassured herself in her dream. *The beast was nothing but a pet.*

With this thought, Eva found herself standing on the forest floor, Bo's arms around her. Tears glittered in his eyes. The angel, the wings, the flight were all gone.

Eva reached up to wipe the tears if they should fall. Bo caught at her hand and pressed a kiss into her palm. She lowered her head to look at the spot where his lips had been and found a pond of tears.

When she raised her face to his again, Eva opened her eyes to bright morning light in her bedroom.

The dust, the decay, the garish splash of sunlight incongruously painting the ruined room with fresh color, greeted her. Eva sat up to study the strange beauty that surrounded her.

I'm happy, she thought. *So this is what it's like to be in love. Pleasure when you're together and joy when you're apart, knowing that, when you're ready, you'll be together again.*

Eva rose to meet the new day.

Her days flowed now. Searing sunlight and steaming heat gave way to the crack of thunderous skies that ripped the horizon and disappeared, leaving chirping crickets and twittering birds in their wake. Strangers swarmed the house in droves, strewing dangerous live cables and gleaming layers of pastel-painted walls behind them, all of it labeled with bright orange warning signs. Plumbing, heated water, and an electric stove were the first signs of the house's new and permanent changes.

The kitchen developed the ability to drain its own water. Anastasia rejoiced that she no longer had to tilt the great tin basin to empty dishwater down the hole that plunged into the earth beneath the pump. Next, the kitchen sprouted polished and painted woodwork, so that its grimy shelves, walls, cabinets, table and benches suddenly emerged like woodland butterflies from chrysalises. Earthy tones and swirls gleamed amid mint green, frosted with the dewy gleam of clear glass cabinet doors and the room's sole window above the new porcelain split sink. Marble countertops sparkling like Gulf beaches before the spill ran all around the room's work areas, echoed by the sandy clay tiles that shielded bare feet from the hopelessly splintered floorboards.

"I love it," Anastasia pronounced as the finishing touch, a screen door to seal out mosquitoes and bats, swung into place.

The fate of the kitchen door had taken some debate to settle. At last, the heavy historic door had been preserved only because a New Orleans artist determined to get out of her Hurricane Katrina trailer had offered to pay her way at the upcoming women's retreat by painting hex signs all over it.

Charley had contacted the up and coming *voudoun* artist to commission some paintings for the redecorated house. Though the woman's bold figures seemed to overwhelm Charley's delicate decor, they had struck a bargain with the painting preservation of the kitchen door.

Seeing the mystical, belligerent production unpackaged, Charley worried aloud that the hex door's brooding burgundy background and vibrant splashes of hands, all-seeing eyes, and spiked crucifixes would destroy the peaceful ambience of the newly finished kitchen. Instead, when the painted door was lifted back into place, "The power of the door gives the softness of the kitchen a sense of substance," Bo decided. "An ethnic connectedness."

"Says this is an African American kitchen," Charley agreed.

"So when are you going to cook us some gumbo in it?" Anastasia wanted to know.

Bo had become unofficial chef. When he had run through the grits and eggs and cornmeal muffin recipes he knew by heart, he produced lovingly battered cookbooks to grace the corner of one marble counter.

"If you see a mob of African American women pounding on the door with their aprons on, don't you let them in," Bo warned Eva when she mentioned the kitchen library he was developing. "Just shout out the window that I'll get their cookbooks back to them after I've copied out some good recipes. I'm new at this, so it might take me some time."

Charley piped up suspiciously, "Would this mob of African American women be any of your relatives, Bo? Because if they are, you can count on it I'm not letting them back in this house. I've had enough of their mayhem. Your people need to calm down."

Eva stifled a smile and chided, "Charley. That's not nice."

"And neither is that man's family. No offense, Bo, but your relatives is wild and woolly. They can't come over here till they learn them some manners, all the money this renovation is costing me."

Bo opened his mouth to defend his extended family, but Anastasia interrupted. "Aunt Charley, didn't we decide that Cousin Bo's relations are our family, too?"

"Eva decided that. I don't want nothing to do with them."

And Bo evidently decided to let the point go for the time being. He had been bringing messages to Eva that Aunt Portia, Aunt Olivia, and Aunt Lydia, whom Eva's little crowd hadn't even met yet, wanted to reconcile. His own parents were proposing a formal dinner at their own home. Bo had put them off with explanations about the dire necessity of the renovations and, Eva suspected, probably some warnings about the misadventures with Uncle Ham and Tansy. But, eventually, what to do about relations leapt onto the mental list of problems to be solved that Eva kept roiling in the back of her mind.

At the top of the list, she believed, was how to introduce to Anastasia the possibility that her mother and cousin might marry. They seemed only very distantly related, if related by blood at all. But would it strike an adult child as incestuous? Eva shuddered at the thought of seeing reproach or disgust in her daughter's eyes.

Bo teased and flirted but had made no more direct requests for lovemaking since the night they'd gone their separate ways. Eva was relieved by his patience and hoped to continue enjoying her almost nightly dreams of flight. She wondered if the vivid and exciting dreams represented the sense of freedom their passion had brought her.

Several nights, when she felt she could not bear to be away from him any longer, Eva had not waited for the dream but had padded softly to the dungeon door and whispered Bo's name into the darkness. Only echoes came back to her and an increase of the terror that those echoes carried.

So she had retreated to her room, rushing through the modernized kitchen from the historic horror that lurked between the corridor's stones. She hoped the room would be sealed off soon. She would have to speak to Charley about it.

Eva never told Bo about her failed efforts to go to him in the middle of the night. By morning, she had always returned to a healthy shame of her superstitious fears.

Bo continued his labored transcription of Baby Joy's cramped and faded pages. He emerged from his labors to brew the morning's coffee and again to cook the evening meal. He and Anastasia sometimes went off together to Cooper College to collect books on African, Caribbean, and African American mythologies coming in through interlibrary loans.

They would walk through the changing house to shove their tomes onto the new library's shelves, loudly debating the reality-bound meaning of some fantastic incident in a folklore tale. Eva was proud that Anastasia held her own.

Other than feeling encouraged that Anastasia seemed ready to leap back into college with a vengeance, Eva paid little attention to the volumes or to Bo and Anastasia's discussions about them. Her mind and heart were taken up in the beauty that spread, like spring rebirth, throughout her ancestral home.

While loveliness renewed their lives inside the house, the outside, like a mirror, became softened and tamed. Wild grass and tangled weeds gave way to bouquets from the surrounding wood's ponds and streams. When these first wild offerings met with murmurs of praise, more cultivated plants appeared until hydrangea and honeysuckle, jasmine and mimosa clustered beneath windows and lifted sheer panels and intricately tatted lace on scented breezes. Bulbs of flagrantly flaunting, vibrant wild lilies slumbered in the damp dark earth, awaiting spring. To her own amusement, by the time Eva could cool each room in the house with its own newly installed window cooler, she regretted shutting out the fragrant allure of its gardens, where antique furniture clustered under tarps and plastic sheets, waiting for its turn to be restored.

The splendor that had begun in the house's chrysalis kitchen now rushed outward and up the reaching staircase on scarlet carpeting that ran through hallways and foyers to fling flowered rugs in shades of rose, moss, and crimson across finished hardwood and parquet. The walls emerged, fine rosewood and mahogany woodwork restored, or antique puckered paper removed to be replaced by hints of cool forests, scattered buds, trailing ivy. Only the upstairs hallway was graced with a replica

244

paper restoring the antique one's scarlet sparkle because Eva couldn't bear to lose the drama of approaching the stained glass floret. The upper hallway's authentic handmade wrought iron candle sconces and darkened ancestral paintings settled back into their accustomed places over the new paper.

Charley asked, dissatisfied and a little disappointed that the hallway seemed only scrubbed, not changed, "Which ancestors do you think those are, Eva? They seem awfully dark to be the landed gentry from Europe. Would the enslaved Africans get their portraits painted?"

Eva said enigmatically, "I'll let you read up on all that when Bo's work with his ancestral records is done. It would be too hard to explain those paintings. Or anything else, Charley, for that matter, so don't even ask."

Charley looked at Eva askance but asked for no clarification. There was enough to argue about without worrying about whether race or quality of paint added depth and tone to ancestors whose portraits lined the upper hall.

The worst debate was over the bathrooms. As rooms were restored, Charley and Eva realized with distress that they had not agreed on two more rooms to be sacrificed for everyone's comfort.

"Well, maybe three bathrooms were ambitious," Charley compromised. "I'd say if we figure out one more, everybody can be okay."

"Not guests," Anastasia argued. "Guests will expect their own bathrooms, per room."

"Not necessarily," Eva said. "Not in such an old house."

"Let's not fool ourselves," Charley conceded. "At the rates we're planning to charge, they'll expect their own bathroom and their own maid."

"Well," Eva quipped, "they won't get their own maid."

"So we better come up with some bathrooms," Charley decided morosely. So two of the seemingly innumerable upstairs bedrooms fell as concessions to necessity, creating two petal-toned, tile-floored bathrooms each.

"Four upstairs bathrooms seem excessive," Eva pointed out.

"They won't be, Mommy, when we start having guests," Anastasia assured her. "Three bedrooms for guests, each with a private bathroom, and one bathroom left for the three of us to share. If women share those rooms with friends, to save money, you'll see lines at the bathroom doors."

Charley laughed. "I hope not, since the doors open into their bedrooms, and I can't imagine where they'd get all the people to make a line long enough to come into the hall."

Eva couldn't quite joke about turning some of the bedrooms into bathrooms. She'd read Baby Joy's stories about the people who lived in those rooms, and Eva wondered which rooms had been used by the ancestors those stories described. Some of the enslaved people had been brought into the house as personal servants and had slept at the feet of their enslavers' beds.

Eventually, as magic and murder evened the power imbalance and drove their enslavers from the plantation to the city, those who had slept on floors moved up onto beds and brought their families in from the fields to live with them.

Eva was shocked to learn that she had become attached to some of the women about whose magical and material struggles she had read. She tried to guess if, from Baby Joy's descriptions of their movements in the house, she could tell which rooms had been used by these women, and whether or not they would have approved of the restorations.

Bo would know best, Eva decided. She took him upstairs one evening to ask if he knew who, in his collection, might have lived in her own room, and what taste that ancestress might have had.

Bo stood uneasily in the doorway and surveyed the rose and vine carpet hiding the burned and scarred wooden floor, the restored fireplace with its newly painted mantel and polished brick mouth, the unbreakable storm glass that glinted behind fine white lace at the window, spilling sunlight onto the still-battered Queen Anne tea table and reupholstered chairs beneath it.

Eva noticed that he kept his eyes turned from the gauzy bed curtains that framed more than they hid her restored box-frame bed.

"You asked me up here to tell you if the plantation owner's enslaved daughter and mistress and granddaughter would have liked how you've restored their room?" His voice was flat. "Yes, I think that, even though they were trapped and trying to escape, trying to fall in love and have lives they could enjoy, they might have taken a moment to enjoy how tastefully you've restored their room."

The words were clearly a rebuke. Eva bristled. "I thought you wanted me to care about your research."

"And about me, Eva." Bo left without waiting to hear her response.

Had she waited too long? Put him off with too little explanation? Standing alone where she had expected to feel encompassed by the house's history and women, Eva experienced a moment's devastation. Meaning to recriminate, Eva rushed out of her room after Bo.

She ran into him at the base of the spreading main staircase. She drew up sharply behind him but said nothing.

For Bo was transfixed in a welter of evident indecision, watching Charley through the parlor door.

Charley must have just come from their post office box, for she held mail in her hands. Or she had held it. Most of it had cascaded to the carpet of flower buds and scrollwork at her feet in the parlor.

The one letter still in Charley's hand caused it to shake. Eva started around Bo to go to her cousin. Bo reached for her.

"Eva, maybe you shouldn't."

The sound of Bo's voice caught Charley's attention. She looked up at him with anguish in her eyes.

Then she noticed Eva, noticed Bo's hand gripping Eva's arm, holding her still, and Charley's face crumpled like that of a child.

Standing as she was in the midst of the ruin and restoration that had become the symbols of her idealism and her audacity, her courage, this strangely frightened Charley terrified Eva with her obvious vulnerability. Bo still held Eva's arm, but he no longer needed to. Eva could not have started forward again into this heartrending tableau if she had tried to force herself. There was something about it too overwhelming, too reminiscent of the days she and Charley had, one after another, learned that they were orphans, for Eva to enter, even to save her cousin from her lonely distress.

Eva cursed herself inside for her cowardice. And still she could not move.

In the pause, Charley looked quickly around her, as though there might be somewhere to run, somewhere to hide. Then she looked again at Eva with the desperation of a creature who has nowhere left to go.

Then Charley, whom Eva couldn't remember ever seeing cry since her parents had died, grimaced and smashed the letter in her hand into a jagged ball. "It isn't right." Her voice, harsh and strangled, was almost impossible to understand. "I've paid. I've paid for everything a million times over."

Charley spun, tottering with the abruptness of the movement, and rushed backward to the room's restored fireplace. She felt frantically along the mantelpiece.

Behind Eva, Bo said, "Oh no," and ran into the parlor.

Eva watched him throw himself at Charley's balled fist. "Give it to me, Charley," he demanded. "You've got to let us help you. Don't burn it."

Eva said numbly, "There are no matches there, Bo."

Low as her voice had been, Charley must have heard. She snatched her head up to look at Eva with eyes searching, frantic.

Bo had not ceased to work at the paper in Charley's hand. She fought to hold the paper. It ripped between them. Charley screamed and looked down at the fragment she still held.

The sight of it seemed to fill her with revulsion. Charley gagged, choked, and flung the tattered bit at Bo. "Take it," she sobbed. "I don't want it. Take it all."

Now Eva started forward, her arms open.

But Charley pushed past her to get to the stairs. She ran up, gripping the slippery polished handrail, slapping hand over hand to haul herself up as though her knees had gone weak.

Eva followed. But by the time she caught up with her cousin, Charley had slammed the door of her bedroom in Eva's face. Eva heard the door's delicate new latch slide into place. And from inside the room, Eva heard the sound of shattering glass.

CHAPTER FIFTEEN
MY DEAREST CHARLOTTE

My dearest Charlotte,

No matter what I am told, I will not believe that your disappearance indicates your utter disregard for the concern you know I feel for you. You have always had rational reasons for actions that may appear irrational. I harbor no ill will for your most recent caper. It has been my duty and my honor to serve as your guide and protector since I met you, an orphan burdened with raising a child not your own.

As you may always expect of me, I assure you of my fullest support in your bid for independence from me. I have had an account opened in Jackson to back your new business venture. The card of the gentleman you must contact to make use of these funds is enclosed. Cease to liquidate your very excellent assets to finance this nostalgic foray into your past. Those investments have cost me considerable sacrifice over the years. While you may wish to forget what you have been to me, you owe me, at the very least, recognition of what I have always been for you. I do not ask for gratitude, Charlotte. Only accountability.

Know that I have never failed you, and I never will.

The letter was unsigned, though initials like slash lines ripped across one corner beneath the jagged handwriting. Eva could not make them out.

Deciphering the writer's initials would have done her no good, anyway. She couldn't begin to guess who would speak to her tough-minded cousin in such a high-handed way.

Even after Eva had reread the letter and begun to study it in earnest for signs of its owner's identity, she could hardly bear to touch it. It reeked of her own willful ignorance of her cousin's life. Who was this writer? What was this person to cause Charley such distress? How long had Eva been negligent of her cousin, leaving her at the emotional mercies of such a manipulator as this writer?

Eva's hand trembled so that Bo was obliged to take back the torn pieces and hold them together before Eva could continue to stare at them.

At last she looked up at Bo. "It's no use. I don't even know where to begin guessing who this person is." Then Eva urged, "Bo, we have to get in there. I heard breaking glass."

Eva was grateful that Bo did not ask the obvious, ugly question, *Does that mean we're afraid Charley might hurt herself?* Eva pounded on the door. "Charley, let me in. This is no time for you to be alone."

It seemed a pulse-racing eternity before Charley's voice came weakly through the latched door. "Eva, I can't. Just go away. I'm so sorry. I'm sorry about everything. I can't do this anymore." Charley was crying.

"Charley, please. Just tell me what's going on. I bet I can help you. You've always been there for me. Let me try. I bet I can see something that maybe you can't."

To Eva's surprise, Bo took up the chant. "Cousin Charley, let's trade secrets. Maybe you can

252

help me. You're good at fixing things. Maybe this once, one of us out here can help you, too."

Charley's voice sounded eerily like that of the sobbing early teen who had just learned of her parents' deaths. For a solid moment, Eva was transported into the Los Angeles Spanish-style bungalow where she had stood in a hallway like this one, listening to Charley cry in her own mother's arms.

Just like Charley had held Eva, when Eva's mother and father were suddenly gone.

Eva returned to the moment, right here and right now with Bo still calling out to Charley. When Eva spoke again, she was stunned to hear the firm persuasion of her own mother's voice coming from her mouth. "Charley, crying is good. You just keep right on crying. And open this door so I can take care of you. I'm not going to stop you from crying. And I'm not going to promise I can fix anything. But I'm going to make sure that, in your upset, we don't make a tough situation any more difficult than it can't help being. Now, all I'm going to do is hold you. I won't talk to you unless you want me to. It's time for you to come across the room and open this door."

Silence. Eva willed Charley to come near, waited, listening.

There was the slightest shuffle of sound, maybe pantyhose on carpet, before the latch slid. The door eased open on lubricated hinges.

Charley's face looked devastated, wide-eyed as a child's, ravaged with ageless distress. Eva's arms shoved the door smoothly open as she reached to pull her cousin against her heart and hold her to the sound and feel of its beating.

They made their way to sit on the loveseat, a reupholstered rosewood and brocade antique, at the foot of Charley's bed. Bo followed in his noiseless way and sat on the floor at their feet.

Charley laid her head on Eva's shoulder and sobbed.

It seemed to Eva that they had waited there for Charley's sobs to cease for hours when they realized that Anastasia was at Charley's open bedroom door. Neither she nor Bo had thought to close it. None of them had heard Anastasia's tread on the carpeted stairs. Now they all three looked up in unison at Anastasia's calm concern as she paused in the doorway.

Anastasia lifted a hand full of letters. "I found these in the parlor. I thought I'd better bring them to you, Aunt Charley. May I come in?"

The gentleness, the well-brought-up manners, seemed to have a steadying effect on the distraught woman. Charley rallied shakily and sat up straight with a wavering smile. "Oh, I must have dropped those," her voice close to disintegrating into sobs again. "Thank you, honey."

Anastasia flowed into the room and joined Bo at Charley's feet. Anastasia raised the letters like an offering. "I think some of these may be about the retreat, Aunt Charley. They're handwritten. Would you like me to open them for you and see?"

"I don't think this is a good time for that," Charley managed to say before her voice broke. Even Eva was amazed. Charley had never, ever even expressed distress or confusion in front of

Anastasia, to say nothing of losing control enough to weep. Charley seemed now to shut her eyes, as if she would block out the sight of Anastasia's alarm.

But Anastasia showed no alarm. In fact, her entire manner seemed to be that of someone who saw nothing out of the ordinary going on. So mild was Anastasia's manner that Eva, herself, began to wonder if her daughter didn't know that Charley was dramatically disturbed right now.

Anastasia looked at the letters in her hand. "All right. But may I read them *for* you, if you don't want me to read them *to* you? Some of them may need answers, and you may not feel like getting to them right away."

Responsibilities could be counted on to strike a chord with Charley. Her shoulders sagged. "Thank you, Anastasia."

Eva lowered Charley's head to her shoulder, surprised that her cousin accepted the comforting gesture. Eva thought her daughter would gather the letters and go, leaving the older people free to talk. But Anastasia didn't. Instead, she shocked her mother by emitting a trill of fairylike laughter. "Aunt Charley, I think maybe you'd better hear this. Maybe we'll want to think about it."

And Anastasia began to read aloud.

The letter was from a woman who earnestly felt that Charley should reconsider the bigotry inherent in offering her retreat only or mostly to professional women. The woman asked, "Professional what? Attorneys? Bank clerks? Bank robbers? Teachers? Prostitutes?"

Bo interrupted. "And her point is?"

Anastasia said, "That amateur pottery, farming, neighborhood babysitting, homemaking, and raising one's own children are also respectable 'workstyles,' though they're not usually referred to as 'professions.'" Anastasia smiled at Charley. "I like that word, Aunt Charley. Don't you? 'Workstyles,' as in lifestyles to make a living."

Eva couldn't imagine a worse time for this discussion. Whatever Charley's professional accomplishments, Eva suspected that her profession might be how the writer of the frightening anonymous letter had come into Charley's personal life and affected it so drastically. Perhaps, at this moment, Charley wished more than anything that she had been a homemaker and raiser of her own children. Eva tried but couldn't think of a way to stem discussion of this woman's concerns.

Perhaps there was no need. For suddenly, Anastasia began to offer her own quips, Charley-style, as possible responses to the disaffected woman. "Would you like me to write back and tell her that we'll consider calling it a hardworking women's retreat? A retreat and roundtable for women who contribute to the Gulf's-no, the world's-future? What's that word you said about Anna Julia Cooper, Mommy? Far-seeing?"

Bo said thoughtfully, "A retreat to the roundtable for far-seeing women. With limited scholarships and partial scholarships, their cost offset by the professional women who pay for each season at the retreat. I like that."

Charley offered a small but sincere laugh.

Anastasia beamed. She rose in one sweeping movement from a leg-entwined Lotus position to stand, bend, and kiss Charley's glistening cheek.

Eva thought, *How does she carry off this kind of normalizing? Has she done this all her life with me?*

"May I write back to her for you, Aunt Charley?" Anastasia drifted to Charley's writing table.

The miniature desk was a masterpiece of antique restoration. The tiny cherrywood escritoire was a maze of cubbyholes and hidden drawers for inks, quills, saved letters, and stationery. Anastasia seated herself on the brocade-cushioned seat.

"All right," Charley conceded. "Just be sure you read it out loud to me before you seal it up," she warned.

Anastasia gleefully availed herself of the opportunity to snoop into and gasp with delight over Charley's collection of delicate Italian stationery. Eva wondered how to get Charley alone to discuss the threatening letter that had sent her fleeing to her room. So far, the recovery was going well. But they'd have to get to problem-solving.

First, Eva tried to get rid of Bo. "Bo, I know I said I'd take over at least some of the cooking, but can you do one more dinner tonight?"

"I'd better," he said cheerily. "It's oxtail soup. I haven't had that since I was a kid, and no way I'm letting you take any chances with it."

Eva ruminated. "Wait a minute, Bo. Anastasia's mentioned going back to vegan eating. What will she have? You have to offer something else, too."

Anastasia piped up. "I'm not a political vegan. I'm a practical ecologist. Every time my history is being cooked and served up for dinner, I want a taste of it. And so far, Mississippi food and me get along just fine. I'm for oxtail soup, Cousin Bo, as long as the bristles aren't still sticking out."

"Mississippi food and *I*," Eva corrected.

"No bristles," Bo promised. "Just gristle, gravy, onions, and potatoes."

"You're making me hungry," Charley pleased everyone by saying. "You don't put carrots in your oxtail soup, Bo? Eva, didn't your mother put carrots in hers?"

"Plenty of garlic and something with color, but I'm not sure it was carrots." Eva hoped to keep Charley talking. "Could it have been tomatoes? Or corn? Maybe okra."

Charley looked disappointed because "Okra's not very colorful," she pointed out.

Bo announced, "I'm following my recipe. Getting that book away from my Aunt Lydia probably took two years off my life expectancy, and I'm cooking it just the way she does because I mean to put those two years back. I remember her oxtail soup could make a believer out of you."

"I have it," Anastasia announced, waving a powder-blue sheet of paper with fine golden tracery around its edges. "Everybody, listen, okay? 'Dear Madam'-I like that formal touch-'thank you for your thought-provoking correspondence.'"

"Oh no," Charley groaned softly.

"Wait. It gets even better, Aunt Charley," Anastasia assured her. "'We'-don't you always wonder who the 'we' is when you write to these businesses?-'have given your concerns due thought, and we have decided to refer to our establishment as a retreat to the roundtable for far-seeing women. This is in honor of the teacher and social ethicist'-I learned that word from Bo, Mommy-'Anna Julia Cooper.

"'If you would like to read her book before you visit us, we are pleased to be able to tell you that most of her work, *A Voice of the South from a Black Woman of the South*, is back in print after over a hundred years. If you book to join our first retreat and roundtable session, please come prepared to discuss the urgent need for mothers to breastfeed and the writing of a group letter to the President, asking him to hire out-of-work fishing and oil industry personnel to construct clean-energy windmills along the Gulf coastline.'"

Anastasia interrupted her letter to gaze dreamily at Charley. "Those windmills are so beautiful, Aunt Charley. Don't you think? And everyone unemployed could be employed right away in a futures industry until the oysters and shrimp make a comeback. Oh, I wish we had the President here with us right now! I'd persuade him, I know I would!"

Then, matter-of-factly, she resumed. "'Please thank your partner for bringing our retreat and roundtable to your attention, and compliment her for the excellent work she did on our electrical wiring. We are pleased to learn of the effect that our plans, and the job opportunities those plans generate, are already having here in the hard-hit Gulf region. Yours sincerely.' Now, do I just sign my own name, Aunt Charley?"

Charley clapped and nodded. "I think I found myself an administrative assistant," she said with real pride.

Eva leapt in. "Speaking of administrative assistants, Charley," she nearly whispered, "would you like to tell me about that person whose letter upset you today? We can go to my room," she said, looking pointedly at Bo and Anastasia, "if you'd like to talk privately."

The two interlopers looked innocently back at Eva and smiled. Anastasia turned back to the desk to sign and fold her letter with a flourish and lick the gummed edge of the stuffed envelope, oblivious to any hint that she should leave. Bo said, "The oxtails are barely thawed. I've got time for you, too, Charley."

Eva said, "Bo, this may be sensitive."

Bo said, "Of course it is. And if the person bothering her is a man, Cousin Charley might benefit from hearing a man say he's on her side, Eva. I'm sensitive, too."

They both looked to Charley.

Charley lowered her gaze to study the muted pastel floral carpet. Her entire room was done in tones of dark reddish wood and the palest sunrise blush of rose on cream. The effect was feminine, elegant, and somehow tolerant of girlish dreaminess in a businesswoman's world.

Charley said, "Bo, I haven't forgotten that you promised to tell me your secret in exchange for mine." Bo nodded solemnly. Charley slanted a glance upward from under her lowered eyelashes, saw his consent, and continued. "I'll go first," she said. "I want to do it this way. Eva, Anastasia, I'm

260

afraid. You're going to find out I'm a fraud. But I want you to know that I've never known what to do."

Eva took her cousin's slender hand. Today, as it trembled beneath her own palm, Charley's hand seemed fragile. Eva marveled that nothing about Charley had ever seemed fragile to her before. "Charley, you're not a fraud. You've always done everything you can to take care of Anastasia and me. There's nothing insincere or inauthentic about that."

"Wait till you hear, Eva. You just don't know. All that money I made, all my success that made it possible for you to come back to me after your marriage," Charley shook her head, "all that was fraudulent. I didn't do it. The man who wrote that letter gave it all to me."

Eva's mind raced with questions. Should she interrupt? Shouldn't she let Charley finish? Eva interrupted. "Charley, do you mean you haven't worked as an investment broker?"

"Oh, of course I have."

"And you're licensed?"

"Of course, Eva. I couldn't have a card and an office and a sign on the door and counsel people and manage their financial investments, otherwise. You've been to my office."

"Well, certainly, Charley. That's why I'm asking what you mean when you say the man who wrote this letter did it all."

Charley had lifted her head to reason with Eva. Now she looked around openly at Bo and Anastasia, too. "I'll start over. Don't say anything. Just listen. Agreed?"

All heads nodded.

The uncontrollable trembling had returned by the time Charley said, "I always thought he killed our parents. Don't make me say his name, Eva. I hate him. I've hated him since I was eighteen, when your parents passed away. You remember I was supposed to get married when I graduated from high school? Well, when your parents died, my boyfriend didn't want to take us both on. In all fairness, I have to say he couldn't. He was nothing but a raw recruit in the Navy. Remember those sailor suits? I thought he was so handsome."

Eva squeezed her cousin's hand. "I remember, Charley," she said. "I'm sorry."

"My loss was nothing compared to yours," Charley said. "I knew what it was like to lose parents. What would happen to you without me? We had your parents' house free and clear with the money both our parents had left. But that's all. I needed a job. I started answering ads. Secretarial stuff, to start with. I could type and file. You know, they used to require that you take that kind of stuff in high school, along with home economics, if you were a girl."

Anastasia said, "I've heard."

Charley said, "At that time, I blessed my lucky stars I had those skills to market. But then I answered this particular ad, which I thought called for skills way over my head, and which I hadn't realized was going to take me across the color line till I got to the office and saw that everybody who worked there was not my race. I just told myself to get ready to be humiliated and chalk it up to experience."

Everyone now grew absolutely still. It took long moments before Charley continued. When she did, her voice was tight and shaking. Tears bubbled up in the elongated corners of her eyes and ran in glistening rivulets down her sun-bronzed face.

"I thought I was so lucky. He came in and excused the woman interviewing me, and he interviewed me himself. I still remember everything. The dress I wore, my favorite color for good luck, my hair in a new cut I was afraid I couldn't afford, also for good luck. My silly little grown-up clutch bag. Grown was the word for me. I felt so scared, but I thought I looked so grown."

Charley's jaw shook, and the tears ran in sheets now. "He asked why a beautiful girl like me was out looking for a job instead of making some man happy. That's how he said it, too. And I told him I was supposed to be getting married, but I had to take care of my cousin instead."

Charley's voice had raced up an octave and broken on the last words. She began to pant, as if she'd been running. Eva pulled Charley into her arms again.

Charley plowed on, cowering in Eva's arms as she told about her long, lonely young years. "He said the man who had given up the chance to take care of me and my cousin was a fool. He said, right then and there in the interview, that he would be honored to take care of us. He said he would start with raising the salary of the offered job. Instead of being his secretary's assistant, I would be his."

"What did that mean?" Eva asked.

Charley calmed as she explained. "Oh, I'd use the same secretarial skills, but I'd sit in on meetings

263

and listen to him advise clients, and generally begin to learn about managing investments. He didn't tell me then that I'd become an investment counselor. He just said I would assist him. I knew nothing, so it made sense to me at the time."

Eva said, "So, is that what happened?"

Charley nodded, drying her eyes, and sat up. She let out a shaky breath. "Yes, that's all it was at first. Except the gossip, you know. It was all over the office, the speculation about what I was to him. I couldn't make any friends. And when his secretary finally threw it in my face one day, I walked back into his office and quit."

"That was brave," Eva said.

"Not brave enough," Charley answered, still wiping because the tears would not let up. "He told me I could go, but first he wanted to show me my investment portfolio. He didn't make it up on the spot. It was there in his desk with my name on all the papers. He was the signatory, but all the investments were mine."

Charley looked around at her listeners, one at a time. "I don't know if you can picture it," she said. "The fear that I would never make enough, I would never get my life together enough to marry and still take care of my little cousin. The house was paid for, but food and meals and clothes and going over to spend the night with friends and taking lessons and everything, all that costs wear and tear, and I still didn't even have a car. We did everything on the bus."

Eva said, "Oh, Charley. I remember."

Charley's inhale staggered down the spasms in her throat. "And here I'd just learned I was rich. I could have liquidated everything and bought one of those huge houses in what they used to call the Negro suburbs, growing up like mushrooms all around Los Angeles. Baldwin Hills. Fox Hills. Shoot, I had enough money to get us into Beverly Hills, thanks to him."

Regret muted her voice again. "He said if I would stay, he would get the gossip under control, and he would teach me to use the interest my investments had already started to accrue."

Eva said cautiously, "How did he get the gossip under control?"

"He fired his secretary. She'd been at that firm when his father owned it. She'd been there forever. He just fired her. The minute I said I'd stay, he called her in, asked me to repeat what she had said, asked her if she'd really said it, and as soon as she admitted it, he didn't even give her a minute to explain. He just told her she would get her two weeks' severance pay along with pay for the two weeks' notice that he was cutting short, given the severity of her offense against him."

"None of what he did was your choice or your fault," Eva pointed out.

Charley looked miserable. "I was frightened by his power over that poor old woman, but I was glad he'd fired her. She'd made my life hell, and I needed that job. But she needed her pittance of a paycheck, too. And who was going to hire her, at her age?"

Eva said, "So, how long were you there before all this happened?"

Charley shrugged. "Eva, don't even ask. It felt like I'd been there at least three years or so, but it had only been a year. Maybe a little over that, if I could draw on the interest from my investments. I wanted to use the money to get a car. But he said he'd rather get it for me." Again Charley's voice lowered. "Eva, that's how we got the Karman Ghia."

Anastasia made a small sound of surprise, for this was the car she had inherited from her mother as Charley's old cars were passed down between them.

Charley said, "I shouldn't have accepted. But when our parents were all dead, I was so afraid of being helpless. All of a sudden, every time something came up that looked like it threatened my job, he had an answer already in place."

Eva didn't ask the question plaguing her. *So when did he tell you it was time to sleep together?*

But Charley had come to that. "He always made it sound like I was his child. I really believed that fate had sent me to somebody who would finish taking care of me. After he fired her, he took me out to dinner. It was the first time we went alone. He didn't say much about-well, what the office gossip had been-except to make it sound like the only thing wrong with it was that we weren't doing it. Like I was using him. When I pointed out I hadn't even known about the investments, he said he hadn't told me because he didn't want me to feel guilty about everything that everybody else already knew he was offering me. He said he wanted me to accept him willingly and not feel obligated."

Charley looked pleadingly at Eva. "My choices were to take everything and stay, or take nothing and go. He fired that old woman, but she had done him a favor. I don't know when he would have

266

come forward with his demands if I hadn't rushed in his office and brought it all up for him."

Bo said, "Don't blame yourself for that either, Charley. He would have brought it up soon enough. He wasn't collecting those investments with your name on them out of the goodness of his heart."

Charley said, "I sound stupid now, but at the time, I believed I was immoral for passing up what he was offering me. He said my parents hadn't lived long enough to make me understand that I was a beautiful girl making my way alone in the world, and I had to learn to appreciate an offer of protection. That's what he's always called it. He was married, and he was of a different race, but he could offer me protection. I believed him when he said anything any other man offered me that was less than what he offered was an insult. He always said that, if I respected myself, I would honor his commitment and be loyal to him."

Eva said, "Did you ever feel protected?"

Charley's voice went dull. "I felt trapped. He could take better care of me and Eva put together than I could take care just of myself. I didn't mind losing our lifestyle, but I couldn't bear taking it away from Eva."

Suddenly Charley's story took a sharp turn. "So Eva, when you left to get married, it was my chance. I left him. My whole lifestyle went downhill, but I was happy. Remember, your husband wanted to support you. So you left me in the bungalow, and every month, I sent you a check for rent. And then when you came back, Eva, so miserable, and worried about your education and your baby, I realized you'd only left because I hadn't done enough for you."

Eva groaned, "Oh, no, Charley."

Charley insisted, "He'd told me when I left that I would come back to him. That the real world would be too much for me. When I did come back, he gave me the Saab, I gave you the Ghia, and he put us in a new house with my name on it. Didn't you realize the sale of your parents' home was what got you through college? Where would we have lived, without his gifts? We lived like queens, Eva, thanks to him. Money for everything including private school for Anastasia. I felt like a runaway wife being placated."

Charley's voice dropped so low that her listeners had to lean in close to hear her say, "I felt unfaithful and ungrateful, and I hated him."

Eva felt heartsick.

What use was there in telling Charley that none of this was her fault? Surely, she knew that by now. Eva's problem would be convincing herself that Charley's entrapment wasn't Eva's fault, either.

Anastasia said unevenly, "Aunt Charley, why did you say that this man killed your parents and my grandparents? What makes you say that? What do you know about their deaths, that makes you think that?"

Charley shook her head. Her eyes were wide and terrified.

Eva wondered if the shock of recounting all this suffocated history was too much for her cousin. Eva realized she, too, was trembling at the thought that this man who had imprisoned Charley all her young adult life, simply by convincing her that he had moral right and power on his side, might even have begun all the tragedies in their lives.

Charley said, "It was how he came into my life, and how he stayed there. Our parents' deaths made everything work for him." She turned to Eva, her eyes pleading, *Tell me I'm not crazy.* "He seemed to know everything. He seemed to take over where they left off, raising me, and then he never let go. When he talked, I could see how their deaths were all he needed to trap me for the rest of my life."

Her voice had been calming, lowering. Charley had wept, and the resolution, the clear-sightedness in her presentation of her painful, shameful story had seemed a good sign.

Now, however, in talking about how she'd always linked this man's invasion of her life to their parents' deaths, Eva feared that Charley's thoughts and voice spoke more of hysteria than reason. "Charley," she said, starting forward, "I don't think you should explain any more just now."

But Bo had, to Eva's surprise, already leapt to enfold her cousin in his arms. "No, no," he crooned, holding Charley so strongly that the sinews of his biceps etched themselves in outline against his sun-polished skin. "He's a wretch, and we'll get rid of him. But I promise you that the one thing he didn't do was kill your parents. Stop now. Hush. No more, Charley."

Bo pulled away and sat on his heels, his hands still pressing Charley firmly into the loveseat. He held her eyes and spoke clearly. "Charley, you remember my father's an attorney? Someone in his firm will know what we have to do to make sure you have no financial strings tying you to this man's control. After that, it's a matter of getting one of my father's colleagues to help us restrain this guy. You've taken the first step, the necessary step that no one else could take for you. You've gotten away, out of his house, out of his firm, and even out of proximity to him. Now you've got friends who'll help you close the door behind you. It's already over. Don't even worry about it."

Bo turned to Eva. "We'll have that dinner my parents have been asking for, so Charley can get to know them. But I'll call now so my father can start looking into how we proceed against this guy." Again he turned to Charley. "You can do this, cousin," Bo said. "On the back of his letter, just write his name for me and the name of his firm in L.A. We'll take it from there."

Anastasia rushed to press a pen into Charley's hand. Charley reached out a stiff arm and scrawled big letters slowly, carefully, as if she could not write them without shaking.

At last, the names were written. Charley looked at Bo as Anastasia removed the pen from her hand. "Bo," she said, "I believe everything you've said except that he didn't kill my parents." Again her face collapsed under the pressure of fighting back tears. "You don't know him," she whispered. "He's vile. He'll do anything. It's not love. He lives for the control. The power to hate and make me act like it's manna from heaven. He's different, Bo, from normal people."

Bo listened until the tide of Charley's terror stemmed itself. Then he said, "There's a simple reason why I know that the man who harassed you and coerced you and seduced you didn't kill your

270

parents, Charley. He couldn't have. Your parents and Eva's were killed by the curse on this plantation."

271

CHAPTER SIXTEEN
GLOW OF THE WITCHANGEL

Eva felt for a moment as if she couldn't breathe. Her mind swam with circular questions. *Curse? I've read Baby Joy's stories, and I haven't found a curse. Is this a lie to comfort Charley? But it's frightening her. Would Bo lie about our parents' deaths? A curse on our new inheritance, after Charley's invested so much in it. Do educated people believe in curses?*

Bo said, "You asked my secret, Charley, and I told you I'd tell it. It begins with understanding that what happened to your parents couldn't be stopped. They ran away from inheriting this house. That's why they fled to L.A. They only came back to protect the two of you, Charley and Eva, from that curse."

Eva was cold with shock. She wanted to hear no more. "No. Bo, you said our history is a legacy. You never said it was a curse. It sounds like you're trying to scare us out of here again. Still trying to get the house. And you've picked a pretty underhanded time to go after us."

"I'm sorry, Eva. But we've got to break Charley's fear of this man, and it's past time for all three of you, even Anastasia, to come to grips with why Ham acted as he did. At some point, you're going to have to learn what everybody but you believes to be true about Tansy."

Anastasia came at Bo, her eyes dilated and reddened. "We have to swallow why Uncle Ham shot Tansy? Is that what you mean?" Her voice

272

became sharply sarcastic. "'Understand it?' What is there to understand, Bo? Uncle Ham shot Tansy because he wants Tansy's inheritance. This property and everything that goes with it."

Bo said gently, "Anastasia, sit down. Listen. This is only the beginning of several things you need to try to hear. What if there is a danger here, and you can do something about it? What if you can free your Aunt Charley of some crippling, unnecessary fears? Wouldn't you want to do that, Anastasia? Isn't that worth hearing something you may not understand right away, but you can come to understand?"

Anastasia sat, glaring, trembling now like her mother and her aunt. "I'm listening."

Eva said, "Maybe we should stop this. We're all too upset. No more, Bo."

Bo said, "We have to take steps, and we can't take them if we don't understand what we're facing. Let me get through this." Bo looked around at his listeners. "Charley, your father inherited this place before your parents ever escaped to L.A. They left to get away from the curse here. It was already a local legend. They came back to clear the curse off of this place because you were coming of age. They wanted you to grow up safely. They didn't want this plantation's legacy following you, sucking you in, maybe drawing you back someday.

"But the curse was too strong for them, and it overcame them. Can you understand that, Charley? That man in L.A. did not kill your parents. He just took advantage of your fear that he had the power of life and death over your loved ones."

Dumbly, Charley nodded.

273

Bo turned to Eva. "Eva, the house and the curse passed to your parents from Charley's parents, not to Charley. Her father wanted to spare her, and he willed the house and property to his brother, your father, Eva, instead of to Charley. My father helped make out that will, just in case clearing the curse off this place didn't work.

"Eva, your parents came back here, knowing what had happened to Charley's parents before them, but feeling they had no choice but to try to free the place of its legacy, for your sake. And like Charley's parents, they tried to put together a will that would protect you, in case they failed. They planned it with my father, and everyone thought that, this time, it was failsafe."

Bo took Eva's hands. "Eva, you were not to inherit this house and its legacy until you were twenty-one. But if by that age you already had a daughter, as in fact you did turn out to have Anastasia," he indicated her brooding adult child with a motion of his head, "then for her sake, you could not take possession until she, too, was twenty-one. She turned twenty-one at the end of this past spring, and that's why you were sent notice of your ownership of the house and property."

Eva said, "So no one died this past spring?"

Bo shook his head. "You inherited this house when your parents died. They hoped-no, we all hoped-that the caretaker might rid the place of Tansy, while you grew up. Until just this summer, since your parents' deaths, the house has remained in the care of a caretaker."

"Who was the caretaker?" Anastasia asked. Bo turned to look at her, but he didn't answer. Instead,

274

he said to Eva, "Your parents and mine all hoped that twenty-one might be an age of reasonable discretion for a young woman likely to be swept off her feet by a charming young man. They were too optimistic."

Anastasia said coldly, "Bo, what are you saying?"

Eva broke in. "Anastasia, this is superstitious nonsense. And I can't imagine why Bo is telling this ghastly story at a time like this. Don't even try to figure out what he means by anything he says."

Bo said, flinging away Eva's hands, "And why not try to figure it out? Look at Charley, Eva." Bo pointed, and Charley cringed away like a cornered animal.

Eva said, "Bo, enough."

But he shouted, "Charley's devastated! She's thrown away her life, her chance to marry and have children, her career, her self-esteem, trying to placate the man she thought made you both orphans. Trying to keep him from killing you and Anastasia, too. Am I right, Charley? This is why you're so afraid of him, isn't it? This is why you thought at last that you could leave him when Eva inherited this house, because he'd never find you out here in Mississippi? Aren't I right, Charley? You thought you could finally get away from your parents' murderer. But instead you ran right to him."

Eva looked at Charley, who was shaking wildly, her breath shallow and rapid. "I think I know," Charley whispered. "I know what the curse is. Oh, God help us, how could I have missed seeing it all this time?"

"Seeing what?" Anastasia demanded.

Charley looked at Anastasia, stricken. "Honey, try to understand. It's Tansy. Of course it is. Tansy is the curse."

Anastasia leapt to her feet, screaming, "He's not a curse! He's a blessing! And he's not here to tell his side of this story. You can't just listen to what Bo says about him."

Bo said, "Anastasia, what's his side? If he's not here to tell it, you tell it for him. What would he say to defend himself?"

Anastasia turned to her mother, pleading, "Tansy can't help the power that's around him. He doesn't ask for it. He can't stop fate."

Eva rose from Charley's side to go to her daughter, who stepped back from her. "Anastasia, what do you mean by fate? That sounds too abstract and too lethal. What happens? What do you think Tansy does or causes to happen?"

A small cry escaped Anastasia. Her voice and face pleading, her hands joined in a gesture of beseeching. "Mommy, Tansy is about love. He's about healing and growing again when everything has been destroyed. He's about seeing into the future, seeing past the suffering of the moment, and knowing that there's more to come, and that we can all get there. What you said about far-seeing, that's Tansy, Mommy. He sees the future, and he makes others see it because it's real. All these people who Bo says have suffered? Look how good their lives have been because of Tansy. Lawyers, teachers, nurses, professionals? They're descended from people in chains, Mommy, who weren't even allowed to read. People who hid in that stone dungeon. People who were afraid to show their

276

faces when they were emancipated. But look at their great-great-grandchildren today and tell me that Tansy has destroyed the people of this plantation!"

Bo said, "It's true that we all prosper while Tansy lies in wait for a bride."

Anastasia stomped her foot and shouted, "No! He's the power of this place, not its curse. He's our inheritance, and, okay, that inheritance costs us something. But Tansy isn't something to fear, and he's not history to be ashamed of, and he won't destroy us. He's one half of a whole circle that has to be complete, Mommy, for all of our sakes. Tansy's bride is a matter of fate. She has to exist. This has to happen. It's an honor! It's a sacrifice that's meant to be."

Bo's voice was now harsh. "Eva, when Anastasia talks about fate, she means that Tansy can't help it that the people who try to come between him and his chosen bride die. Isn't that what you mean, Anastasia?"

Anastasia said desperately, "Mommy, it's a power that he can't do anything to stop. It's like when we looked up the herb tansy, Bo and I, in all those books at Cooper College. Tansy, the herb itself, is used to bring lovers together, and it's also used to abort their babies. That's what I mean about a circle. It's life and love and death all together, complementing and completing each other, and tansy the plant can't help that any more than Tansy the man can help it. Mommy-"

Bo shouted, "Tell it all, Anastasia! You mean that Tansy the man couldn't help killing Charley's parents and your mother's parents because they tried to keep him away from their teen-age daughters.

277

And while you're at it, warn your mother that he'll kill her too, if she tries to keep him away from you, Anastasia!"

Eva said, "Oh, my God."

Bo was relentless. "And isn't this a good time to explain to your mother and Charley that Ham risked his own life to save them from being killed by Tansy, because you're the daughter of this house now, Tansy's 'chosen bride' as you put it, and he's chosen you? And stupid, loutish, clumsy, drunken Uncle Ham didn't know how to stop the cycle of violence and evil, but he thought he'd rather take the curse on himself, get killed himself, than stand back and watch another mother die trying to protect her daughter, as he did twice in the Seventies."

Eva had caught her breath and turned toward Anastasia, to come between her and the barbarity, the insanity of Bo's words. But as Eva moved to protect her, Charley moaned, holding herself and rocking back and forth. "Please, let's stop this. I can't hear this. I don't believe in things like this. Bo, this will drive me out of my mind."

Eva turned back to Charley, frightened for her and torn over which woman to comfort.

Eva said, "Bo, you're tearing everyone apart. Shut up! You're making no sense, and you're doing no good. I'm beginning to think you've lost your mind in that dungeon."

Anastasia looked hopelessly from Bo to Eva. "Bo isn't crazy, Mommy, but he is wrong. Tansy isn't the violence or the evil. He's the charm against the violence. He's our chance to heal and to see ourselves in a promising future, Mommy, like I've heard you say, and to move forward!"

Anastasia's earnestness tore at her mother's mind and heart. *How do I stop this? What in heaven's name have Bo and Anastasia been talking about all summer, while I was worried about being in love?*

Eva scrambled for something to say to ease the sledgehammer impact of Bo's theory on her impressionable child. "Anastasia, Bo's misused your faith in him. None of what he's saying means anything to you or about Tansy. Tansy is just a homeless young man out in the woods. He's too young to have met my parents or Aunt Charley's. He couldn't have killed them because he wasn't born yet, and I don't know what's happened to his body since he was shot, but he can't harm anyone now because he's dead. What you and Bo are saying is all nonsense."

She neared her skittish daughter. "Everything you've both said is magical and impossible, honey."

Just as Eva's fingers touched her daughter's arm, Anastasia turned and fled Charley's room.

Eva called, "Anastasia," and ran after her.

It was useless. By the time she had chased her daughter down the stairs, through the kitchen door, and across the fallow cotton field between the house and the woods, she was winded and stumbled to a stop, gasping for breath. She bent double, clutching her knees.

Eva's heartbeat pounded in her ears, and her lungs burned. She was unable to catch her breath enough to call out again. She managed only to raise her head and watch her daughter's fleet, slim shape slip away between the trees.

Strong hands grabbed Eva's shoulders. She cried out.

It was Bo, and his grip on her arms steadied her. "Let her go. I can help you find her later, Eva. I promise you, I'll take you to her. I know where she goes. Anastasia will be safe. Right now, I need you to help me with Charley."

"You wouldn't need help with Charley if you hadn't said those insane things. How could you be so outrageous? What did you think you'd accomplish? You really thought you'd make Charley feel better by telling her that Anastasia's homeless friend killed our parents?" Eva spat the words breathlessly into Bo's face, panting open-mouthed as he held her near him.

Bo looked skyward as if summoning infinite patience. "Then you come calm Charley down while I get my parents. We can agree, can't we, that Charley needs my father's legal advice and help? Or maybe I should send for Aunt Olivia first? Aunt Olivia is a nurse."

Eva recalled the hypodermic and shook her head violently. "No. I'll help with Charley. But how do you know my daughter will be safe? If you know where she's going, why don't you go after her now? Why are we waiting?"

Bo said, "We're not waiting. We have two crises and we're taking care of one of them at a time, based on which one can't wait. Charley can't wait. I can't calm her down. I'm trying to get you back inside before Charley loses her mind behind all this. What she told us today about the last thirty years of her life is enough, Eva, to destroy her. Let's get her some help as fast as we can. I promise you, Anastasia will be all right."

Eva sat with Charley and held her still and quiet while Bo telephoned his parents and explained their emergency. He had to use Charley's cell phone in her bedroom, so that she could monitor every word he chose to describe her plight. Charley listened and nodded, staring and expressionless, while Bo talked. When he was done, she collapsed against Eva as though she had exhausted herself.

Eva was appalled that putting off meeting Bo's parents, her potential in-laws, had come to this. Foolishly, she talked to Charley about how they should wash their faces in the new upstairs bathrooms and maybe put on a little lipstick or brush their hair. "You'll feel better," Eva coaxed Charley. "Really, everything is just about all right now. If only Anastasia would come back home."

Eva kept looking through the lace-curtained windows of her own and Charley's bedrooms for a sight of her daughter.

When the two women had washed away the streaks of tears and cooled their swollen faces, the three of them, Eva, Charley, and Bo, sat in the parlor to await his parents' arrival.

Bo's parents, the Wolfsons, came in a sleek black Rolls-Royce. Eva would have been impressed if she'd had any emotional energy to spare. As it was, she floated distractedly through polite greetings with a small, straightforward woman in a creamy silk pantsuit and a man with neatly trimmed hair and a goatee more gray than black, in a gentlemanly summer suit of dark fawn. Like a child, Eva noticed the visual details of the meeting, but she could bring her mind to focus on none of the conversation.

Eva remembered only later that the warmth of the Wolfsons' embraces brought renewed tears to her eyes.

Eva was so restless, as they settled into seats in the parlor, that Bo soon interrupted his explanation of Charley's situation to ask if they couldn't talk in the kitchen, where Eva could watch for her daughter. His parents rose and made their way there as though they were very familiar with the house. His mother complimented the new decor, all along the way.

Through the kitchen screen, Eva watched for Anastasia while Bo led Charley to answer his father's questions. Bo set his oxtail soup to bubbling. Eva noticed, as she fought down her worries about her daughter, that Bo and his mother joked quietly about Bo's being forced to cook for a houseful of women. Eva noted dimly that she liked the sound of their banter. *What went wrong between Anastasia and me?*

Where was her daughter? And why should Bo know where to find Anastasia when her own mother didn't? Had he seen her in the woods? Tracked her down before, without alerting Eva? *Or did Anastasia confide something to Bo that he kept to himself, until now?*

Bo's mother came to Eva as she paused in her pacing by the kitchen's screen door. "You mustn't fret, Eva," Mrs. Wolfson said, taking her hand and patting it. "This will be all right. I have a feeling that it's time all this upheaval and suffering should

282

end, for you and for all of us. We'll get through it this time."

This time? Eva considered how to answer. Did Bo's tastefully understated mother have any idea what wild stories flew through the family about this house and the people who had lived in it? Could she speak for Bo's irresponsible theories about curses and legends come to life?

"I would like to believe that that's true, Mrs. Wolfson."

"I've seen a lot, baby. When I was much younger, things would happen, and I would think, 'This is the end. Life can't go on after this one.' But you learn that life is more extreme than anything you ever imagined. Everything you thought was impossible can and does happen. And when it does, life goes on anyway, with you and the people you love, or without you and those people. You have to adapt how you see things, Eva. You have to make yourself believe that you can handle whatever happens. That's how you cope and survive. You'll survive this, Eva. And so will your daughter."

"You haven't met Anastasia, have you, ma'am?"

Mrs. Wolfson shook her head with what appeared to be real regret. "No, I haven't. But I'm sure I will soon, and we'll all make up for lost time. Next time, I think we should meet at my house. If Bo will give me back at least one of my cookbooks, I'll even make us some fresh pecan pie. Would you like that, Eva?"

Eva managed to smile. Bo defended himself.

"Mama, you always said you wanted me to learn to cook. Well, better late than never. And better your cookbooks than some of those other women's that you hang around with. Isn't that right, Eva?"

His mother teased, "Bo, you don't fool me. You're just trying to impress this good-looking woman, here. Eva, you take my word for it. Bo's a good son, and I think he'd make a great catch, but don't you think for one minute that he's going to touch those pots after he gets married. He's too much like his father for all that."

Eva laughed politely, but she wondered, *Do they know? Did Bo tell them he's asked me to marry him? What will they think of my family and me now?*

Mr. Wolfson spoke up from the kitchen table, where he and Charley still murmured over glasses of iced tea. "What's that I hear about myself? I can't cook?"

Bo said, "Not as good as I can, Dad. Don't worry about it, though. See these books here? I got your back."

Charley laughed.

Charley looked young again. Not young and terrifyingly vulnerable, as she had upstairs, revealing her hidden history. She looked young and hopeful, as she had over the last few weeks.

Eva called, "So, what do you think, Charley, after talking with Mr. Wolfson? Do things look manageable?"

"Please," Bo's father said, "we are extended family, after all. It's Samuel and Hetta. Aunt Hetta and Uncle Samuel, if that's not too familiar for your comfort."

Eva said, brightening, "Samuel? That's my father's name," and Mr. Wolfson assured her, "Yes,

284

of course. Tends to get used a lot in this family. Hasn't Bo told you about the first Sammy? Brought his name all the way from Africa."

"Sammy doesn't sound like a name from an African language."

Bo explained, "Baby Joy spells it S-A-M-I."

Eva said, "Kind of like inheriting Boye and changing it to Bo? I wonder what tribe Sami's name came from, and what it meant, and what we mean when we pass it down to our children. What were my father's parents thinking when they named him Samuel?"

Charley said, "You know what, you all? I'm starting to like having family and history. It feels good not to be alone, figuring out how to get through, how to get by. I admit, I'm more than a little afraid of what that man's going to do when he finds out I've gotten legal advice and started to take some kind of action against him, to get rid of him. But thank you, Bo, for calling your parents. And thank you, Uncle Samuel and Aunt Hetta, for coming right over."

Samuel rose, folding the torn letter and sliding it and the card into his wallet. "Tomorrow we'll take you to meet my associate, and we'll get started clearing up your finances and your right to privacy, so you can get on with your life. Now, are you coming home with us, young lady?"

Aunt Hetta smiled. "Please do. I never had a daughter. I'd welcome all of you, but I imagine you want to wait here for Anastasia, don't you, Eva? Well, when she comes home, tell your daughter that I went to Cooper and loved it. Bo says she'll start there this fall. We need to get together and let me show her my yearbooks."

Anastasia. What would her life be like, by the time a few more weeks had passed, and fall arrived?

Worry assailed Eva afresh now that the evening drew to its dusky close.

Bo's parents wouldn't stay to eat. He turned off his simmering soup and put the scandalously hot pot in the refrigerator as Aunt Hetta persuaded Charley, "You just need a good night's rest, and a simple dinner like my chicken soup. You can try Bo's oxtails the next time he cooks them. Let him get some practice."

Uncle Samuel said, "Bo, you and Eva might as well eat that oxtail soup, after you've done all that work."

Bo said, "We'll be going out to look around for Anastasia. We'll bring her home and eat together."

The Wolfsons, all three, shared a discreet glance.

All in all, it seemed to Eva that the Wolfsons were so determined to take Charley away-or was their goal to leave Bo and Eva alone?-that she became uneasy. She was sure she saw a look pass between them again when they finally got Charley to agree to come away with them.

As Aunt Hetta and Bo shepherded Charley into the depths of the Rolls' luxurious back seat, Uncle Samuel lingered on the porch to take Eva's hand. "Trust my son, Eva. If anybody knows what's needed to get Anastasia safely through this, Bo does. That's why we consented to let him start caretaking here so young."

Eva was startled. "Bo was caretaker of this house?"

Uncle Samuel looked over at his son, his gaze a bit askance. "He hasn't told you all that? Well, it's time he did. You ask him when we're gone. I think he'll see you're ready to understand."

Bo re-joined Eva on the porch, and they stood together to wave as the Wolfsons and Charley pulled away. Watching the darkness grow into the woods all around the house, "It isn't safe out there at night," Eva said.

Bo said, "Anastasia is safe."

Eva had had her fill of other people's secrets. Impatiently, she turned to look at this man whom she had taken as her lover for passion, she now thought, and not for trust. How could she have thought she trusted him when she did not know him? Yet, irresponsibly, thoughtlessly, Eva had let this stranger stay in her home, had him here feeding such fearful stories to her cousin and her daughter that they had scattered in fear and distress. I'll *bring them back, and I'll get rid of him.*

"Now take me to my daughter," Eva said.

Bo took Eva's hand. She let him hold it though she looked away from him. "Eva, you need to know that what Anastasia said was true."

Eva's head snapped around toward Bo. "What do you mean?"

"Anastasia's right. Tansy's original nature is to be united with a bride who joins him in the water, in rivers and streams. He dies to be reborn as power and healing that she carries to the people. In West Africa, America, and the Caribbean, when she dies,

287

too, there's a feeling that her death ransoms his and saves the community from suffering."

Eva said acidly, "You're making no sense."

Bo said, "It's crossing the sea that changes things. I mean that the Middle Passage that changed people from enslaved citizens of warring kingdoms to beasts of burden in America, to chattel, also changed their gods and goddesses."

Eva pulled her hand from Bo and started down the porch steps. "You said you'd take me to my daughter," she flung back at him over her shoulder. "It's getting dark. I've heard enough of these folktales already."

Bo caught up with her as noiselessly as always. "You haven't heard enough to get you through this safely, Eva. Listen to me." He grabbed at Eva's hand again and pulled her up short.

Eva snatched her hand back and faced Bo. "I'll listen while I walk."

They had reached the stone angel's rose bower. As they passed under the angel's wings, Eva reached up to touch one. *Lifted, about to take flight.*

Eva thought of her recent flying dreams. The odd thought struck her, recalling her conversations with Bo about the winged women in Baby Joy's writings, that perhaps this angel, modeled on a young enslaved woman, was meant to represent an African witch.

What is an enslaved woman with wings? A witch, the follower of a goddess? Or an angel, empowered by a god?

Was it right to assume that power was wrong in the hands of a downtrodden person? Were only the advantaged to be entrusted with power? Was power in itself good or evil? What about choice?

Uneasily, Eva remembered reading in Baby Joy's stories that this statue was made for a young woman owned and murdered by her own father. And if she returned from that death with wings, what was she? Why fear Tansy and not the witchangel?

Against her will, Eva took the time to pause and look up at the statue's peaceful face. *She has been kind in my dreams. An angel. She helped Baby Joy find half the freed community, though they were in hiding. Is she real? Can she help me find Anastasia?*

Eva shook these thoughts away. *Now Bo has me thinking about his madwoman's fantasies.*

If Bo noticed Eva's preoccupation with the statue, he gave no sign. He caught up with her beneath the statue's lifted wings and, once again, took her hand. "Eva, when the mermaid and merman lovers come from the West African rivers to the sea of the Middle Passage, they become something else. They're separated. They're two different entities. They both stand for love, always yearning, and for healing and children, just as Anastasia said about Tansy. But they also become destructive, Eva. It's in their nature."

Bo placed Eva's hand over the beating of his heart. "I think it's the separation that creates a vacuum of need between them, like the vacuum of loss felt by the people enchained in the hold of slave ships. It's a pull into emptiness that can't be resisted. It destroys whatever gets in its way. An emotional black hole."

Eva pulled away and kept walking toward the woods.

Now they crossed the fallow cotton field toward the deep blackness of the canopied woods at nightfall. She had never been out here at night, and she was unprepared to be as afraid as she felt. *It's not like in my dreams. But then, in my dreams, I'm flying above the darkness with moonlight and stars. And the glow of the witchangel holding my hand.*

Walking through the woods with Bo, Eva was aware of danger. Fallen bits of forest broke under almost every footfall. Rotted things collapsed in gaseous puffs as they deflated. Stink and flowering growth mingled and sickened Eva in their entanglement.

Creatures called in warning and pain as they fell prey. But Eva could see little that was not at eye level, scurrying shadows among the blackened tufts of green, just above the ground.

Bo hulked in the lowering darkness. Eva had never thought of him as bulky, but his lumbering silhouette blotted out pricks of light filtering through enclosing trees. His shape distorted, his head huge and long, snouted as he sniffed at air, a hunter without weapons. His top-heaviness dwindled to slimness at belly and flanks, all sinewy curves like a racing hound's.

Where was Bo leading her? Surely, Anastasia could not have gone so far. How would a young woman born and raised in one of the world's largest cities have come to know such a wild tract of wilderness so soon?

Suddenly Bo stopped. Eva paused beside him. *I might as well confront him now.* "I don't believe we're after my daughter," she called low.

Bo's voice drifted back to her. "What do you mean?"

"I don't trust you. I'm sorry, Bo."

There were soft sounds, perhaps padded feet on mulch and moss, drawing near. A whisper. "Why don't you?"

"I've figured it out, Bo. Your father said that you were the caretaker. You should have told me that, and you didn't."

"I had my reasons."

"I know. You said yourself today that the caretaker was supposed to rid the plantation of Tansy. So, why didn't you? Because you knew that if you let him live, he'd kill me, and then he'd kill my cousin. And poor Anastasia would kill herself, loving him."

"Kill herself? How?"

"Bo, I've listened to you and Anastasia arguing about the folktales you read together. The bride always dies in the stories. She's human and is either drowned as a punishment or drowns herself, for love of the merman."

There was movement, as though Bo turned away. Eva called to him, "Bo, you knew the myths, and you knew what would happen to all of us, if you let Tansy live. You wanted all of us dead so that you could inherit everything. But you would never be blamed for our deaths because Tansy is nothing but a folktale. You stayed here and protected Tansy, as caretaker, instead of protecting us. That's why you didn't lead us to him, after he was shot. That's the secret Anastasia sensed in you."

Bo's intake of breath was sharp in the dark near Eva. She couldn't see him. "What you say makes sense, Eva. But you seem to forget that Tansy is also human. You tell me. When you held him, bleeding, was he a person? Maybe I couldn't kill him because, like you, I couldn't make myself believe what I knew must be true."

Eva laughed, a short bitter bark of sound. "Oh, no? But your parents have taken away Charley, and your awful accusations have driven my daughter into the woods in the middle of the night. And now I'm out here in the woods and swamps alone with you. You've split us up, and we're at your mercy."

Bo spoke softly against Eva's ear. "And what will I do with the three of you, at my mercy?"

Eva trembled but spoke between teeth clenched to still their chattering. "You'll let Tansy destroy us, however he does it, one by one. And then you inherit that accursed plantation and sell it for the worth of the land and Charley's renovations."

Bo sighed. Eva felt the heat of his breath prick at the tender skin running behind her ear to her collarbone. "Good theory, as far as it goes. But why are you saying all this? You don't believe in Tansy. If he doesn't exist, how can he destroy you?"

"Whatever you're doing is tearing apart Charley and Anastasia. You're using the myth of Tansy to break us down and drive us apart, so we can't help each other. Can't get away together. Have to keep choosing and leaving someone behind."

He's messing with my mind. Bo brought me out here to kill me. Will he let me say good-bye first to my daughter?

CHAPTER SEVENTEEN
WHAT IS REAL?

"Why won't you take me to her?" Eva asked. She hadn't heard such bitterness in her voice since her long-ago, distant marriage. She was shocked at herself and caught her voice up at the end of the question, as if fighting a sob.

Bo turned toward her in the play of silver beginning to lighten the darkness, his silhouette burnished bronze against the sparkle of stars breaking among the trees to expose vast sky. "I've been waiting for you to ask yourself what is real."

"What is real?" Eva repeated. Scorn scraped her voice, slowed down the words, and forced her to hear the question.

Bo's frustration, his discouragement, seemed profound. But the rage that alarmed her before was gone. "I've already brought you to her, Eva."

Though Eva still saw nothing, her repetition of Bo's question, "What is real?" opened caverns in her mind, where it echoed, and now she could hear other sounds that had escaped her. Light splashes of water. Laughter like a breeze in tree leaves.

Anastasia's laughter?

Eva pushed past Bo, stumbling urgently toward that silvery, starlit sound. Her daughter? Out here in the woods in the dark of the night? What could have gotten into her?

And suddenly, she was there. Eva brought herself up short, her hand plastered to the trunk of a tree that blocked her headlong dash. There before her in the dark, lit from inside with profound happiness, sparkling with the cosmic fires of millions of stars burnishing her skin and burning streams of water that flowed to her and around her, eddying and buoying up her lithe body, was her daughter.

Eva stared. She thought at first that it was this inability to breathe that kept her still, kept her from crying out, "Anastasia!"

But as she calmed and caught her breath and still said nothing, she realized she was thinking. Hard. Fast. Trying to understand something that had escaped her long ago.

For now she knew why Bo's question, "What is real?" had slapped at her mind with such force, had sent her crashing ahead through the underbrush. That was the very question that had forced her to leave her husband.

She remembered now. Her mind raced, panicking, to grasp its meaning. What had she missed? Eva forced herself to wait and let the pictures, the memories, catch up to her present moment.

It was her only remaining friend who had asked the question. The friend was really only an acquaintance, a woman whom Eva only happened to meet because they lived in the same apartment complex. The woman was homesick for the Apache reservation just south of the Sangre de Cristo mountains-*blood of Christ*, Eva thought at the time, translating the Spanish-and the terrifying cliffs of Wolf Creek Pass. Eva had met her-Lania was what she called her "American" name, though Eva had never heard of it before-because they both kept ceramic pots of herbs, flowers, and vegetables outside their apartment doors.

"No room on the balcony," Lania had explained in her straightforward way one day when she and Eva both opened their doors at the same time to pour water from pitchers and jars onto their plants.

"No balcony," Eva had confessed, thinking herself trapped in a poorer apartment than her neighbor's. Lania had laughed, for she too had no balcony.

Now Eva could see that it was this first interchange that should have told her everything about what Lania had tried to communicate, as if it were all a gift for the present moment. Lania saw what was not there, like her non-existent balcony, and considered it part of the situation. For Lania, nonexistence was a valid state of being. For Eva, until that moment, nonexistence had meant nothingness, not potential.

By the time Eva had let Lania into her apartment, her own face swollen from crying, her forehead shot between the brows with what was becoming a perpetual scowl line, Eva had thought she should say something about the screaming fights that must be keeping her neighbor up at night. Should Eva explain that there was no wifebeating, despite the horrid shrieks and the sounds of precious things breaking?

But Lania had said, "Eva, I think I have to tell you something. I want to ask you what is real."

When they were seated together in the living room, looking out at the meager scraps of L.A. rooftops that made up Eva's view, Lania had still said nothing more. Handing her patient and only friend a glass of iced tea, sitting cross-legged on the floor to sip her own and calm down as she nursed her baby, Eva said, "I don't know what you mean, Lania."

"What is real?" Lania insisted. Eva felt her own impatience rise. Didn't she have enough to worry about without some flaky friend with nothing better to do than ask esoteric questions dropping in to meditate in the middle of the day?

As Bo had just done moments ago, all those long years ago, Lania watched Eva unblinkingly and seemed to be thinking. "I think I'd better tell you a story about myself."

Only because Lania never talked about herself did Eva decide to quell her irritation and listen. Perhaps, she reasoned, it would be a good story to settle the nursing Anastasia back to sleep.

Lania said, "In L.A., what was real to me on the reservation may not still be real." Her voice was heavy and low, as if weighted with loss. When she had first come to Los Angeles to accept a college scholarship, Lania failed two of her classes simply because she did not show up promptly enough to protect her grades. "Here I was, you know, the Apache genius who had gotten all those scholarships. And I was failing. Not because I didn't understand the material. I was probably the person in the room, next to the professor, who understood it best. But I just couldn't make it to those damned classes every single day at the same time. It just seemed so unnatural."

When Lania had gone home at the end of her first semester on academic probation, she felt as if the university decision makers had conspired to humiliate her and teach her a lesson. "Stay on the reservation," she explained to Eva. "Or you'll wish you had. I felt like they were after me, pushing me to fail and go back home and stay in my place, you know?"

Lania knew she had to tell her parents about the failing grades. But she couldn't right away. She had gone off alone to a small pond near a cave of rocks where she and her brother used to play when she was little.

"I hadn't seen that place in forever. There was nothing special about it. But I knew that being there would help me."

She had closed her eyes and sent her ball of explosive hatred of her professors hurtling from deep inside her toward the university that been the site of her shame.

Lania felt so good when she finally opened her eyes that she had a plan. She wouldn't tell her parents about the academic probation just yet. She would go back to the university right now and spend the break getting up every day at some ridiculous, monotonous time to get to some arbitrary spot on the campus at some arbitrary, fixed time. She would do this every day of her vacation, forcing herself to learn that this kind of behavior was her new normal.

When Lania told her parents she was driving straight back to L.A. that same night after dinner, they told her not to. "There's a flash storm out there. Flooding everywhere. The roads are dangerous. It's a miracle you got out of there in time to get here safe. Don't go back until it passes."

Lania had been sure that the storm was her doing, the result of her burning bundle of rage.

She had waited until the end of the winter break to come back. But when she got back, the practicing she had done in her mind, picturing herself showing up at the same time every day to arbitrary spots on the campus, worked. She was now on time, and her grades rocketed back to scholarship status.

"I didn't know when I did it that some people can do things like that," Lania had explained to Eva as Anastasia's mouth let slip her mother's nipple.

"Like what?" Eva asked. "Learning to be on time?"

Lania shook her head, black hair a river against her shoulders, in her lap. "Sending storms," Lania said, her tip-tilted eyes steady.

Eva looked down, unsure how to respond to this tale of something like witchcraft.

"But on the reservation, where I come from, some people believe in things like that. It's real to them. That my anger sent that storm and changed things."

Eva looked back up at her friend and nodded.

Lania's voice dropped again. Her next story was about her abortion. "That was my second year. I wasn't in love, but he made me feel secure. He was a reward I gave myself, you know, because I was doing so good in my classes. But I was lonely. I was still out of place."

This Eva could understand.

"But it was a mistake. When I got pregnant, I found out who I had given my body to. He made me a whore. He accused me of other men. I couldn't keep the baby, after that. I thought it was his baby."

"Wasn't it?" Eva asked, confused.

Lania shook her head. "No. After I got rid of it, I realized it was mine."

Eva felt heartsick. She looked down at her own sleeping baby, Anastasia's open pink mouth tinged white with milky drool. She was so beautiful. What might have happened if Eva had ever thought of Anastasia as her husband's baby?

Eva looked up at Lania with deep compassion, but this was not what Lania wanted. "A year after the abortion, to the day, I wanted to go lie down on my couch, like I had done when I came home from the clinic, bleeding and grieving. I wanted to lie down there and hold onto my belly."

The intensity in Lania's relentless, slow voice sent aches of suspense and uncertainty through Eva's own gut. She doubled forward, over Anastasia, and wished her friend would stop.

"But I knew if I lay down, Eva, if I went and lay down on that same couch, in that same position, at that same time as I had a year before, following my abortion, I knew my baby would come back to me."

Eva could not be silent. "What do you mean?"

Lania said without inflection, "I knew if I lay down on that couch, my baby would come back, and when I got up again, whenever that might be, I would be three months pregnant with that same child I had given up a year before."

Eva had sat open-mouthed.

She knew that what Charley called "the old folks" somewhere in a place called "back home" had strange tales that they swore were true. Vaguely, she remembered that Charley used to

300

regale her with these tales when their parents were alive and they were both quite young.

But here she was, an adult with a baby of her own, and here was her only remaining friend, the one woman whom Eva had trusted in her married life. And this woman would tell her such nonsense.

Eva stared at Lania. And Lania, unblinking, stared back.

And Eva realized that, for Lania, this was true. She began to really think about Lania's question: "What is real?"

If Lania had thought her baby came back, if Lania had thought she was pregnant, wouldn't she have lost her mind?

Eva said nothing, but Lania voiced these thoughts herself. "I thought to myself, 'I'm here in L.A. This is where I wanted to be. I'm here, but here, I didn't know that was my baby. I didn't recognize it. And now that it's come back to me, to give me another chance, I do recognize it. But I'm still here in L.A., where people don't believe in things like that. In ghost babies.'"

"Is there anybody who would believe in things like that back on the reservation?"

"Oh, yeah. Plenty of people. But it's not like they would have had to believe in my baby. They would have given me room for whatever was happening in my world. I would have had that baby, real or not to anybody else. And I would have healed."

Eva digested this. "Healed?"

It was good to talk to Lania. Even if she didn't understand the depths of Lania's esoteric message, the power of Lania's faith in her words, in her other worlds, pulled Eva in and suspended her, as if weightless, in possibilities.

"It was my baby, Eva, and I sent it away twice. The first time, away from my body. And the second time, away from my spirit. I wouldn't let it come back to me, even in spirit."

"Why not?"

Now it was Lania's turn to look at Eva as if she were out of her mind. "I was afraid. What would happen to me in the middle of L.A. if I got up one day three months pregnant, telling the doctor it was my aborted baby come back for a second try?"

"Well, if you really were pregnant, I mean so that the doctor could see it, he would think you were confused."

"Crazy," Lania said flatly.

Eva conceded with a nod.

Lania prompted, "And if he couldn't see the baby? Couldn't see the pregnancy?"

Eva admitted, "He would think you were crazy."

"With grief," Lania softened the phrase. "But crazy, all the same."

"Yes." Eva was dying to ask, *So what did you do? Lie down? Stay awake until the magic hour had passed?*

Lania said, "I sent my baby away a second time. I sat there in front of my couch all afternoon, into the night, till I knew my baby was gone away again. I sat there and waited for it to give up on me and leave. Not because it wasn't real. Not because I didn't believe in it. But because I was here. If I'd been home, where people give you room to go

302

through what you have to, I could have kept my baby that second time."

"Were you afraid of it?"

Now Lania's old half smile almost came back. "Of my own baby? No. I was glad it was here. I wanted to keep it, now that I understood it was all mine. But I couldn't risk getting kicked out of college. And what good would my social work degree do a crazy woman?"

Eva was sick to the pit of her stomach with confusion. All she could get from this grueling story was that when you were in the wrong place, you couldn't do what you believed, all by yourself, to be right.

Eva, young and self-centered, had looked at the story as a parable to tell her that she could not stop screaming like a madwoman unless she left her husband. And it seemed so true, so clear, in the murky half-world of Lania's story.

Eva could see that she had married her husband because he was a blank page she could rewrite her father on. And then she would become her mother, and all would be well. Her unbearable loss would be healed.

Only, her husband was not a blank. He was a stranger. And living with him had thrown her back into those mindless, screaming years when she had railed against the world for casting her parents out of it.

She had been happy, calm, with Charley. Eva decided that the point of Lania's stories was to break through her static tantrum and propel her back to Charley.

Eva said as much. And Lania, like a fount of infinite tolerance, had invited her to go camping in the mountains above her reservation.

They had stolen Eva's husband's old clunker of a car and escaped to the reservations linked by Colorado's Wolf Creek Pass.

It was a welcome break from Eva's reality. Until high up on Wolf Creek Pass, standing on the edge of a precipice that hurtled, sheer and unguarded, a mile down into a canyon where a river trickled like a thin silver stream, Lania had turned to Eva and said again, "Eva, have you thought about what I asked you back in L.A.? What is real?"

Eva had been holding Anastasia. The toddler was heavy with sleep, having just nursed, and was groggy all the time from the thin, clear air. Eva was troubled deep in her mind because, after Lania turned to her, she was afraid that she, down-to-earth Eva, would not resist the urge to leap out over the green, dizzying depths of the canyon and fly.

Eva could have flown. At that moment, trapped in the world that lurked, dark and profound, in Lania's question, Eva was as sure of her affinity for flight as she was of her need for air.

She could fly. She would fly, if she stood with this unanswered question for one more breath of time at the cliff's edge, a mile above the canyon floor.

Eva forced herself to hold on to the baby. She anchored herself to Anastasia's safety.

She had to get away from Lania.

Eva had, by force of will, resisted the pull of Lania's spell. But she was troubled now to recall that the trip up the mountain with Lania was the first thing Anastasia had mentioned to her, their first morning here at the plantation. It was impossible that Anastasia could remember Lania and the visit to the reservations! She had only been a nursing toddler at the time.

That same evening, driving down from the Pass to get back to Lania's parents' house on the reservation, Eva slammed on the brakes at the sight of a woman in a hospital gown walking along the road with a nursing baby in her arms. Eva had been sure the woman was Lania.

But Lania was asleep beside her on the front bench seat.

Anastasia had wakened in her car seat in the back and squealed in alarm from the impact of the sudden stop. Shaken, Eva turned to calm her. When Eva faced the road again, there was no woman. The road stretched, empty and starlit.

Once Eva escaped to Charley and success, she had never gone back to see Lania again. Lania let her go.

But Anastasia had recalled Lania, brought her question forward into the test of the present moment. And now Eva could feel Bo making his stealthy way up behind her, his breath hot and needling her skin as she watched the incredible scene he had brought her to see for herself.

In the stream where Baby Joy recorded that so much evil took place long ago, below the cave and cliff where magic and murder had happened, Anastasia splashed happily with Tansy.

It was clear that they were in love. Their eyes shone even in the darkness, lit by joy. Their laughter bubbled up, unstrained. Their hands met, emptied of water, and clasped, and they circled each other, danced around each other, bobbing up from the depths to embrace and hold on.

Eva watched her daughter, who had disappeared, cavorting with Tansy, her lover, who did not exist, and asked herself, "My God. What is real?"

Eva watched, yearning to call her daughter to the safety of their known world, to pull her out of the mysteries of the starlit stream. Eva wanted to demand of Anastasia how she'd found her inhuman, inexplicable lover, and if her daughter had any idea what had resurrected him.

In the face of an impossibility, Eva strained to perceive another level of reality implied in Lania's question. Perhaps it was not so much that only one thing was true, and it was true everywhere and for all time. What if, in a certain space, one thing, incredible anywhere else, was undeniably true? What if it were true all the time, but one could only see it in that certain space?

"Do you see it, too?" Eva whispered to Bo.

"Yes."

Eva wanted to rush forward, embrace her daughter, berate her for her escape and the incredibility of finding her like this, in the arms of an ancestral myth. *Get her out of there! She's in danger!*

But Eva couldn't just burst through the trees, calling to her daughter and screaming at the interloper to get away. *Anastasia, do you have any idea what you're tampering with?*

Anastasia would turn those gleaming, joyous eyes upon her mother and say, "What am I tampering with, Mommy?" Anastasia had already heard, understood, and accepted all of Bo's wildest theories.

And suddenly, Eva too saw the legend clearly played out in front of her. The aquatic merman lover, risen from water and death to claim his soul's bride. Her vivid, brighter-than-life daughter, infused by this marriage and resurrection with the power to heal nations of shattered peoples.

The cost of being the bride of the resurrected savior?

In all Bo's and Anastasia's research about that haunting, horrible mythic love story, the chosen princess's mother or father interfered and killed the fish-prince. The savior was killed and, just as in a Catholic mass, consumed.

"If he is our inheritance, then we eat him down. We eat our heritage. It becomes us as we destroy it."

And what happened to the merman's bride when her family came between them, even for her safety? "She always dies."

Eva ran through in her mind all the possible endings of the fairy tale that she had heard or read while Anastasia and Bo argued their perceptions of reality. It never changed. In the West African, Haitian, and African American versions of the tale, the fish-prince always won, she thought with dismay. He claimed his bride in life, and she followed him into death.

Now tears flowed down Eva's face. She turned in a burst of outrage to the man who had brought her to this scene of choice and desolation. "What right does he have to claim my baby? I gave her

307

life! Who is he to come wandering along and take it from her?"

"He only offered himself, honey. It was up to your daughter to accept him or let him go."

Eva's hand had snaked out and whipped a cutting slap across Bo's hard cheekbone before the idea had even reached her brain.

She gasped at the astonishment on his face. She whirled to see if she had interrupted the lovers. Did the noise reach them? Break up their tryst?

Bring death, drowning, loss upon them both?

Eva clung with trembling hands to the trunk of the tree and watched as her daughter laughed and frolicked like a child with the stranger. If they had heard anything, it had not alerted them to Eva and Bo's presence.

Eva could not break them apart. She would not risk the danger to Anastasia. What would have happened in all those myths if the mother or father did not kill the merman, sent no one to harm him?

The impetus of her outrage and horror were lost, spent in her futile physical attack on Bo. Eva leaned against the tree and dreaded leaving this spot, surrendering the possibilities of this moment. In the morning, she would rail against her gullibility, her cowardice.

She couldn't do it. She couldn't separate them.

How long had she watched? Eva couldn't be sure. But she came to herself when the two lovers abruptly stopped their play. Mesmerized, staring into each other's ocean-hued eyes, they drew close, pressed golden chest to gleaming breasts, and kissed. Their arms went around each other in a tangle of coppery limbs and burnished masses of wild black and bronze hair.

Only then did it occur to Eva that her daughter was a grown woman, though a very young one, and the two were not naked children, but lovers.

Eva let go of the tree trunk that had braced her up all this time. She longed to look back at the lovers before she turned and withdrew. But she couldn't.

Eva realized only when she got to her house's kitchen door and could not open it that Bo had followed her. He reached to help her shove the heavy door. She turned to him. "Please don't leave me alone with this."

He let her in and followed her on silent, padding feet to her room.

In the hallway, Eva thought the restless stained glass rippled as if made of water. But Bo seemed to see nothing amiss.

Eva kept her silence.

CHAPTER EIGHTEEN
WHAT LOVING YOU HAS DONE TO ME

Eva and Bo didn't make it as far as her bed before she collapsed. "I don't know what that thing will do to my little girl." Eva pounded the carpet with her fists.

Bo held her, rocked her. Murmured, "This is all my fault. I let you down, honey."

Eva snatched up her head. "What do you mean, Bo?"

"I didn't kill him, Eva. I was sent here to be the caretaker, and I let him live. What a fool!" Bo's voice grated up his throat, burst out between distorted lips. He bent his head to hide his shifting face inside his hands.

Eva was afraid, suddenly, of his distress.

She covered his hands with hers, lowered them so that she could gain eye contact with him. "What is this about being caretaker, Bo?"

Bo was brusque. "There is always someone watching over this house. Someone has to be caretaker. It's an old abandoned property, full of . . . never mind, Eva. Because of your and Charley's parents' deaths, I was assigned to watch the property, even though I was too young for that much responsibility. My parents didn't realize then that it was a mistake."

"How could they not realize? How old were you, Bo?"

"Eva, don't ask."

"In what way was it a mistake, then?"

"Eva, I said don't ask me these questions!" Bo turned from Eva. He rose in jagged stages to his knees, then to all fours.

"Bo, is this about the secret you've hidden from me?"

Now Bo stood. Against the speckled starlight piercing the lace at Eva's window, Bo seemed to twist, contort. Battle with himself.

"Bo, what is it?"

Bo threw back his head against the pricks of distant light and roared.

The sound coiled up from his abdomen, slammed against his ribs, strained his lungs to emit a howl of rage and pain between distended lips.

Eva's first move had been toward Bo, to comfort him.

But as the sound shredded the damp air with its ferocity, flung itself around the room and down from the upstairs hallway, her skin prickled as fine hairs lifted. Flight. *I've got to get away.*

In one sweep, she was up from the floor and at the door of her room.

Bo was with her.

Eva felt his fingers clamp her arm, squeeze, and hold her helpless. She screamed and tried yanking back.

Bo watched and held on. When her scream died for want of air, he drew her to his liquid face, *Molding into something else as I watch it,* Eva thought with horror.

Bo's voice was not his own. "You refuse to understand, don't you, Eva? Not a thought for me in that busy, pretty head." Anger without inflection. As though his hatred was matter-of-fact.

Incredulous, Eva listened.

"I put the pieces all in front of you, Eva, I tell you everything, I wait, and still there's nothing!" He spat the last word. "You can't be bothered to figure out what I'm trying to tell you, can you, Eva?"

Eva responded at last. "Why are you saying this?" She fought down the rising note of panic. "My daughter's out there. I only want to help my daughter, Bo." She jerked, snapping at the arm trapped in his hand. Eva willed Bo to be persuaded by reason.

Again Bo threw back his head in that bellow of abysmal hurt and hopelessness.

Is there really a hell? Eva stopped resisting Bo, paralyzed. She had never seen anything like what she saw now.

Bo swung his head, ejecting something vile from inside him. He spewed it from his mouth, retched upon the loss of breath, and ended in a guttural wail that left his face distended like a muzzle.

Panting, he turned, hideously transformed, to Eva.

No! He said it's not like this. Shapeshifting is when the spirit travels, not when human bodies turn into monsters.

The thing that panted where Bo should have stood said, "Is this what you want of me, Eva? Is this what I have to be for you? Look what loving you has done to me."

Bo flung Eva from him.

The force sent her flying into the hallway. She struck the stairway railing and bent backwards over it, flailing her arms.

312

Howling, the distorted thing that had flung her now leapt above her, beyond her, snatching her from midfall to carry her with it as it hurtled through the empty space beside the stairs.

Eva cried out as they flew and fell. The raging thing was huge, much bigger than Bo, its muscles harder, bulging. Even its gentleness was a trial of her endurance. Its clawed hands raked her skin as it dropped her safely to the lower floor. She stumbled from it and fell, faint with vertigo and nauseous with terror.

"Do you see?" Its voice rumbled as she tried to raise herself to her feet. Eva turned. That last note of dismay was surely Bo's own clear baritone.

It was true. Now it was Bo who stood behind her near the stairs, crouched as if he were hunted and ready to run. "Bo? Is it you? I thought you were . . . something else."

"No!" he shouted. "Not ever again." He looked wildly at Eva. "You're all right? I didn't hurt you?"

Bo sank to his knees, his head in his hands again. He bent until he cowered on the floor.

Eva crept to him. "What happened? Bo, what was that? What happened to you?" When she reached him, she extended a hesitant hand.

His skin felt smooth, his muscles lean. He raised his head to look at her.

In the wash of starlight from the parlor, Eva saw his face swept with tears. Bo groaned with the effort to weep. "Eva, I can't control the beast. You don't understand. It's more than I am. It was fully grown when I was still a child."

Eva resisted her urge to pull away.

313

"Eva, this is why my parents locked me in the stone room when your parents died. I went mad. I loved your father and your mother. They understood the curses of this place, and they were kind to me. I wanted to avenge them."

"You remember my parents?"

Bo threw back his head and cried out his agony. Eva forced her hand to lie still on his shoulder.

As the hoarse howl dwindled to a whimper, Bo drew in shuddering breaths. "Spare me. This is why my parents brought me here, taught me to lock myself into the stone corridor. Blood everywhere. Wild animals. Pets. Mangled in my bedroom in the mornings. This is how I killed my bird. Chasing Tansy. Letting myself be the thing that could kill Tansy."

Bo fixed his eyes on Eva, rage building again. "Hunting Tansy. Night follows night, and I followed his scent. Killing anything. I could have killed my own parents, so mad with the bloodlust."

Eva withdrew her hand.

Bo rocked back as he sat on his heels. "I swore I wouldn't let it happen again." He swung to look at her. The rage had drained from his face and left it beseeching her to understand. "You see how you pull away? All these years, there has been no killer here but me. I had just decided there is no Tansy, no curse. Just a kid believing scary stories. I am the only killer. I saw no one and nothing until my uncle tried to kill him for me." Again Bo struggled with the resistant tears, gasping them out, spitting out salt and water with weak sobs.

Bo shook his head and held out his arms. "I've let you down, Eva. But how was I to know that

Tansy really existed? That you existed. That you would bring your daughter to him."

"Bo, of course you couldn't know."

"You see why I can't let the beast out now. Do you understand? I could have killed you on the stairs. It's too powerful. It doesn't think."

"I don't understand everything I've seen, Bo, but I believe you. Whatever it is in you, don't let it out."

"It's useless, anyway. Nothing can kill Tansy."

Bo's voice was weaker now, hollow from the release of the beast and the tears of a lonely boy. "Eva, all those years, I could scent him but I couldn't see him. But now I know the stories are true."

Bo had crawled close against her. He seized her hands. Soon, she thought, they would be in each other's arms again, and tonight's nightmare would vanish as if it had never been. Disgust shook her.

Bo was caught up in his own realization that, "Tansy is invisibility, so that's why I could never find him. Tansy is immortality, so he always heals. Tansy is suffering, so he never dies. Resurrection, so he'll always live again."

"I don't believe any of that, Bo. Tansy is a homeless vagrant in the woods."

Bo sprang from her, crouched, ready to spring again. His eyes caught light and flared. "You can't believe what you see?" Another gut-wrenching bellow.

Eva huddled away from him into a ball to fight the mindless terror. The floor beneath her shook as Bo stomped to her. She felt his claws slice air, felt the thick wet summer air split as Bo reached

315

through it for her. Then she felt herself weightless and sickened with helplessness as he swung her above his head.

Bo turned, still holding Eva, and bounded up the stairs. He hurtled to a stop at the landing and flung Eva at her bedroom door. She struck the wall and sat, stunned.

"Get away!" Bo roared, backing down the stairs in jerks and starts. "I'll do it. Just stay away from me. Stay away from him. We're death, and I can't stop that."

And he was gone.

Eva watched the jagged, swift steps of the beast in Bo circle, snuffling, and clamber on all fours headfirst down the stairs. It reached the bottom of the stairs and halted, splay-legged, scenting its unseen enemy, snapping at nothing.

As Eva watched, the creature that had been Bo worked itself into a rampage. It doubled back on its haunches, howling above its hunched shoulders. Maddening itself for the hunt.

Eva huddled away into the shadows of the hallway when the frenzied thing swung its reddened eyes up to scan the stairs.

It will kill anything. It might kill my daughter. Yet Eva feared to call it back. It might kill her. But what if her own death could save Anastasia?

Eva crawled to the railing. "Bo, come back."

But the great black beast, sinews enwrapping curved vertebrae, slipped through the kitchen doorway. Eva heard the new screen hiss into place.

I can't stay here. But can I follow the werewolf to Anastasia?

Eva pulled herself to her feet and ran to the stained glass at the end of the hall, to see which direction the werewolf might take.

Face pressed to the brittle glass, Eva saw Bo as a sleek black streak across the fallow field. What remained of the man paused, lifted its head, stood on two sharply bent hind legs to turn and peer toward the stained glass window.

It told me to stay away.

Eva slammed her back flat against the hallway wall. She stood motionless, blood rushing in her ears. She pressed herself out of Bo's sight and wiped at the gashes he'd left on her arms and torso, trying to stanch the seeping blood.

Still she lingered, wretched with dread, until her eye was caught by a play of light in the stained glass. *Is the rosette changing? Another sign.* Eva focused on the images.

Blue water rippled. A man rose, dripping water from locks of matted hair around him in the stream, at the man's hips the aqua scales of a fish. His fins lifted and swept down.

A woman came and stretched herself out along his wet, long body. They swam together.

Toward where a man waited to scoop the fish from the stream. Suddenly red shimmered through the blue. Beside the crimson flow, all that was left of the merman was bones and a weeping bride who sank into the stream.

What had Bo told her? That she had all the pieces but never put them together.

Bo is my lover now and my daughter's mentor. Through me, he's become Anastasia's father. He must not kill Tansy.

317

Eva stared at the whole, healed woman now rising from the crimson stream in the stained glass. Why had she and Bo never discussed what would happen if the lovers were left alone?

Raked and aching from the body slams she'd endured at the hands of the werewolf, Eva made her way down the stairs. *I'll never get to Tansy before Bo finds him. I don't even know how to find the stream.*

By the time Eva made her way to the kitchen screen door and peered through the obsidian night to the waiting, distant trees, she was reeling from shock and pain. She peeled off her shredded, bloodied clothes before she slipped to the floor.

She willed herself to rise, to push open the door. Her urgency swept her into the night air. *The dream. Flying.*

I am flying.

Or was she falling? Her head was as light and her vision as blurred as though this were a dream.

I can save her.

Below Eva the wolf streaked to the silver stream. Above her, the lovers had climbed to the cliff Baby Joy described in her stories. Scenes of love, escape, and vengeance loomed in Eva's mind. She shut them down.

No one will die tonight.

Eva found herself standing on the cliff. Below the wolf sniffed at the stream, lapped at it. Raised its head, its nostrils and tongue full of the scent and taste of the merman. Sighted Eva above it, waiting.

The wolf began to climb.

Eva watched the black fur undulate above the creature's muscles as it worked its way up the hill.

318

Behind her, the lovers stirred, cried out at the noise of the huffing beast closing in.

Tansy said, "I always knew someday he'd come after me. You stay here, Anastasia. I'll go out to him."

The slender young man came forward from the cave to the bright cliff, awaiting his killer.

Perhaps, in the nature of dreams, no one could see Eva. Tansy seemed to walk to her and through her, his green eyes fastened on the edge of the cliff.

What had Anastasia said about fate? For this was a young man who believed it was time to meet his destiny.

Would Bo see her? *If this is a dream, do I have any control?* Eva flew to the cliff's edge to confront her lover.

But it was the savage-eyed thing that clawed its way to the crest of the cliff, not Bo. The creature dragged itself up onto the cliff's landing and squatted low.

Eva thought of Bo's tears for the death of his bird. *I fly. I am like a bird. When I interfere, will he kill me?*

She turned to face her daughter. Anastasia, eyes distended with disbelief at the sight of the thing that had consumed Bo, was working up her courage to join Tansy.

Anastasia, stay back. We all want to save you.

Eva swept toward her lover, who had given himself up to the beast that he despised. Eva wrapped her wings around him, pressed her ethereal body to him. "Bo, you can't kill Tansy now. You're going to be my husband. That makes you Anastasia's father. You remember the tales. You'll kill her, if you kill her lover. You have to let him go."

The grunting thing that had stalked up the side of the hill to kill a mythical enemy was no longer quite Bo. But Eva could see her intelligent lover in the depths of the creature's eyes, trying to think.

But the creature's power was beyond Bo's. If it heard her, it disdained her and crept past her, snarling and snapping at Tansy, lifting and dragging its clawed pads across the rocky ground.

It balanced delicately above the backward-pointing bones of its long feet, perched high on massive haunches, thick glutinous ropes of saliva dangling from yellowed fangs down between its spread legs, anticipating a bloodfeast.

Again Eva swept before the creature, reached for it, stroked its grating fur.

The thing swiped. Curved claws connected with feathers and fragile bones. Eva was thrown to the ground.

It moved on to Tansy, a growl rattling in its throat. The trail of drool laid a glistening path beneath its lashing tail as it passed Eva. It huffed at its prey, not quite a bark, but an unmistakable challenge.

Tansy stood his ground.

"Boye," Eva called. "Here, Boye. Good, good Boye."

The werewolf reared and turned toward the sound. Then it ran at Eva, slamming the resistant ground with tendoned feet, striking claws and pads into the rocky soil, gouging its way toward her.

The creature's next blow drove her into the air. Eva fluttered at the end of the awful trajectory, above the cliff's edge, too far out. Her bruised wings beat the heavy air, and for seconds, she hovered.

Her arms slapped air, scrub and dirt, fighting for a handhold on the cliff's edge. Her struggling wings lifted her once more.

And there was Tansy, green eyes wide, hand extended, trembling, to pull her back to safety. She clasped his two hands in her own.

Tansy's eyes widened with dismay. Shock. Eva threw her arms around her daughter's lover, drew the remaining power of her failing wings in a sweep that lifted her and the young man beyond Bo's furious lunge, plunging together over the edge of the cliff.

Bo's werewolf howled and leapt to swipe at its quarry again.

Fluttering above the stream, Eva could no longer hold on as Tansy struggled against her. She opened her arms and released the glittering fish that twisted, flapping and mouthing, its glassy eye still fixed on her as it hurtled toward the water below.

Anastasia crowded Bo, human again, at the cliff's edge, and screamed as her lover fell.

Eva woke from the floor with a start. Cold. Dark. The faintest trickle of light coming through the kitchen's single window.

Eva sat up. *What a nightmarish dream.*

And no wonder.

She'd fainted from hunger and shock and pain right here at the kitchen door, and here were the bloodied scabs slashed across her torso to prove it.

Impossible. Bo would never harm her, of that Eva was sure. *But the werewolf?* Nonsense. That was just a dream.

Something terrible had happened. Anastasia had run away. Was out in the woods in the black of night.

Bo had gone to look for her.

But what had happened to Eva? Why was she on the floor, bloody and faint?

The problem with dreams was that they always felt real until one awoke from them. Philosophically, Eva began to work her way up to her feet and to the bathroom built on the side of the kitchen. She would wash up, find fresh clothes, dress, and telephone the police about her missing daughter.

But when she came out of the bathroom, aching but clean and wrapped in Charley's peach-colored terry robe, Eva found Bo sitting at the kitchen table.

CHAPTER NINETEEN
GHOSTS AND DEAD MEMORIES

Will anyone ever find these words? Why have I spent my waning years with ghosts and dead memories?

I ask myself if anyone could ever understand the world we lived in, the way it was. Or how we lived, and how we felt about our lives? We were not brutes acted upon, too coarse to dream and ponder. The horrors we sustained transformed our souls.

We plowed this hostile, fertile land with our terror and sowed it with our triumphs. We soared hope-filled skies each time we rose from desperation and survived. But why would any who were not among us attempt to resurrect such suffering as ours and understand it? Will not the future be content to leave us in its past?

I write to fight despair.

Bo sat at the farthest end of the hand-hewn table, the end nearest to the door, as though he wasn't sure he would be welcome.

"Good morning," Eva said.

Bo nodded.

"Do you know if Anastasia is coming home? I have something to tell her."

Bo rose and came slowly around the plank table toward Eva. He kept his eyes on hers and his hands where she could see them, as though he were under arrest. When he reached her, he said, "I don't ever mean to hurt you again. Let me see, Eva."

He untied the bathrobe and pushed it open.

There was nothing she could do about the slashes. She had washed them sitting in tepid soapy water, but it was clear that the wounds were fresh and would need attention.

Eva said, "I thought I'd ask for your Aunt Olivia, since I'll have to make peace with my new in-laws sooner or later, anyway. She's the nurse in the family, right?"

Bo dropped the edges of the robe into place and fumbled with the sash. "I can't let you do that. I can't let you marry me. I thought it was over, or I never would have let myself get near you. But you see what I've done."

Eva took the sash and tied it. "Bo, I can't believe that any of that was real. Don't bother to argue. You won't persuade me."

"How do you explain the wounds?"

She shrugged. "I don't. At least, not today. I just want to speak with Anastasia. There are things I should have told her long ago, with or without Tansy coming into her life."

"Will you rest? I'll make you something soothing to drink, Eva. Then I'll go find her. It won't be hard. I've tracked her before."

"I know. I've figured that much out."

"Now that I'm myself, she might agree to come back with me."

"If she doesn't agree to come with you, send her home alone." Eva saw Bo wince and made up her mind to address the issues with both of them, separately or together, at once.

After she'd sipped at a cup of chamomile tea, Bo followed Eva to the stairs. She couldn't manage more than two, even holding his arm.

Bo lifted Eva gingerly, as though he feared that her wounds might bleed if she were moved. "The wounds are long, but they're not deep," Eva said.

"Don't minimize what I've done, Eva. That won't help."

Eva's head dropped against Bo's shoulder. The long, slow climb was more wearying than she had expected. She murmured as they moved through the faint light, "That's not the problem anyway, Bo. Who can help me figure out what's really happened? It's like we're all caught in a dream and can't wake up."

Bo laid Eva on her bed. She lifted the new apricot-tinted satin coverlet and slid beneath it, still in Charley's robe.

"I'm so tired. Please find Anastasia."

The next words Eva heard, as if she'd awakened in the middle of a conversation, were Anastasia's. "I didn't mean to risk your lives. I didn't see it that way."

Charley's voice broke in. "Honey, your mother will understand."

Eva's eyes flew open. "You're back," she said and held out her arms. Both Anastasia and Charley crowded inside the embrace. "You're both back. I have so much to tell you two."

Charley said, "We've probably heard it already. You've got to do something, cousin, about that habit of talking in your sleep."

Anastasia joked gently, "Especially when you're going to sleep for days at a time."

Eva groaned. "Days? Don't tell me Bo let Aunt Olivia stick her needles in me again."

Charley clicked her tongue. "Worse than that, Eva. Aunt Lydia this time."

"You're not serious. Not another nurse."

Charley looked sage. "Worse, honey. Aunt Lydia's a doctor." Charley shook her head. "I'm telling you."

Eva laughed. "It's so good to see you two."

"It's so good to be home," Anastasia said quietly.

"Oh!" Eva sat up, alert now. "That's what I meant to tell you. Anastasia, I'm so sorry."

"What about, Mommy?"

Eva took her daughter's hands. "I'm sorry it took all this to bring me to realize something you and I should have agreed on long ago. I didn't think you'd ever had a boyfriend before."

"Not what we'd call a serious one, Mommy."

"No? Excuse me for not passing on to you sooner something that Charley taught me about parenting a young woman."

Charley said brightly, "I taught you? I don't know a thing about parenting. I've got to hear this!"

"Anastasia, none of this panic and violence ever would have happened if I had made this agreement with you, so I want to make it now. If it's Tansy, or if it's anybody else-and I'll be honest and say I hope it's somebody human, next time-"

Charley interjected, "Look at the pot calling the kettle black, to judge from all the confessions Bo's been making around here lately."

Eva lost her train of thought. "You know Bo's secret?"

"You damn skipping, Eva. That man better tell me what's going on in my own home, when I come

326

here and find my cousin tore up to shreds and passed out in the bed with all his aunties and their hypodermic needles and cookbooks all over her."

Eva laughed. "That does sound bad, Charley."

Charley snorted. "And it looked worse! You know how wild Bo's people can be. I didn't know what those women were cooking up here, if you'll pardon the pun."

"Speaking of cooking," Eva asked, "Did Bo ever get his recipes copied out before his aunts took their cookbooks back?"

"He was still writing even while they stitched you up."

"You made that up."

Charley smiled, "Yes, I did, little one. He couldn't have seen a piece of paper to put a pen to it, the way he was crying while they worked on you. That man got too many guilt issues. I know some people could use some of Bo's guilt, and it would make a better world, if they did."

Eva said seriously, "The worst, for me, is picturing that little boy whose own parents moved him into this big abandoned house, so he could lock himself up in the dungeon whenever the werewolf took over. It couldn't have been true. It's some kind of hallucination or something. What did you think about his situation, Charley?"

Charley said, "That it's *our* situation, cousin. We're in this together, now."

Anastasia said, "Don't believe all that mushy stuff, Mommy. She bolts him into his stone corridor every night, and he's in there alone."

327

"Sliding the bolt on *his* side of the door, so I can't haul him out to chew him out about getting his wolf under control."

Eva had to laugh.

Charley said, "Well, I couldn't have you waking up accusing me of getting rid of your fiancé. What was I going to say? So I thought I'd best keep that bad boy here in some kind of condition where he couldn't pull none of that werewolf nonsense no time soon."

"I love you two so much. And Anastasia, that's what I want to say. Whoever you choose to love—and I hope someday you'll choose someone without a curse attached to him—I hope you'd feel free to leave him and come home at any time or for whatever reason."

"Mommy, you think you know that kind of thing about your own family, until the problem comes up. And then you realize that you feel like it's life and death, you know? I thought I'd die if you wouldn't see Tansy the way I did. I couldn't leave him and come home."

Eva heard the word "did." "Are you home now, or is this a visit?"

Anastasia looked puzzled. "I'm home, Mommy. Where else would I be?"

Nothing for it but to plunge into the fray. "I thought you might have run away to live with Tansy."

"I thought you saw what happened, Mommy. He's a fish these days."

The phrase was flat and Anastasia's face expressionless. "Come on, Mommy. You're not going to pretend you didn't know. You made him do it."

Through Eva's mind hurtled the twisting, flipping, sparkling turquoise-scaled fish, its unblinking eye fixed on her as it fell. *That was just a dream.*

Anastasia folded her arms and tilted her head at her mother. *Play along.* Eva said, "A fish, huh? Well, I guess we could run some water and keep him here in one of the bathtubs."

Anastasia was the first to laugh.

Charley offered, "Your mama's man locked in the dungeon, howling, your little friend locked in the bathroom, swimming, and my dirty old man locked in the jailhouse, cussing. We three really know how to pick them."

Anastasia shook her head. "I think I've had my fill of romance."

"Why is that, honey?"

"Because I have other things I want to do," Anastasia explained.

Charley said, "Like starting college in a few days?"

Eva said, "And opening Anna's Academy?"

Anastasia added excitedly, "And helping Aunt Charley run the Retreat for Far-Seeing Women. Do you want to see our new stationery?" And she bounded from the room.

When they were alone, Charley turned a sober face to Eva. "Why didn't you tell me what you were going through? Bo, and the angel, and the flying. All the crazy things I've been hearing, lately." Charley reached and squeezed Eva's hand. "Couldn't you tell me anything?"

"Ditto back at you, Charley, for all these years with your supervisor."

"Point taken. Let's make a deal, okay? No more superwomen keeping secrets."

Eva smiled. "No more superwomen, cousin. I just have one question. Who told you about the angel? Or was it a witch? I've been calling her, in my mind, a witchangel."

"Didn't I tell you that you talk too much in your sleep? Make that sleeping or waking," Charley quipped.

Anastasia leapt like a gazelle back into the room, trailing a reluctant Bo behind her.

"Eva." Bo sat on the edge of her bed opposite Charley and took Eva's free hand. "So you are pulling through."

Anastasia plopped between them and waved a pastel green sheet of paper scrolled with golden curlicues and embossed with a delicate letterhead. "Green for growth," she said and waved a powder blue sheet, "blue for serenity," and a rose sheet, "and light red for the blood of sacrifice and renewal."

Eva said cautiously, "Whose ideas were those?"

"Mine and Charley's and Aunt Hetta's. She was here taking care of you for a while, so we let her have a vote, too."

"Aunt Hetta wanted the blue," Charley explained.

Eva said, "Blue is the color of the goddess that made me figure out what I needed to tell Anastasia. Anastasia, Bo, do you remember the mermaid who makes it all the way across the Middle Passage without her merman?"

Bo and Anastasia said together, "Yemoja."

"I saw her in the stained glass. She looked like Anastasia, rising from drowning over Tansy. That's how I realized that the person I needed to try to save was Tansy, so Anastasia could decide for herself if and how she was going to live beyond him."

Anastasia said, "I didn't mean to make everyone risk their lives. I didn't understand what I was dealing with. It just wasn't real to me until I saw-" Anastasia shuddered, broke off.

Gently, "Honey, what did you see?"

"Oh, I saw my mother's boyfriend go ballistic and break out in fur and fangs. I saw my mother fly over a cliff and my boyfriend flip into a fish, to survive the fall."

"Did you really see all that?"

"Mommy, sometimes I'm not sure." Eva took both of Anastasia's hands. Anastasia brightened. "At the next place, Mommy and Aunt Charley, let's not get any new boyfriends until we've finished fixing up the house. Okay?"

Bo said, "Anastasia, I think your mother and I have something to tell you. I don't think your mother will be having any more boyfriends anytime soon."

Charley said, "Eva, are congratulations and best wishes in order?"

Eva looked distracted. "What next place, Anastasia? I don't plan to move again in my foreseeable future. Especially if I can finish my dissertation, now that I've learned a thing or two about ancestral memory and storytelling. I might even get a job at a college in this state."

"Well, I guess you better change your plans, cousin." Now Charley was in her stride, amused and confident. "And along that line, Eva, why didn't you warn me about that other property?"

"Other property?"

Bo said, "Charley, you didn't tell her? No wonder she's so cheerful."

"Tell me what?"

Anastasia took over. "Let me do it. Mommy won't mind. She likes adventures."

Eva had a terrible feeling. "I'm waiting. What should someone have told me?"

Anastasia said with enthusiasm, "That this isn't the only property you inherited. Isn't that great?" And Anastasia squealed with joy. "There's another property that goes with this one, Dennison land won in some kind of gambling, off in the swamps of southern Louisiana. I figure that, after I finish my degree at Cooper, we might want to see about opening up another branch of the retreat over there. I'll run it, of course, if you'd rather stay here and not move." Anastasia glowed.

Bo said, "Eva, I'm surprised if you didn't know about the other place. Didn't you read about the freed people who trekked off to start a commune, in Baby Joy's stories? It's a pretty solid historical recording of some little-known problems suffered by those emancipated during the enslavement era."

Eva flopped back onto her pillows.

Charley said thoughtfully, "So, nobody knows the address over at the new place except us. And if I do all my transactions through the address here, nobody will be able to trace me, while I'm fixing up that place over there. Bo, I trust your dad's legal partners to protect me. But some added insurance against my stalker, like a few acres of swampland filled with alligators and poisonous snakes, might give me some peace of mind."

Anastasia said, "Brilliant!"

Bo looked concerned.

And Charley turned a radiant smile upon her cousin. "So, Eva, when are we going into the cane swamps to fix up the new place?"

THE END OF VOLUME ONE